Heather —
Keep it always,

xoxo

Tyler

Tahoe. Badass. SEAL. Player. Powerful. Jerk. Available.
All words used to describe me for the past ten years. Wrapped up in the war, running and gunning constantly, has taken its toll on me. My next assignment is supposed to be a break, something to aid in taking the edge off; help open a new base in the miniscule, coastal, Florida town of Bronze Bay. A non-deployable position, I can work-out, decompress, and handle the mundane tasks of structuring a new SEAL command. Or, in other words, enjoy my free time with the tanned, toned, country women of the south.

Mission accepted.

Falling for a southern belle wasn't supposed to happen. In fact, it's more stressing than any challenge in my sordid past. Especially when she uttered the words, "I am a virgin."
Someone cover me, I'm going in.

Caroline

My first memory is in an airplane over the waters of the Gulf of Mexico. My daddy sitting beside me and my heart full of joy. When I was sixteen, I made my first solo flight over those exact same waters. My daddy owns and operates the little airport in Bronze Bay, so my eyes have been skyward for as long as I can remember. Things like men and college, never appealed to me. My days are spent waitressing in my Mama's diner, counting down the hours until I can head to the airport.
Then the SEALs came and changed everything. Big, brutal, jerks, forcing themselves into our little slice of paradise. Demanding use of our airport. One man in particular, aiming to take more than I'm ready to give. He is beautiful. Magnetic. Strong. Convincing. For the first time in my life, I'm flying in a different, exhilarating way. Keeping it isn't going to be easy when merely looking at the man makes me think of four words.

Foxtrot. Uniform. Charlie. Kilo.
Bless my heart, I'm in trouble.

PRAISE FOR RACHEL ROBINSON NOVELS

"Rachel Robinson knows SEALs better than SEALs know themselves."

Natasha Madison, Bestselling Author

"INTOXICATING. Absolutely consuming! What a ride. And it's such a different story! It really is. I just loved it."

Angie, Angie's Dreamy Reads

"Rachel Robinson has penned a flawless story of pain and heartache, damaged pasts and uncertain futures mixed with soul searing heat, all consuming love and breathtaking beauty. Black and White Flowers is a stunning novel worth an infinite amount of stars."

Sophie, Bookalicious Babes Blog

"Achingly beautiful. This book will haunt you in the very best way."

J.L. Berg, *USA Today* bestselling author

"In Life Plus One, Rachel Robinson delivers a captivating romance with characters you easily fall in love with. Harper and Ben's story is a heart breaking love story I never wanted to end. Her best yet!"

Josephine Brierley, Author of *Delicate Lies*

"I loved this book so much that I want to shout it from the roof tops. A beautifully written love story that will keep you wanting more."

New York Times Bestselling Author, Aurora Rose Reynolds

TITLES BY RACHEL ROBINSON

CONTEMPORARY ROMANCE
CRAZY GOOD SERIES
CRAZY GOOD

SET IN STONE

TIME AND SPACE

THE REAL SEAL SERIES
BLACK AND WHITE FLOWERS

HERO HAIR

LIFE PLUS ONE

THE BRONZE BAY SEALS
KEEPING IT

ROMANTIC COMEDY
FROG HOG NOVELLAS
Frog Hog – Valen and Hutch

EROTIC ROMANCE
THE DOM GAMES

Visit Rachel Robinson online

www.racheljrobinson.com

facebook.com/racheljeanrobinson

A NAVY SEAL MEETS VIRGIN ROMANCE

keeping it

INTERNATIONAL BESTSELLING AUTHOR
RACHEL ROBINSON

ISBN-13: 978-1983998300
ISBN-10: 1983998303

NOTE FROM THE AUTHOR

As always, writing a heartfelt novel is a painful self-exploration, tinged with moments of pure elation and sorrow so real, it depresses me in real life. After that painstaking, beautiful process is over, it takes a village to get this into your hands.

Thank you to Lindee Robinson Photography for the amazing images that grace the cover and all of the teaser images. You brought Caroline and Tahoe to life. Quite literally, in the most beautiful way possible.

J. Wells. The extraordinary editor that questions every single sentence I write. My timeline will never be tighter than when you have control of it. Thank you for fixing this story, and in the end, loving it, just as much as I do. Tahoe is secretly, and always, yours.

My family deserves thanks, because writing a book (or 11) takes time away from them even if I do my best to spread it evenly. My husband: bless you, and that AWFUL mask squeeze that you wore around like a Halloween mask for months. I mean, I'm glad it happened so I could write about it, but you really did scare the shit out of me. I love you, and our small hometown. Forever.

I grew up in a small, coastal town in Florida. It gave me so much more than a larger city could. Of that, I'm certain. Bronze Bay is my way of tipping my hat to the beautiful town that still to this day I call home. It's the same place I met my husband (and grew up with him), and the town I return to visit my family and friends. If Bronze Bay feels real, it's because it is. Kind of. I mean, it's fiction, but my hometown is truly inspiring. Thank you for reading Caroline and Tahoe's story, and I hope you enjoyed the adventure and love. If you want to know if you'll see more Bronze Bay SEALs, the answer is yes. Leif and Malena are coming up next in TOSSING IT.

DEDICATION

For the small town girls...

keeping it

Prologue

Caroline

If this island was an organ, it would be my heart. Isolated, lost, and misunderstood. Oh, and broken into jagged, sharp pieces. How could I forget that? Shell Island. I know exactly where I'm at. The airplane went down about seven minutes after I took off. I didn't know the storm was coming in or I probably wouldn't have gone up. I love the horizon before a big, nasty storm, but try to avoid putting myself into one. The thunderheads look as if they're leaking love letters from heaven. The colors in the clouds are this magic mix of reality and the supernatural. It soothes me to go for a quick flight before a storm, but that was not my intention today. Today, I needed the mental clarity being in the air provides more than I have ever needed it before. Maybe that's why my plane is destroyed, mangled in shiny bent pieces in the distance. I didn't pay enough attention to my gauges—the warning signs.

The crash landing was bumpy and I should be grateful the island was in my landing field or else I'd be sinking, and halfway to the ocean floor right now. A fate I'm not sure wouldn't be preferable at the moment. My arm is broken, and if I was a betting woman, I'd say I have a cracked rib or two. The seatbelt harness did its job a little too well. The rain started—a thick, soaking pound about the same time I crawled out of the cockpit and made it a safe distance away from the smoking, metal heap. The plane slid in hard after the stray bolt of lightning struck. The falling wobble was terrifying, taking all my strength to control it through the rough, wet sand. They talk about crash landings during flight lessons, but it doesn't prepare you for it happening in real life. I might still be breathing, but if I survive this, the whole thing shaved years off my life in anxiety alone.

Worse still, I didn't tell anyone I was going up. It's the number one rule. The only rule my daddy gave me with regards to the airport and the planes. I'm rain soaked with tears streaming down my face and completely alone. I sent out a mayday on the way down, but the electronics may have burnt out with the lightning strike so I don't know if it went through. It's a small plane without the fancy bells and whistles of the other planes we have. Some may say I was asking for trouble.

Maybe I was.

Maybe I knew this was some big, ironic conclusion to the relationship I knew was going to cause me pain and heartbreak. I suck in a sharp breath and wince when my ribcage expands. The smoke stream seeping from the plane grows as each second passes and I'm confident it will go up in flames. Not that I'd have the tools to fix it if it wasn't going to explode, nor the ability to get the thing back in the air without a runway. I'm stranded. Heartbreak keeps me company. Deep, perforating, soul searing heartbreak. I was careless, reckless in falling for a man obsessed with perfection. No one can live up to those standards. The betrayal I feel for my own decision is the second-string gut punch. Why did I let him in?

Standing, I swallow a sob and use my good arm to support the other, like a sling. *My bag. I had my bag.* Logic slips in for a brief moment and I remember I threw it into the cockpit when I rushed the hangar.

The cell phone is in it. For once, I have the stupid electronic device with me. The service might be spotty, but I know the phone works. In high school, we would pile into boats and come out to Shell Island to drink and party. Well, they would party, I was mostly the designated boat driver and people watcher. It was about a thirty-minute boat ride from Crick's Beach docks. Phones worked out here then, and service must have improved since high school.

Moving as quickly as I can, I hobble toward my airplane. The steaming and hissing grows louder with each step. Tripping on a piece of metal that used to be a beautiful wing, I pull myself up with my good arm. The bad arm stings with pain without support and a pathetic whimper escapes my lips.

The purse is wedged on the passenger seat side, next to the door. The straps are barely visible from this angle, but it's enough to let me know it's still intact. I make the decision to dive in quickly despite the sear of mangled bones, and make a grab for the handle. A few tugs prove it's stuck, which makes perfect sense, because why wouldn't it be? I bet the phone is crushed to bits. "Try Caroline," I whisper to myself. "You can do this. I can do this. I have to do this."

A sharp noise draws my attention away from my purse to the dark orange flame rising from the corner of my aircraft. Swallowing hard, I understand what's happening. My fight or flight response kicks in, my heart racing along in a disconnected way. One hard wiggle and tug, and my bag is free. I check the radio system one last time and confirm it is down, then turn from the airplane and run toward a grove of trees in the distance. Hoping they will provide shelter from the rain, I dump the contents of my purse on the sand. I see the familiar glow of the cell. I snatch it up with shaking fingers, open the first message on my list and tap out, *Shell Island*. I send it, and then try calling the airport, but it rings and rings. There's no White Knight coming after me. Those only exist in fairytales told to pacify children. The realities of life are far crueler, and littered with lies and unintended consequences.

I've always followed the rules—a good southern girl, a friend, a daughter. A person worthy of respect. This is what happens when good girls don't follow rules. I can't cover my eyes, count to ten, and take this back.

My whole body is shaking. I look at the rest of my belongings in the bag. An apple. A crumpled note that says, *you are perfect*, my wallet, and a bottle of water. I'm thinking, bitterly I might add, about the irony of this combination of things while lying down in the sand, adrenaline coursing through my veins numbing the pain I should be feeling.

Another sharp pop sounds from the plane behind me. I stand quickly and my head thwacks a low hanging branch. I see stars. More pain. Blackness goes in and out of focus.

Then I see flames, not just a thin rising, but a harried wildfire of destruction.

The explosion ricochets and I see nothing.

Because this is the hard truth about love.

It always goes up in flames.

Chapter One

Caroline

I found him there. In the space between who I was and who I wanted to be. In the place I've always been, the same small town I grew up in, surrounded by the people who love and loathe me in equal measure. He was sitting in a corner booth quietly, alone. His face a mask of contemplation. His body was more massive than anything I've ever seen in my lifetime, probably more chiseled than anything I will ever see in human form again. I've seen his kind lately, though. They opened a base on the water. It's secretive, small, and wrapped with barbed fencing so high it seems to touch the sky. I know they're here to protect our nation, but I can't help but be bitter at the intrusion. They remind me of everything that's been stolen.

The terror attacks that spanned the entire world rocked America right down to the core. Years later, we're still recovering, still rebuilding. We are still hunting the terrorists responsible for stealing hundreds of thousands of lives, and trying to keep it from happening again.

Our world changed that fateful day in a forever kind of way. While my small town, Bronze Bay, wasn't affected directly, the next town over had an entire shopping mall that burned to the ground. Two suicide bombers made sure there was nothing left but ashes. The Homecoming Queen from our rival high school was doing charity work there that day. Every single person in our country was affected in some way or another.

Martial Law lasted for what seemed like forever and the grocery store shelves were barren for months. It's lucky we're in a small town on the water with farmland surrounding us. We fished a lot, and I ate more seafood in that time period than I'll ever admit to. My mama's old diner closed for several months and the small airport my daddy owns and runs temporarily became a museum. A place for him to tinker with engines and work on small projects to keep his hands busy.

While it's hard not to stare at this large, out of towner, I intentionally look away. I do my best to avoid anything I'm not familiar with.

Shirley nudges me. "Do you see that cool drink of water?" she asks, leaning over to whisper in my ear. A pointless act, since every customer sitting at the bar top can hear her. They turn their gazes toward us, then away, knowing smirks on their faces.

Slicing a generous piece of apple pie, I keep my face neutral. "I saw him," I whisper, letting a fork clank against the hot plate. "He's been in twice this week."

Anytime an unfamiliar person enters our town for longer than a stop through, people notice. Anytime a man with the physical presence, and looks of a Hollywood action movie star shows up, people, especially my friend Shirley, are frothing at the mouth to know more. A man like the one in the corner booth is little more than fresh meat. One of these women will stake their claim soon enough, and it won't be me. Men like that don't notice women like me. A hint of embarrassment washes over me as I internally admit I've noticed him at all. When he's come in, he's never sat at one of my tables.

Shirley clicks her tongue. "He's in my section. I'm going to go give that man what he wants." She grabs a tray off the beat-up Formica counter, tucks a strand of bleached blonde hair behind her ear, and sets forth on her mission. I laugh to myself and pass the ketchup bottle to Bob, a regular, seated in front of me.

He winks at me, overhearing Shirley's departure. "You don't need no fake hair and brazen walk, Caroline. You've got it all in spades over all of 'em."

Smiling wide, I stifle my irritation. No one wants to be compared to other people. I give Carl, another regular, his pie while saying, "Thanks, Bob. I appreciate that. Can I get you anything else? No mustard with your fries today?" Shaking his head, he mumbles around a bite of food.

"Tell me if you need anything else," I say while turning my smile to Carl. He winks at me, and I take a quick glance at my full counter to make sure no one needs a refill before checking for orders in the kitchen behind me.

I've worked at my Mama's diner since I was old

enough to balance a tray and I've seen it all before. Secrets can't hide in a place like this, not in this town, anyways. They are whispered, passed from friend to friend, given life even if they aren't true. Botched proposals, cheating spouses, blackmail, stolen property—I've heard it all, even some things that will stay in my nightmares as long as I live.

Shirley comes up behind me, tucking her face close into my neck and says, "He. Is. Delicious. Caroline."

I laugh. "You think every man is delicious," I return, rolling my eyes so she can see my irritation. Shirley ignores me completely while she grabs an order, shaking her head to herself, a grin permanently affixed to her face. Glancing at the wall of a man briefly, I know he is a little more delicious than the standard Bronze Bay man. He's not wearing a fishing shirt, cowboy boots, or a cocky smile. His face is angular, stony. Thick lashes line his narrow eyes and his jaw is covered in a dark black scruff.

"Order up," Caleb calls, breaking me from my quiet daydream. "Caroline. It's yours," he adds on, grinning when he sees he's caught my attention.

I smile. No teeth. "Thanks, Caleb."

"What are you doing this weekend? Any big plans?" he asks, eyeing a few orders hanging in front of him. He's twenty-one, and he's been here since he graduated high-school. He's always been nothing except kind, but I also know he'd jump at the chance to be more than my friend. No one gets that kind of chance though, so I nod his way. "You heading to the spot tonight? Heard there's going to be a big party." Caleb throws three patties of meat on the grill, and then returns to the window.

I hang up another order while saying, "Still working on my apartment. I want to get it finished this month, so it's crunch time. No time left for much else. You should go to the spot. I bet it will be a blast!" The spot is a place in the woods off of one of the main roads in Bronze Bay. It's cleared for the most part and it's a never-ending tailgate party every single weekend. Usually there's a bonfire, someone ends up burning themselves, a dozen throw up in the woods, and at least one couple gets caught having sex by the canoe docks. I went a time or two when I was younger and I was shocked enough to stay away after that. Some nights the cops bust it up, other times they join in the debauchery. That's the charm of a small town. It's also the curse of it.

"I can help at your apartment. Got a set of hands that are at your disposal," Caleb replies, while laying cheese over the crackling meat.

I clear my throat. "That's okay. My Dad helped with the more in depth woodwork, and now it's stuff I can handle. Thanks for offering, though. I appreciate that." Because of my skills in tinkering with airplane engines, I'm really good with all household projects. I only needed my dad to help install the cabinets. I made them on my own.

Caleb's smile falls. "Oh," he grunts.

Damn basic bitch guilt. "Maybe another time though?" I add, internally groaning.

He brightens. "Sure thing, Caroline. Hope you get

everything finished and it comes out how you want it."

Sighing while simultaneously smiling, I turn back to the bar and fill a few glasses while checking on my customers. Pocketing a couple tips, I wipe off the counter and Shirley catches my eye. She's leaning over *his* table, elbows bent, butt in the air. She's laughing, presumably about something he said, but his face is flat, no telling signals if he's welcoming of her attention. Sipping his mug of coffee, his eyes leave her face and his gaze finds mine. Steely. Magnetic. A knowing smile tilts his mouth and just like that he turns to reply to Shirley.

Taking a deep breath, I realize I've been holding my breath while staring at him. I startle when someone lays a hand on my back. "You can leave whenever you want, sugar. I know you've been here since before the breakfast rush," Mama says, patting my back. At the reminder, my feet ache a bit.

"Why are you here so early? Is Daddy still at the airport?" I tell her, hugging her quickly before clearing Bob's plates and taking the twenty dollar bill he left under his plate. I talk to her while I cash out his tab, and pocket my tip. She tells me about her day with her friend Gloria. I love that I can help out here when she needs me. It's what I've always known. The diner is my safe haven.

"Daddy's there. He'll be there all night tinkering with heaven knows what. He said the apartment upstairs is almost ready. Y'all going to finish it this weekend then?"

Shaking my head, I tell her all we have left to do as excitement swells in my chest. Finally, a place of my own. A place I already love. It's two-thousand square feet of space above the enormous airplane hangar on our property. I'm about to tell her about the shade of white I picked for the exposed brick wall when Shirley saunters over to us. "Did Caroline tell you about my new boyfriend?" she coos at my mom.

I roll my eyes and wipe the counter. Again. Carl waves, and I wish him a good day.

Mama laughs. "Which one now?" she asks, humoring my friend who she's known almost as long as she's known me. It's been a friendship of a lifetime. I never left after high school and neither did Shirley. It was for different reasons, though. I love the airport. And flying. And I could never leave Bronze Bay behind because of it. The airport will be all mine one day soon. I've already taken over almost all of the business aspects. Shirley stayed because although she was smart enough for college, it wasn't anything she wanted. After that decision was made, staying made the most sense.

"His name is Tyler, he works at the new base off Island Run Trail and," Shirley says, jerking her head in his direction, "he's single."

I sigh. "Of course he is. Look at him. He doesn't look like the type of guy that keeps a woman. Not one, at least."

"You're such a sorry sport, Caroline. One day you'll realize what you're missing," Shirley says, her lip turning up in a snarl. "I'm going to ask him out," she finishes, her chin high.

"You should. He's perfect for you," I return.

My mom nudges me with her shoulder. "Why don't

you ask him out instead?"

Shirley laughs and I turn to look at my mother dearest. "Not you too!" I nearly shout. "Come on. I can't catch a break."

Beside me, Caleb appears his dirty apron hanging over one arm. "Everyone thinks you should go on a date then, huh?" he asks, his voice low, stance wide. "I tried!" He exclaims.

"Oh, Caleb, honey. It's not you. It's her," Shirley says, turning her charm onto the short order cook. I have to give her credit. She's a horny chameleon. I'm used to everyone discussing my lack of relationship status. That's nothing new. If it gives them something innocent to talk about, so be it.

Mama saves me by making small talk with Caleb about his upcoming shifts, and Shirley clears one of her other tables. *Tyler*, I think. My best friend doesn't get a chance to ask him out. He stands and his sheer size is overwhelming. More than one person turns to look in his direction.

He's at least 6'2 and his clothes pull against every chiseled muscle on his body. No, he's definitely not a Bronze Bay man. This man-beast is in a league all of his own. His hair is dark, and the scruff on his face says he doesn't give a shit, and he knows it looks hot. He has big blue eyes, a jawline that is magazine worthy, and a straight angled nose. In other words, he must be a horrible person because his exterior is pretty damn close to perfection.

Tyler's boots are heavy against the tile as he makes

his way to the front door. Before he opens it, he glances at me long enough to give me a smug, crooked grin. No teeth.

The bell bangs on the glass door as he leaves. I swallow hard.

"Oh, my God. He totally wants you," Shirley says, witnessing his barely there grin.

I raise one brow. "Right. Of course he does," the sarcasm dripping as I speak. Changing my tone and being serious, I say, "I bet you get that date the next time he comes in."

Shirley is swearing under her breath as she goes to clean the beasts table.

Taking off my apron, I put it in the basket under the counter labeled with my name. I grab my messenger bag, kiss my mama and throw a quick goodbye to my disgruntled bestie.

Once outside, my eyes turn to the sky. Hopping on my bicycle, I ride, half distracted by clouds to the airport. The roads are never too busy here and we are close enough to the coast you can always smell the saltwater no matter where you are.

Someone honks, but I ignore it.

I'm almost to my happy place.

Chapter two

Tahoe

They made me come here. It was under the pretense that only my particular expertise could serve this command. In reality, my bosses sent me here because I slipped up. Overworked, and dog tired, my mistake got a brother shot. As if living with that knowledge isn't enough, I'm now forced to associate with the small-town folks of Bronze Bay that look at me like I'm the statue of David. Or a pariah, I can't really be sure.

Relax, they told me—focus on making sure everything runs smoothly. Work-out, keep my aim sharp, keep my ears open and my eyes wide. Terrorists lurk everywhere and I know this first hand. It's why I'm a heap of muscle and mess. It's why all of my brothers in arms are busy hunting people down. It's why I'm burnt out, why I haven't had a true life outside of work in years. A decade?

My new motto is three words. Keep it simple. It should be easy in a place like this. No one moves very fast and it almost seems life exists separate from rest of the world here. The people are friendly, the beaches are nice, and the women are rabid for fresh meat. I went to the solitary bar in town last weekend and could have taken home at least five different women. I didn't, though. It wasn't that kind of night. I'm still getting the lay of the land, trying to figure out where I fit into the scheme of things, absorbing the details most gloss over. This weekend I'll go back for other, more selfish reasons.

After glancing over a report about an incident back home in San Diego, I head into the conference room for the daily meeting. It's a run down on who is doing what and who is allowed where, a never-ending list of small tasks that need to be accomplished. With a base on this side of the Gulf of Mexico and another on the East coast of Florida we've been moving boats all over the place so we can be as fast acting as possible. Pensacola took a huge hit in the attacks and those in charge felt it was safer to have a new base for us to operate out of rather than try to move in on the destruction. Knock on wood, it's been slow days at the office since we got here.

"I want to secure an airport," Leif says, leaning back in his chair and propping his feet on the long table.

"For jumping?" I ask, narrowing my eyes. "Or?"

"Yeah, for jumping, and it would be nice to have something closer if we need to get somewhere quicker. The main airfield is quite a distance away. We always planned on building an airport here."

I pick at my thumb nail. "We aren't on the first call list. We're not going anywhere fast, bro. I can see having something for jumping though. That would be fun." I nod, thinking about skydiving. There's little else that thrills in the same way. Wind hitting my body, the black of night encasing me, my very existence teetering in my hands only to save by the pull of a string.

"The May Airport? Down on the other side of town?" I ask, keeping my eyes on the nail.

"That's the only one," Leif says, sliding a printout across the table. "Our budget was upped again so buying it outright won't be a problem. This will be much easier than building one."

"Hasn't that been in their family for generations? What makes you think they'll sell?"

Leif opens his oversized arms to the sides. "Look around. If the price is right these people will do anything." He fails to realize the people of Bronze Bay love their lives and wouldn't change a thing. I haven't been here long, but something like pride in your family establishment is an easy understanding.

I nod, shrugging my shoulders. "Sure. Okay. I'll feel him out. I can head over after this, I brought the truck today." Honestly, most days it's easier to bike in to work, but I bought an old jalopy of a truck when I first arrived. I'd sold all of my possessions before I moved across the country. What I didn't have time to sell, I gave away to my friends. "Anything else? I read the reports about the incident in San Diego," I say, changing the subject.

Leif shakes his head and tells me a few other tidbits

of information he's gleaned and we start wrapping the meeting.

"Call me and let me know what you find out about airport," Leif calls at my back.

I throw up a hand, and nod. "Diving tomorrow?" I toss back on second thought.

"Yes. Then the range. Check out the weapons you'll want before you get in."

A day full of my favorite things. Bonus points for not doing them while my life is on the line.

My truck doesn't start when I turn the key. Hopping out of the tattered cab, I pop the hood and mess around with the spark plugs I know are on their last leg. Sure enough, a little twisting and the truck rumbles to life. It will be a fun weekend project—something to keep my hands and mind busy. The mundane. Something I've only had in insignificant doses over the last decade.

There's no need for GPS or navigation in Bronze Bay. There's the water side and inland. Now that we're here, we've taken up a huge chunk of the water side, securing government water for our boats and our diving. The beaches are fenced off on either side of our compound. I'm driving inland now, toward May Airport. There's tall grass growing on the sides of the roads and the houses are few and far between. I turn down an unpaved road that's half seashells and half dusty rock pieces. The only indication this is where I need to be is the large rectangular sign proclaiming this as May Airport. The font is square and large in a bright shade of red. It reminds me of something you'd see in an antique shop.

The landing strip comes into view as does a cluster of airplane hangars, one larger than the others. I pull into a spot that looks as if other vehicles have parked before and hop out into a cloud of salty dust. I traded my uniform for my standard black tee and jeans before I left work. Not that it makes me any less conspicuous. The word outsider might as well be tattooed on my forehead. The residents know I'm not the standard fare newcomer. I'm an intruder.

A loud engine roars from somewhere in the general vicinity breaking up the silence.

"Can I help you?" A man calls over the noise.

I turn toward the voice and see an older man wearing a bright Hawaiian shirt. I put up one hand in a wave. "Hi sir, I was hoping to speak to the owner," I say, approaching slowly.

The man perches both hands on her hips. "Depends on which one you're looking for and why, but I suppose I fit that description," he says, grinning while extending his hand in my direction. I don't miss the way his eyes scan my body from my head to my toe. "What can I help you with? We don't get visitors very often."

What he means is he doesn't get visitors like me.

Shaking his hand, I ask if there's somewhere we can talk with a little less noise. He tells me it's an airport and I should expect some degree of noise at all times. I laugh, grin widely, and pretend not to be annoyed. It probably doesn't work well. I've been told my smile resembles The Joker, Heath Ledger style.

"Let's head to the office," Mr. May inclines his head to the large hangar beside him. I follow warily, taking note of everything around me. Running an airport has to be tiresome, but I imagine the only people using it are the extremely wealthy or the hobbyists. The light metal exterior of the hangar belies the contents. After I walk through the door I'm met with air conditioning. That's the first surprise. The second is that it's actually really nice inside. There's an office to the right and a spiral staircase to the left of the office. A door straight in the back ostensibly leads to the portion of the hangar where actual aircrafts are stored. "Right through here, Mr.," May pauses, waiting for me to offer my name.

Clearing my throat, I say, "Tyler. Tyler Holiday. It's nice to meet you," I say, walking into the office. May leaves the door open and walks to the other side of the room where a small mini fridge buzzes in the corner.

"Can I offer you something to drink, Tyler Holiday?" I don't want anything, but rejecting hospitality is bad form.

"Sure. Please," I say, nodding to the bottle of iced tea in his left hand. A can of *Bud Light* is in his right.

After he hands me the tea, he cracks the beer and downs half. "I'm here on behalf of The Bronze Bay Naval Compound," I edge.

He nods. "Of course you are, son." He lowers his chin while staring at me. "The question is what are you doing at my airport?"

He knows. He must have anticipated something like this. "We were hoping to inquire about the procurement of your fine facilities," I say, setting the bottle down on a table next to me. I don't take my eyes off his face, eager to glean any tells he may give. Nothing. "We are prepared to pay you handsomely."

May laughs loudly, bringing one hand to his chest, covering a smudge of grease marring his tropical ensemble. "I thought you might say something like that. You know this land has been in my family for generations, right? I'm sure you've done your research so that means you're plumb crazy." He's still shaking his head, disbelief washing every feature. I stay silent, as I know he's not finished. "Rent. I figured you'd come here and want to rent some time or perhaps even a hangar to store a plane or two. Never, in my wildest dreams, did I think you'd come here asking to purchase my crown jewel."

I told Leif. I knew this would be the outcome. My goal now is to figure out how to sway his mind. "I can assure you, if you sell May Airport to our command, the memory will live on. We won't change the name," I say, grasping at straws.

"Sell the airport?" A woman screeches from behind us.

Turning quickly, I see the person from which the squeal came from. "Caroline, honey. It's fine. I've got this under control. Mr. Holiday, may I introduce you to my daughter. She's half owner of the business and property you're wishing to purchase." His laughter trips his words and I'm left feeling like I'm lacking armor and weapons while lying in wait for a killing blow.

"Did I hear you right?" Caroline says, leaning against the doorway, one tan leg propped on the other like a flamingo. Her shorts are short and her dirty t-shirt is knotted, exposing a sliver of sun kissed stomach. Several strands of golden blonde hair that escaped her pony tail fall into her face. "My airport? First you take over my favorite beach. The very one where I took my first steps and block it off to the public, but now you want *my* airport? I don't think so. Take your beast body and your handsome offer and leave. There's not a fiery chance in hell you'll get your mitts on my family's airport." Her face is red, and she's leaning forward now, like a lion about to pounce on prey.

I hold my hands out in front of me. May laughs, and a vision of a torture device pops into my mind. I hear him drain the rest of his beer. "Sure you didn't mean handsome body and beast offer? Cause that would make a lot more sense. No need for the hostile measures. I came here in peace," I reply, using a calming voice.

"Peace?" Caroline nearly yells, stepping toward me, one finger extended. "You represent everything except peace. You're not even allowed to say that word. Who are you exactly? One of those SEALs?"

There's no need to lie. "Yes. I'm one of those SEALs. You know, the men that protect your freedom, your nation, the ones that keep the peace," I say, emphasizing the last word. "We're here to better protect America, Caroline." At the mention of her name, she calms, swallowing hard. "I came here to merely ask about negotiations. We need facilities such as yours to train. Skydiving and what not. Skills that help us do our job. That means peace for *you*."

She backs down immediately and her eyes change. For the first time, she looks at me instead of what I represent and she's affected. Her huge, crystal blue eyes land on mine. Yes. Familiar territory. I flash her a small grin, teasing my bottom lip with my top teeth—a small gesture the average person wouldn't pick up on, but something someone attracted to me will zone in on quickly. "Negotiations. Fine," she says. Taking a huge, visible breath, she walks into the office and leans against the wall to the right.

Caroline blows a strand of hair off her face. Recognition dawns. "You work at the diner," I say, narrowing my eyes.

"Mrs. May owns the diner and Caroline helps out. This is her primary focus though. She's building a right fine apartment upstairs. I'm retiring!" May exclaims, rummaging the fridge for another beer. This town is smaller than I ever imagined. Everything and every person is interconnected in some form. Lesson learned.

Caroline rolls her eyes in her father's direction. "I'm taking it over willingly. It's my dream," she says quietly, like her dream should be silenced. "I'm the main pilot these days. Daddy, I mean, Mr. May is a master engineer and mechanic. Between the two of us we can fix anything." May takes this as his cue to exit the office.

"It's a fine dream," I reply, standing straighter. "Perhaps I can help make it happen quicker?" Leif can suck my cock. I know what I'm capable of getting from these people. I also know how I'm going to get it.

Her arms folded across her chest she widens her eyes. "I'm waiting," she exclaims.

"I'm prepared to rent the entire airport for one day, every week. This is what we'll pay you annually," I say, grabbing a pen from the small desk, I scribble a number on the sheet Leif gave me with their information. The math was done in my head and double checked in mere seconds. It's one of my gifts. Keeping the paper in my hands, I show her the number, holding it a foot from her face. "Deal." I say, instead of asking.

Her eyes widen as she takes in the offer and all the zeros following it. "What if it's no deal?" she asks, her eyes finally flicking up to meet mine.

This moment is important. It's more important than

anything money can buy. I run my eyes down her body, slowly, and all the way back up. Her chest heaves as her breaths come quicker—her cheeks flush, and huge doe eyes belie an innocence I haven't seen in a long time. Her gaze fixates on my mouth. I lick my lips.

I shrug my shoulders up and down once. "Then I'll be here every day trying to get what I want. It's up to you."

Chapter three

Caroline

He's waiting outside the diner for me to finish my shift, tossing an apple from hand to hand like a bored, annoying twelve-year-old. Every day this week he's been standing out there waiting for me. I even tried to switch my shifts around to catch him off guard, but that persistent bastard figured it out. Mama swears she didn't tell him anything and Shirley uses her big smile whenever I ask her what the ogre is doing peeping in our windows. Something she does both when she's telling the truth and lying, so I can't be sure what is going on. The only reason I haven't given him an answer about using my airport is because I honestly don't know if it's the right decision. What if it's the first step in total domination? The whole saying "give someone an inch and they take a mile" scares me.

If the fervor in which he's pursuing me means anything, the man wants the airport badly. All of it. Not just rented time for a sum of money that would make an oil tycoon's eyes widen. For the most part I've been cordial and kind. I'm southern, those traits are bred into me, but I can't help the snark that comes after a long day. He's a welcome sight, don't get me wrong, it's the second he opens his mouth that the mystique goes out the window. Something in the way he speaks—the tone of his voice tells me not to trust him. That's another southern specialty. Sniffing out lies.

"He didn't even ask about the airport yesterday, Caroline. Why don't you just give in and go out with the man? Did you ever think he might just want to get to know you?"

I smile. "You think a man like that wants to get to know me? Come on, Shirl, you're too smart for that."

Shirley drags a rag over a table, leaning over, eyes to the window in thought. "What if you believe the best until he proves you wrong?"

It's easy for a beautiful woman like Shirley to assume the best until the worst rears. She has options. Limitless options in men. For someone like me, a woman who is a slave to her hobbies and passions, I hope one day to find a man who will put up with being second fiddle.

Sighing, I take a bite of the pizza in front of me. Caleb made me a quick lunch before he left for the day and Daniel took over the kitchen. Daniel is far less jovial—with hard lines creasing his face like scars of anger. "I need to make a decision and then he'll go away."

"Or be in your business constantly. He'll be at your house for crying out loud," Shirley says, accent twanging. "Have a passion filled day…and night with that man and get this over with. I can't think of a better person to pop your icy cherry than that man." She nods at the window, at Tyler. He's shirtless now, balancing the apple on his chin. "That takes skill." She's shaking her head, like she's actually impressed.

Laughing, I finish my pizza, tell Desmond a few things and ditch my apron. "It takes something. Not sure if skill is the word I'd use."

"Commend the man's persistence! I've never been on the receiving end of something like that!" Shirley coos into my ear, leaning close.

"Because your morals are as loose as your," I whisper into her ear.

Shaking her head, she leaves me to steel my nerves. Business Caroline needs to bubble to the surface. Savvy. Confident. Willful. Qualities I don't have. In high school I let a rumor swirl for months because I was too meek to correct anyone. It was easier to be silent, take the path of least resistance. I can find my voice now because something I love is being threatened. My short, white, dress uniform is miraculously still clean as I freshen up in the bathroom.

"He's just a man," I tell my reflection. One that wants more than I'm willing to give, the practical side of my brain reminds me.

When I push open the side door the hot, swampy air coats me. A light sheen of condensation takes hold of every exposed skin cell on my body. My white bike is parked in the rack on the side of the restaurant, a pile of empty cardboard boxes stacked next to it. There's no need to put a lock on my bike here, not anywhere in Bronze Bay, actually. I wheel it to the front of the restaurant, ready for Tyler's daily joke. He has a new one every day and they've progressively gotten worse. My guess is he doesn't have a humorous bone in his body. He probably googles dad jokes and uses the ones that come up first.

"Shouldn't you be working or something? For someone who has such an important job, you have a lot of time to waste," I say, putting a hand on my hip, my gaze focused anywhere but his shirtless chest. We're in Florida so it's common place for men and boys to run around without shirts on. It's a beach town. Somehow he makes shirtless seem triple x. From my peripheral vision I see a red bike with a large basket in the front, the same as my cruiser, but larger, and older. "Got a bicycle, huh?"

"Yesterday I ran behind your bike all the way to the airport, remember? This will be a little easier on my lungs. It's so humid here. How do you deal with it? I feel like a fish, sucking in water with my oxygen."

Laughing, I let my guard slip. "I don't know anything else. It's what I grew up in."

"You don't even sweat," Tyler exclaims, gesturing to my body. It's true, I don't. A dewy glow is all I get. Even after a workout, a thick sheen is my sole sweat reward. I heard it's good to sweat, so it's not a quality I'm proud of, but it is convenient.

Shrugging, I throw a leg over my bike as daintily as I can with the kitschy dress. "Is that an opening for today's joke?" I ask. "You don't have to follow me home today.

My daddy isn't there so you won't be able to work him."

I meet his eyes for the first time, and it's a mistake. "Who said I was trying to work *him*?"

Swallowing hard, I take a deep breath. "How long are you going to do this?"

"I don't know what you mean," Tyler replies, not missing a beat. "I was just working out yesterday. It's a free country. I can run anywhere I please." He grins. I don't miss the joke. "Are you going to come out for a drink with me tonight?" he asks. "It's Friday."

"Oh, there's the joke. I was starting to wonder if you'd lost your impeccable touch."

Tyler winces, an exaggerated gesture, while flashing—white, perfect teeth and dimples. "That wasn't a joke, but I didn't have one for today so it can be if you want." A bead of sweat slides down his neck and cuts a path down his rippled, tattooed chest. A slow blink cuts my view and I suck in a deep breath.

"What if I get a drink with you? Will you leave me alone and let me make a decision about the airport in peace?"

"I enjoy your company," he replies, hopping on his bike, facing me. It looks ridiculous. He's so enormous. His bathing suit is hung so low on his narrow hips I know he's wearing nothing underneath. "Give me a chance. That's all I'm asking. Let me be useful. I saw the paint cans yesterday. I'm a monster with a paint roller. What do you say?"

Even if he's only paying attention to me because he

wants something, I can't deny how it makes me feel. I've never felt like this before. This sort of mix between lusting for something I know is bad for me, and the vulnerability of knowing I don't have the first clue how to deal with a man like Tyler. He's sweating everywhere now: face, arms, legs, and his gleaming torso. I tilt my head to the side and narrow my eyes. "You help me paint the harder to reach areas, I get a drink with you, and then you leave me alone. No more bad jokes, or stalking me at work," I say, waving my arm to the diner, and then back to him.

"Deal. Can we get going now though? If I don't get some airflow, I'll melt."

I smirk, and start peddling for home. His bike squeaks behind me until we reach the hangar. I didn't lie about my daddy being gone, but I forgot what that would mean. I'd be here by myself with this man. Parking my bike, I try to ignore the flip-flop sensation in my stomach. Tyler reaches over and grabs his shirt out of the basket on his bike. I hold the door open after I unlock it and enter. "You need to grease your bike. It sounds like something out of a horror movie," I remark, making my way to the office to see if there's anything pressing I need to deal with. This building has a faint smell of oil covered in the vanilla scent I use to pretend my house is normal—not an airplane hangar.

Tyler uses his t-shirt to towel off the sweat while standing in the office doorway. "I bought it at a yard sale while I was walking to the diner today," he admits. "I'll get it fixed up."

"You sure are adjusting to small town living rather quickly," I say, thumbing through the stack of mail, eyeing his muscles as be bends to wipe his legs.

I pull out one of the envelopes I know is a bill, and rip into it. "The whole reason I'm here is for a change of pace. I figured it would serve me best if I took full advantage of everything Bronze Bay has to offer." The double entendre was covered well, but, of course I heard it.

"What's it like?" I ask, unable to keep my curiosity under wraps.

"What's what like?" Tyler replics, without looking up.

I clear my throat, and hot shame rises for asking something so personal. "The war? Living in a big city? Life outside of here?" It's personal on my side, too. It rips the small-town girl wide open, showing all my stereotypical cards.

Tyler stands, sighs, and walks away from the doorway, toward the paint cans at the base of the spiral staircase that leads to my home. "You show me yours and I'll show you mine," he says, picking up the four cans, two in each huge hand and starts up the stairs. "I have to know what a house inside a hangar looks like," he states, like he's actually, truly curious.

I follow behind him, grabbing the brushes, rollers, and the bills I need to sort later tonight. "It's homier than you would think. It's taken a couple years for me to get it to this point, but I'm living here full time now. Finally out of my parent's house. They live just over the hill to the east."

Tyler laughs, and presses himself against the railing so I can get by to unlock the huge, black, iron door. "What's funny?"

"I guess that everything is so perfect here. It's like this place is unaffected by everything. It's hard not to get caught up in the mirage of safety, that's all. Your town, Bronze Bay is the exception, not the rule. You talk about your parent's house over the hill, and everyone rides bikes and no one gets shot at and I'm wondering what planet I'm living on." He shakes his head. "I guess that must be the whole point. Why I'm here instead of back there." He didn't say, instead of home, and I wonder what that means.

He inadvertently answered my questions about the war and city life. "Are you trying to be offensive, because like I said, I don't need your help." I push open the door and motion for him to enter in first. He does, leaning over to drop the cans by the front door. He keeps his head up as he takes in the huge room before him.

Shaking his head, he says, "Didn't mean to sound offensive, it's a big change, that's all. For me." His gaze widens as he takes in my pride and joy. People looked at me like I was crazy when I told them I was building this apartment, in an airplane hangar, at the airport. They don't understand me. Not one bit.

The floors are salvaged hardwood from an enormous

shed and stable that was destroyed by a hurricane a few years ago. I hauled most of it in here by myself after taking months to sort through it. The walls have been painstakingly lined with brick to make it more secure and the exposed pipework curves around the ceiling like a maze. "This is amazing. I've never seen anything like it," he says, walking in further to look out of one of the huge back windows. It's one of my favorite features. It has a view of the runway and I can see planes take-off and land in the distance. There's green as far as the eye can see, and a sliver of beach off the coast side. The view holds everything I love in a snapshot. Leave it to an outsider to *get it.*

"I love it," I admit. "I plan to stay here forever so I wanted it to be perfect."

His eyebrows raise and lower in surprise. "I can't say I blame you and that's pretty shocking."

I look at him sideways. He's wearing his sweat soaked shirt. "How is it shocking?"

He shakes his head, as if he's day dreaming. "No, I didn't mean it's shocking you'd want to live here forever. It's shocking I can understand why. I've been everywhere, you know? All over the world and there's never been a place I've wanted to be for longer than a little while. This place is really beautiful," Tyler says. "I can't wait to skydive over it."

Reality crash. "I haven't agreed to anything yet."

He shrugs. "We'll build an airport somewhere else in Bronze Bay then. Figured you'd want the income, though." He nods to the stack of bills I haven't put down. I should have known he'd know the debt our business carries. The government knows everything these days.

My face heats under his gaze, and I'm too mad to say anything at all and that fact infuriates me even further.

"Call me Tahoe, by the way. All my friends, do." Right now I want to call him a string of ugly swear words. He slides a pocket knife out of his shorts pocket and stoops to open a can of white paint, the view and my parent's house all but forgotten. I have a drop cloth and everything ready to go. "You're painting all of the brick, white?"

"I'm not your friend so I will call you Tyler, and yes. Start at the top, close to the pipes."

He pays me no mind and just starts painting. I watch him for a solid fifteen minutes to make sure he's doing a sufficient job and then retreat to my bathroom to change into a pair of board shorts and a tank top. I throw my hair in a messy bun and try to calm my rage. Why am I so angry?

Because Tyler is right. We do need the money, and my thought process has led me to realize I need to be nice to this man even if his presence makes me madder than a poked rattler.

"I don't need your help with any of this. I just want to make that clear. You've been driving me nuts and I figure this might relieve some of the…annoyance," I say, when I return mostly so he knows I'm back in his vicinity.

He grunts. "Everyone could use a hand. Even the

people who refuse it time and time again."

"Are you talking about yourself or me?" I say, picking up a clean brush and dipping it into the bright white. "I'll work on trim."

Tyler nods. "I'm talking about anyone who the statement can apply to. I'm really not big into talking," he says, flicking his gaze down to meet mine. A shiver rakes my whole body.

I laugh nervously. "Okay. Are you some kind of robot? How do you live without speaking to other humans?"

He sighs. "All the humans I'm surrounded with don't ask me questions...like that," he explains. "It's easy that way. Less complicated. You seem like an uncomplicated person and you also seem like you could use a hand."

Carefully, and slowly, on my knees, I brush the baseboards until the standard cream color turns white. I'm not sure if being uncomplicated is a compliment or an insult, and I think it was a purposeful tactic used to confuse me even further. "Maybe if you talked more you wouldn't be here," I say, trying to engage in a different direction. It's rude to dodge questions, but he didn't ask any questions. Not flat out, anyways.

"It might be a good thing I'm here," he replies almost before the statement left my mouth.

"I talk all the time and my life is easy," I argue.

He grins, it's sharp and full of an emotion I can't put my finger on. "I think you just proved my point, darling. That said, it seems your life isn't well rounded either. You don't have a boyfriend or he'd be here rolling paint, and you have a hard time making decisions."

My brush drops into the paint tray. "Excuse me? I make thoughtful decisions. You're just a brute and a bully." I have to remind myself how this man got inside my house to begin with.

"Ah, so no boyfriend. Gotcha'. What happened? Was it him or was he just not that into you?" he grins.

"I didn't invite you in to let you insult me," I snarl. "You annoyed your way in here. The least you can do is act like a civil gentleman!"

He drops his roller so the end hits the floor and faces me. "I didn't come here to be interviewed," Tyler replies, and his eyes narrow as he lets his gaze slide from the top of my head down to my feet, leaving a trail of fire on my skin. "And I'm not civilized." Tyler licks his lips, then shakes his head. "Not anything even close to a gentleman, either." He leans his head to one side and then the other, like he's stretching after a workout. I'm left breathless, in a state so unfamiliar, my body feels like a traitorous enemy.

"Why did you come here?" I raise on brow, challenging him to do something he doesn't want to do. Talk. And because I'm breathless, wondering how in the world this man can affect me so swiftly when no other man in the past has, and surely they've tried, right?

He pauses, stares me down once again, and then turns away and starts painting again. I clear my throat and sigh to the roof. "Boyfriends take time. Time is precious to me. I'd rather be doing other things. Like flying planes or working on engines, or helping my parents. It's my choice to be single, and quite honestly I enjoy doing house projects on my own," I say, slinging one hand on my hip. "Key words: on my own."

He nods, his face thoughtful and dips the roller again. A drop of white paint lands on his burly, tattooed forearm. I watch it slide a few centimeters as he works the roller up and down.

"I came here because it's fun to…annoy you, and believe it or not, I don't have very many friends here," he replies, smiling. That brings my gaze to his face.

Pressing my lips together I remark, "You don't say? Most people respond better to kindness than intimidation. Just for your information." I offer him something to drink and he declines, I offer him to sit down on the sofa and take a breather and he declines. I give up on trying to talk to him or trying to get anything more from him than an arm with a paint roller in it.

After I finish painting the baseboard against the longest wall, I start making dinner. "Are you hungry?" I call across the room. It's an open floor plan. One huge room with everything except my bed and bathroom which is behind a half wall in the far corner. My damn southern hospitality kicks in as I envision my mother telling me to be a good host.

"Does a bear shit in the woods?" Tyler replies, appearing from the side. "Please, that is. If you're cooking. I would love to eat." His smile widens, then he pulls his bottom lip in between his teeth.

Before he sees me blush, I look away. "So you're nice when I leave you alone for a while? Noted. I was going to make a grilled chicken salad," I explain, opening the fridge, and then the freezer just to see what supplies I have. "Is that okay?" I pull the ingredients out before he has time to respond.

"Not so much leaving me alone, more about talking about things I'm agreeable to."

"Food is okay to talk about, but anything personal is off limits?" I ask. "Where I come from it's rude to be in male company without a buffer. I don't even know you, other than you want to take my airport from me. I feel like you should offer me something of substance." I light the pilot on my oven and pull out two plates from above the sink. Tyler's gaze pierces through me. "Or you can stand there and stare at me like a creep," I add on, opening the drawer for the silverware I'll need.

I feel him then, his body heat against my back. Tyler smells like dried sweat and a faint hint of sweetness mixed with paint. I swallow hard. "I told you I'm not a gentleman, Caroline. I don't play by the rules. For me, there are no rules, just what I want and what you're willing to give me."

I spin to face him and I lose my breath. He looms large, his massive chest at eye level, his crystal blue eyes challenging me—taunting me. "You can't have my airport," I say.

Tyler throws his head back and laughs, his muscular neck widening and rippling as I watch in awe. "What do you want to know?" he asks, when he finally stops laughing.

Folding my arms across my chest, I ask, "Are you making fun of me?"

He shakes his head. "No. Not at all." Backing away from me, he releases me from his masculine spell. How confusing, how embarrassing.

"Tell me the basics. Where are you from, your family, you know? Typical things friends discuss."

"You said you weren't my friend." Tyler tilts his head to the side, hitting me with a smarmy grin.

My stomach flips, and my heart rattles against my chest. He saves me from responding by humming briefly. "I am the product of the Navy. My dad served and we moved all over the world while I was growing up. The longest time I've ever been somewhere was when I lived in San Diego, after I became a SEAL. The Teams gave me my first true home. The brotherhood provided me with the only siblings I'll ever have. My Dad is retired now and him and my Mom live in Northern California." Tyler pauses. "I visit them every once in a while, but they know my life. They respect my decision, so they're less needy than other families." He leans against the counter with one large hand, his fingers tracing the edge of the white marble.

I swallow, surprised by his honesty. "You weren't lying about traveling everywhere, were you?"

He laughs, shakes his head, and then leans his back against the spot where his hand just was.

"No girlfriend then? You'd be rolling paint at her house if you had one."

Biting his lip, he blinks slowly. "Well played," he replies. "I saw how the military broke families. I've avoided as many relationships as I possibly could because of that first-hand knowledge." His face changes, then. Almost like the guard he keeps in place wilted a touch by telling me something personal. I can tell he wasn't lying before, he doesn't talk about this kind of stuff. "I like to keep things simple now." He drums his fingers on the stone behind him.

After an awkward pause he tells me a story about how as a young child he rode a subway alone to school when he was in Japan. I marvel at his tale. With my interest, he continues to tell me tales of his amazing life. His bravery transcends that which most would label brave. His stories are surreal given my limited experience with traveling. He can tell I'm eating up every word because he keeps talking, keeps my mind spinning. Sometimes he uses his arms when he talks and he reminds me of Thor, or some WWE wrestler because he looks so big in here—like maybe a horse or a bear found its way into a house on accident.

I serve the salads on large plates and set them on the table. He watches me move, and I'm a little less self-conscious as time passes. I still hate him and what he stands for, but I guess he's not the most horrible of company. Especially when he's telling me cool stories.

"Grab a couple napkins from the holder behind you,

Tahoe, and give me a month to decide" I ask almost on an impulse, trying my best to keep a grin off my face.

He nods, turns and grabs the napkins, and smiles, his face aimed at the floor, all the way to the table.

Chapter Four

Tahoe

The water is so fucking clear and warm compared to the west coast. Diving is much easier when that's the case. In order to keep up on my dive qualification, and get paid for it, I have to do a major dive every so often. Today, the lot of us went out and did a dive with full gear. I'm always surprised by how tired I am after a long day of diving. While I'm suspended in the water, my flippers on, it's like I'm as light as a feather. I'm at peace in the water, a quality that most SEALs have, but some don't. Some hate the fucking water with a passion. They are the ones that struggle through BUD/s training and only the strongest will make it through. It's the end of the day, and our sleek, matte gray boat is carrying us across the glassy water back to our docks.

As we pull closer, I see her sitting on one of the old wooden docks to the left, tan legs a mile long, bare feet kicking the water back and forth. She sees us, but she doesn't see me—can't distinguish who is who while we're all wearing the same black wetsuits and gear. She brings a hand up to shield her eyes from the setting sun as she seeks me out.

"Your puppy looks lost, Tahoe," my teammate Aidan remarks, mirth tainting his observation.

I shake my head as I walk up the deck of the boat, dripping water as I go. "Aren't dogs supposed to obey?"

He replies, "Puppies don't. They chew up everything in sight for months. My buddy got a lab and that thing ate the legs off a goddamn table!" It's like a light switch with most of us. We're finished working. Now we can talk about dogs, puppies, and beautiful, unnerving woman who sit on docks. I merely shake my head at his analogy.

"Leash trained, then. Job well done, Tah," my friend says. It's a joke meant to make me laugh, but it makes my empty stomach swirl with unease. I've never been around a woman quite like Caroline before. I thought the innocence was a front, a gimmick to make a man interested. I tested it a few times and came on to her hardcore—full on Tahoe wants to fuck, but while her body responded—her cheeks pinked, her breathing harried, and her eyes widened, she didn't act on it. No, she wasn't sure what to do with any of it.

"Shut up, bro. She doesn't do what I say. She doesn't do anything I want," I remark, sliding the shoulders on the wetsuit down. On a second thought, I make a snap decision to lie. I tell him how she sucks amazing dick. We're grown men and yet I feel the urge to hide the fact I'm spending so much time with a woman in a platonic way. Like maybe they'll realize I really am truly fucked up and belong in Florida instead of in San Diego with my best buddies. San Diego Tahoe would have a different meaningless brunette every day of the week.

He leans against me as he shimmies his own wetsuit down, like a sticky second skin. "Ah, so the truth is finally freed. All it took was a little southern dime piece to tell you no snakes in the grass. I'll write it in my calendar," he growls, lowering his voice as we approach said dime piece. His sentiment isn't entirely untrue. She's not telling me no for the reason he thinks. Caroline isn't answering *any* of my questions.

I catch her eye, finally, and she smiles, her pink lips tilting to one side. "Don't bust my balls. Caroline does that enough for ten people. She owes me a decision today," I remark, aiming my words his way. Checking my watch, I confirm it's been exactly a month today. A month of me trying to get a read on her, 30 days of trying to get into her pants, two fortnights and two days of challenge and entertainment, of house projects and laughs and stupid arguments.

"You need to seal that fucking deal. I need to get in the air. I'm surprised Leif didn't break ground on a new airport. We're all itching for sky diving." The same time they sent me here, to Bronze Bay, Florida, they opened up several other small SEAL bases in coastal states. San Diego and Virginia Beach are still the main bases, but our reaction times are quicker now that we have smaller ones staffed around the U.S.

"These things take time. You know that. This is taking even less time because we're handling the deal in first person instead of a middle man coming in here and complicating everything that much more." I clear my throat. "She's going to agree to it. We'll be jumping by next week." As I say those words, I let my gaze find Caroline. My teammate slaps me on a wet shoulder and heads for the office. I veer in the opposite direction, toward her still sitting on the dock.

Dropping my flippers next to her flip flops, they splash water on her ripped jean shorts. She doesn't complain or squeal like a typical woman would. The pockets of her shorts are hanging out, exposed against her thighs. With her sun kissed skin and white tank top, she is my favorite definition of Florida. "They let you in here," I say, joking. When I told Caroline she could come in to my work to talk about the airport arrangements, I made sure I put her name on the approval list.

"They did take my driver's license and gave me this badge thing," she says, holding up a lanyard and a plastic card. "Like I'm going to steal secret intel or something," she scoffs, turning her eyes to the setting sun. "You stole this beach. I learned to walk here, you know?" Caroline nods to the right, toward a long section of beach that now sits untouched. We bought all of the land, including the beach when we established our base here. "The question is, why did they let you in here?" Her gaze rises to meet mine. Crystal blue. Her eyes are almost see through in this light—the color of a pale blue, fluffy cotton. She raises one brow, urging me to answer.

I pull my arms out of the sleeves and push the wetsuit down my torso until it's resting low on my hips. "Because I always get what I want," I reply. She studies my tattoos for a moment and then turns away like she's committing a crime by looking at my bare body. These southerners have rules I've never heard of before. It makes me smile.

Leaning back on her elbows she says, "You can use our airport. I came to tell you that. Not because you always get what you want, because it's a sound business decision. My dad is clearing out hangar five for you. If you need more space than that, let us know. I'm sure three would work as well, though that one is a little closer to my house than I'd like."

"Yes!" I exclaim, jumping in the air. When I land, Caroline startles and then gasps. "Excellent. Thank you," I say, my enthusiasm surprising both of us. Maybe because it took more convincing than I thought it would, maybe because I count any victory as something to be celebrated.

"Don't kill me, dear Lord in heaven, you about scared me to death. You can sign the paperwork the next time you're over my way." She pulls her feet from the water and perches her heels at the edge of dock and hugs her knees up to her chest.

Sitting next to her, I scoot until my wetsuit covered leg brushes against hers. "Aren't we going to your house right now?" Almost every day ends at her house. It's become an unspoken routine. "I was going to put up the lighting fixture in the living room area." I started following her around to convince her, sexually, into giving us the airport. It was a challenge and this is such a small town there really wasn't much else to do. As I got to know her better, it turned into something else entirely. A friendship founded on opposites. "It was the last thing that needed to be done. I need to finish it." It's the hanging chad of house projects and I've taken more ownership of her place than I had any right, but it's given me something I didn't know I needed. Companionship.

Caroline shakes her head and turns her face my way. "We're going out tonight. I owe you one real date, remember? Then you can be free of me. No more doing me any favors to win my good graces. You sign and the deal is finished. We'll be business partners at the airport, but I'll stay out of your way and you'll stay out of mine."

Pride is an awful thing. Right now, it keeps me from demanding a friendship and her attention. It's also what won't allow me to give up. "You're going out on a date with me?" I ask.

She brushes her long, wind-tangled hair out of her face and juts her chin into the breeze. "One drink," she replies, cheeks blushing.

"I do have a question for you, though," I say loudly, trying to get her full attention. Caroline makes a hmm noise and crosses one tan leg over the other. "Did you know this entire time you were going to agree to the airport terms?" What I'm really trying to determine is if she's so stubborn, she'd wait until the last possible moment to give in to my demands.

With one hand behind her head, holding her hair into a makeshift ponytail and the other holding her flip flops, she walks by me, my sheer size forcing her to brush against my body to get around me. "I didn't know what I was going to do." I hear the lie in her tone. She goes on, telling me different reasons for her hesitation, but I don't hear truth in any of them.

While her back is to me, I pull the wetsuit down my hips and bend over to get it down off my legs and feet. When I'm bare but for the tiny, black speedo I wear under the skin, I say, "Admit it, you just wanted to watch me work on your house."

Dropping her flip flops, she whips around so fast that her hair has to catch up, her face a mask of anger. Then her blue gaze dips to the lower half of my body. Slack jawed, and wide-eyed, her temper rises. "You know that's not the truth. I told you I didn't need your help." Stabbing a finger in my direction, she tries and fails not to look at my body. It's not her fault, I'm taking up all the space in front of her. I hold my hands out to the sides and let them fall. Water laps against the dock and a seagull cries off in the distance. Caroline swallows hard. "I guess that answers *my* question," she whispers under her breath. "What's under the kilt? What's under the wetsuit? Valid questions I never knew I'd know the answers to."

I laugh, flexing my pecs and shoulders to make myself appear even larger. "You have something else to wear out, right?" Caroline stutters, forcing a reason for her blatant appraisal.

"Do you?" I return, nodding toward her body—the wet spot on her shorts I created.

She looks down, confused. "I didn't plan on changing my clothes, why?" She walked in to my trap.

Stepping forward, I enter her space and lean down, so

my lips brush the curve of her ear. "You're wet, Caroline. Shouldn't we take care of that?" I swallow, slide my face into her neck, barely touching her warm, sweet skin. With my lips scarcely brushing her collarbone, I feel her pulse, and can taste her breaths. I'm rapt in my game, so entrenched in my thoughts of fucking and tasting and having this woman as my own, that I forget where we are.

She doesn't jump away from my touch, the reaction I expect. Caroline eats it up, leaning into my chest with the faltering grace of a woman undone, a woman who craves the touch of something destructive and powerful.

"Hey, fucking Phelps! Take that shit home! Not on my dock!" Leif calls out from the doorway of the office. I don't pull away, not from something that feels this good after a month of keeping her at arm's length. Caroline startles at the disturbance and pushes away from me, but leaves one palm flat on my flexed stomach, her fingers curling into my skin.

At her absolute mortification, I heap some more on top. "Your shorts are wet, Caroline. Do you want to change?"

A little line appears in between her eyes and she works her bottom lip with her teeth. "Oh. Oh, of course that's what you meant," she says, dropping her hand to the wet spot, taking another step away from me. "They'll dry. I'll be fine. Get changed and we'll go then?" she says, looking over her shoulder to see Leif smiling, waving his hand in the air like a southern mama greeting her child. Cringing, she waves back and stoops to pick up her flip-flops. In a town full of water loving individuals I shouldn't be surprised by the amount of flip-flop wearing, but it's even worse here than in San Diego, and it's year round summer there. "I'll wait for you up there," she mumbles, pointing toward an overhang by our office. "I have to trade this thing in for my driver's license anyways." I stare at her, narrowing my eyes, as I realize what's happening. It's utterly mad she assumes I was talking about her *shorts*. I could stop her now, take her body into my arms and kiss the shit out of her, let her feel my hard cock straining to get free, but I don't. That would be me, but now, more than ever, I'm convinced it's definitely not her.

This will be more entertaining anyhow.

"I'll meet you at the guard shack," I say, heading inside to grab my bag, doubtful she heard me over the quick pace of her walk of shame. I shower quickly, rinsing my body of the salt water and make a round of shampoo all over my body for good measure. When I'm dressed in jeans, a black tee, and flip-flops, I go to meet Caroline.

Her laugh is loud and gleeful and I hear it before I see her. Leif is leaning against the guard station, one arm tucked behind his head. Three other guys are standing around her, their lips in varied degrees of smiles. The heat wraps my body, both from my jealousy and from the humidity in the air. Caroline is talking with her hands, shifting from one bare foot to the other. Her blonde hair hangs down her back and skims the top of her jean shorts. Anytime she raises her arms, tan skin plays peek-a-boo, and every one of those bastards see it too. My pace falters when I get close enough to hear the last statement thrown Caroline's way.

"Consider yourself one of the wonders of the world. Tahoe has left every single woman he's ever been with. You must be something special," Aidan says, running his eyes down her legs and back up again. "Or something even better than special," he finishes after his appraisal.

"Better," Leif adds on a second before his eyes flick up to meet mine. The sound of ocean drowned out my approach. His eyes widen. These assholes are easily blinded by distracting beauty. Caroline's back stiffens and she takes a small step away from their semi-circle of testosterone and hard dicks.

My pulse takes over where the ocean left off, drowning my thoughts. With one sentence, he's destroyed my game. It's not his fault, no. He's telling the truth, but I wasn't honest with him. I told him she sucks my dick. "Fucking vultures," I say, trying on ambivalence, pretending I didn't hear what was said, praying Caroline's delicate manners dictate she doesn't rat me out. "You ready Caroline?" I ask.

"I think you have the wrong idea about me," she replies to the men, looking them in the face one at a time. Sliding into her flip flops she says, "Tyler is just my friend." A bead of sweat breaks out on the side of my face and slides down to my chin when she turns to look at me. "Right?" One brow is raised, daring me to say anything different.

"Sure. Just friends," Aidan answers, chuckling under

his breath extending each word in obvious sarcasm. "Whatever you say."

These men are like me. Or most of them anyways. We're here because we don't have attachments in the way of wives and long term girlfriends rooted in San Diego. By proxy that makes us the players, the flirts, the men who don't settle down or get serious. We're good at this. My friends think I've had a piece of Caroline and now I'm willing to share the wealth. They will continue to think that until I tell them otherwise. Until I show them.

I wrap an arm around Caroline, and can feel the anger leaking from her pores. She's seething, once in the past she called it, *spitting mad*. "It's not whatever I say, it's the truth," Caroline hisses, pointing one finger at the group. Their lazy smiles vanish when they realize she's not of our normal variety. "I am sincerely offended you think I'm sleeping with Tyler. Or doing anything with him, actually. I'm not. I won't. We are just friends." *I won't. I won't. I won't.* Nothing else registers as truth except those two words. "Business partners," she adds to drive her point home. "Insinuating anything else is purely bad form."

That's when the ocean stops beating against the docks, and the gulls stop crying, and my oxygen fizzles into something that isn't conducive inside a human body. Their faces say everything I'm not. I don't have to. Until she tells me to. "Tell them, Tyler." She uses my given name instead of my nickname and I think about how long it took for her to get comfortable enough to drop the legal name. Glancing at her, I see her red cheeks, and the tears of betrayal pooling in her eyes.

There's no way to salvage this, and at the very least I'm staking my claim. "She's *my* friend," I say, emphasizing the middle word through tight lips. They mutter their understanding, and confusion under their breath. "Mine. Got it?" I say again, meeting their eyes one by one.

Uncomfortable silence descends and with their heads down and their tails tucked, my brothers depart for the office. Caroline slaps her driver's license against her palm as she shrugs out of my grasp. "Such gentlemen. My word, I've never in my life been so thoroughly embarrassed." Her shoulder is warm under my palm as we walk to the parking lot. I don't bother replying to anything she's saying. I'm too busy wondering how long it's going to take for the guys to tell the entire troop that I'm hanging out with a chick I'm not banging and what that means for my cred.

We depart, her bicycle in the bed of my truck, Caroline sitting next to me stammering on about their rudeness. My stomach does this dance—the salsa of death and nerves. Unknowingly, she's exposed me in a raw, jagged way. I don't have too long to deal with that feeling because she connects the dots quicker than I thought she would.

"Did you tell them we were sleeping together? Is that why they said that?" She licks her lips, as her gaze dances over the side of my face. We're almost to the dusty turn in for Bobby's Bar, and I keep my eyes focused on the prize.

"If I did?" I throw my hand down on the turn signal and let off the gas pedal. No one is behind me, in fact only two cars drove by going the opposite direction during our short jaunt. "What if I did, Caroline?" I ask, while pulling into an empty gravel parking space marked only by a lime colored post.

She sniffles and looks out the window. "Then I made the right decision being finished with you after tonight. After all of my obligations are fulfilled."

I tsk. "You'll be seeing me every Friday, remember?" I correct.

Caroline shakes her head, blonde waves moving over her bare shoulder. "That's business. Why would you lie to them? I don't understand." When she shifts on the worn-out cloth and meets my eye, I almost cave. I almost tell her the testosterone filled truth.

I lie instead. Mostly to preserve the integrity of our night and hopefully salvage my dignity. "I didn't tell them anything. It's guys being guys and they were telling you the truth about my sexual history." If she knows one thing, she should know what kind of sexual monster I am. I'm not afraid of scaring her off at this point. I'm afraid of not having her.

Blushing, she turns away. "You've never had a real girlfriend?" A topic we've never broached before. Blessedly, it's not about the guys anymore. I have had a girlfriend. Once. It's why I've never had another one again. The burning inside my chest and the wound she left when things ended, made a gaping, black hole that proved how much power I gave her without realizing it.

I take a deep breath. "Are you offering?" I return, sliding my palm across the truck seat to cover her hand.

Chapter Five

Tahoe

Caroline rears back, pulling her hand away from mine like I've burned her. "What is with you guys? Is everything an invitation to be lewd and rude? Let's just go inside and get a drink so I can go home. My slippers and Netflix are calling, and they're a million times more polite than my current company," she sasses.

Throwing my head back I examine the loose layer of fabric hanging from the ceiling. It smells like mothballs and I almost didn't buy this truck because of it. I make a loud gurgling noise. "Are you done killing me yet?" I moan, clutching my neck with one hand. "You have to at least attempt to have a date with me. That means you have to like me."

"Pretend to like you, you mean," she spits back, folding her arms under her glorious tits. I check my line of vision back to her face.

Resting my arms on my steering wheel, I put my head against them. "Are we back to this again? You like me, Caroline."

"I do not," she quips, tilting her chin up.

Frowning, I add, "And I like you too." I want to tell her how hot I think she is when she's arguing with me. How I'd love nothing more than to rip off her clothes and fuck her in the cab of this old ass truck—until her ass cheeks smell like my Grandma's old sweater closet. "More than *like* I'd fathom a guess," I add, when I become aware she's waiting for me to say more.

That gets her attention, her posture lightens and the lines between her eyes relax. "I've heard enough lies for today, I think. How about that beer?" Her words don't match the expression on her face.

I sigh. "Look. No one is even here yet. Let's allow the town drunk to get going before we go in there. I'm not lying to you. I do like you. Maybe you don't like me, but you're attracted to me, and that's enough to stroke my ego enough to live another day. What do you say? Truce for the night? Not even the night. Just this one date. Technically, you did promise."

Caroline sighs, a heavy emotional heave that tells me she's done with me and this conversation. "That's a lofty assumption. One that stinks of a serious ego problem. You don't have to pretend to like me, Tyler. I was perfectly fine before you arrived and I'll be just as fine when you leave." *What if I don't want to leave?* The thought comes to mind quickly, like a bolt of lightning striking, the thunder following is me realizing exactly what that means. I've found something I want. Strike. Boom. Blast. Silence. I need to find a way to make Caroline mine.

"Bronze Bay has its finer points. Don't count on my leaving anytime soon," I say. "I'm sorry my friends were…rude." The apology tastes like chalk, but I know it's necessary.

She relaxes a little. I knew manners went a long way in this small, southern town, but now I'm thinking I can *yes ma'am* this woman until she lands on my dick.

Caroline faces me, bending one leg under her body. "You never answered my question about having a girlfriend. You deflected, like you always do when you don't want to talk about something." She meets my eye when she asks, and I realize how rare that is. She talks around me, never really engaging me directly. She's trusting me to give her honesty, trusting me enough to let me know my answer matters.

I smirk. "No harm in the truth if you don't want to be my girlfriend, I suppose." "You don't want me as a girlfriend," Caroline says, shaking her head, eyes narrowed in skepticism. She fires off a statement that basically says she won't believe me if I do tell her I've had a girlfriend because even if my friends are crude, they had no reason to lie about my promiscuity.

I shrug. "It's true, I did have a girlfriend, Stella, for three years. It ended badly. So, technically they didn't lie, they just didn't tell you why I am the way I am."

I implore her not to ask any questions about the relationship. She's thinking about it. "Why do you want to hang out with me, then?" Caroline asks, gesturing to herself. "You throw the girlfriend word around so casually you have to be joking."

I swallow, and I taste the battery acid from the breakup with Stella, the panic when I realized the pain wouldn't go away, ever. Even now that she's married and pregnant by some investment banker in N.Y.C. "I haven't spent so much time with a woman since then," I admit. "Pretty sure you already qualify as my girlfriend regardless of if I want that or not."

"Why are you so," she replies, closing her mouth, "so hot and cold? There are so many other girls in Bronze Bay that can give you what you want. I've given you the airport you needed. You've helped me with my place. I'm not...that kind of girl."

"I know." Scooting closer, I take her hand in mine. "That's your draw."

I watch her neck as she swallows hard. "It's not smart to mix business with anything other than numbers." *What about sixty-nine, Caroline?*

I shake my head. "Those rules don't apply to me. No rules apply to me. I'm quite fierce when I'm pursuing something I want." I lean in closer. There is a small smattering of freckles across her nose you can't see unless you're in kissing distance. Her blue eyes, on mine, reflect a mixture of fear and wanton desire. "I want you." I skim my hand up her arm and across her exposed collar bone. A trace of goosebumps rise behind the trail of my fingers. "Say the word and the g-word is yours for the taking." I haven't felt an adrenaline rush this strong, and state altering since the last time I almost lost my life. I have a scar to prove it, a long narrow grazing mark tearing across my ribcage. The internal scars from Stella are worse than anything a bullet could produce and here I am giving Caroline the power to kill me without even knowing why I am doing it. A taste of her is worth a lifetime of torture. That's the rational I'll embrace—the only logical reason I'd give someone this power again, and she really is different. There's no pretenses, and I'm pretty sure she hates me as much as she likes me and that's a dose of "fuck you" I've needed for a while.

I'm lost in the moment, in my asinine proposition, and the wonder in how she'll reply. I don't see the cock-blocking intruder coming. Someone raps on the passenger side window, tearing us out of the breathless moment.

Caroline spins, recognizes the face, and cranks the handle to roll down the window. "Malena you scared the rice, beans, and pepper out of me!" she exclaims, one hand on her chest. A pretty brunette, all teeth, and high glossed lips leans around Caroline to peer at me. I don't react with a smile or otherwise. To be quite honest I'm furious. "How have you been?" Caroline croons, seeming pleased her friend has saved her from answering my question.

"I thought that was you, Caroline. I was gonna' ask what you were doing out here, but now it's clearly obvious. I'm Malena," her friend says, trying to get me to respond. I don't miss how her eyes rake over my body and face. "You two coming in?"

Why else would we be here? "Tahoe, this is my friend Malena. We went to school together," Caroline says, turning to me without meeting my questioning gaze. "Malena this is my friend Tahoe. He, ah, he's working with me now. At the airport. They'll be using one of the hangars and airspace for their training." That's all she says, and I want to shake her, then kiss her, then stake my claim on her. Airports have nothing on my dick.

"Nice to meet you, Ta-hoe," Malena drawls, looking at me. "I know of his kind, Caroline. No need to say anything further. Any of your friends joining us tonight?"

She winks, like a damn poker shark.

I grin, tip my head in greeting and reply, "I'll send them your way if they do." More and more cars and trucks and bicycles pour into the small parking lot.

Caroline notices. "Something going on here tonight?"

Malena clicks her tongue. "Don't you know? It's Britt and Whit's engagement party!"

Caroline falters, but catches herself quickly. "Of course. Of course. Why didn't they have it down at St. Ives? It's so much nicer than here."

Malena shrugs. "You know how Whit loves his drink. I'm sure they gave him a deal for the night." Caroline nods. She then asks about her family, as politeness dictates, and then promises to catch up inside. She rolls up the window, cranking hard at the end because it's a piece of shit that barely closes, and sighs.

"I take it this isn't good news? Come on, it's a party! Think of how much fun this could be." I tug on her hand, a stupid, goofy smile on my face. "Let's go wish Britt and Whit the best of luck!" I say it in the most sarcastic voice as I can manage.

Caroline rolls her eyes to the ceiling. "They are the town stereotypes. Well, I guess they used to be. Now it's just kind of pathetic."

"Caroline May are you talking bad about people?" I croon. "Tell me more." My tone is still joking, but a little part of me wants to know merely because something is bothering her. I've yet to see her annoyed with anyone except me.

"Shut-up, Tahoe. You seriously want to know?"

I nod, and steel myself for trivial drama I'm sure to forget in five minutes. "Okay, well he was the quarterback at my high school and obviously, she was a cheerleader. They were together all four years of high school. They broke up a couple of times, but everyone always knew they would get back together so girls wouldn't date Whit because they were afraid of Britt's wrath and all the popular jocks steered clear of Britt, because, well, Whit probably would have killed them had they touched her. You get it? They were meant to be. Written in the stars. In true fashion, Whit cheated on her with most of the popular girls from the town over and Britt cheated on him. She'd banged the whole band by Senior year. The percussion section twice."

I laugh at the imagery that creates. "Wow. I have a feeling that's not the worst part?"

She shakes her head and licks her lips. She's getting to the juicy part. "Whit wanted to break up for good after prom. It was because he wanted to go to college and be single. I think he had scholarship offers, but Britt went crazy when he mentioned it. She took a whole bottle of headache reliever and wrote a note professing her undying love. She ended up at the hospital getting her stomach pumped."

I raise my brows. "They've been together ever since?" It's a foregone conclusion. People attach themselves to those they think they deserve—to the comfortable agony of false truths.

She nods. "Insane, right?" Caroline's eyes are wide as she nods her head. "They deserve each other, but I still can't believe they're getting married." She says the word married like a spoken reverie and I know her stance on the subject without asking.

"I can't believe they haven't gotten married *yet*.

Idiots like that usually do stupid stuff sooner. They don't make people wait to show their true colors." I proclaim. "Ready to go in?"

"Marriage is not idiotic," Caroline hisses. "It's romantic and sweet and it's one of the only things that's the same as it was way back when. It hasn't changed." I knew it. Unsurprising, but a conversation I'd avoid having with another living human like the plague.

The word spoken aloud makes my heart race. Perhaps it's because I've never considered marriage before, or maybe because it's something so permanent in my world of impermanence. The divorce rate among the Teams is nothing to shake a stick at either. Last time someone spouted off that as a reason for staying away from it, it was over 75%. Those are about the same as BUD/s drop out odds. Even with Stella, after years of dating, I wasn't ready to take the plunge and I thought she was my forever. I've lived a wild life full of change and variables. A constant never appealed to me. "It's an old-fashioned way to tie a ball and chain around balls. Just think, back in the day you wouldn't be flying your airplanes or twisting a wrench. You'd be pregnant in the kitchen resenting the very institution you deem so worthy."

She crinkles her forehead and purses her lips. "I'd never resent love. The real kind that makes you want to do things like be pregnant in a kitchen. Lucky for me I can also turn a wrench and fly a plane as well. Marriage is love and I have to believe in that. If I don't what else is there?"

The determination in which she makes this proclamation shakes me to my core—makes me want to believe in something just as fiercely. Something more than life, death, breathing or not, good or bad. I can't help it. I let my guard slip and I envision what Caroline wants. It's not Stella who I picture in my life, wearing my ring, either. I swallow hard, noticing how her eyes are dancing over my face. "Okay," I state simply.

A megawatt grin splits across her face. "Okay? That easy, huh? You don't want to argue."

I can't help but smile back. "Or you're right. I'm the first to admit when I'm not an expert on a certain subject. Given our current subject matter, I'm definitely not. You could be right."

She presses her lips together. "I am right." This is all it takes to lighten the mood. Caroline's face falls. "Guess we should go in."

My throat is still tight, and my mind still fuzzy with images I'd like very much to get rid of, but I'm not sure how. "You talked mad shit about them. Pretty sure meeting these two is going to be the highlight of my evening. Let's go." I open my door, when she hops out.

She waits for me at the tailgate. "Can you behave in the mildest manner you're capable of?" she asks, clasping her hands together in front of her stomach. "I wasn't talking bad about them, either. I just told you the truth."

I wrap my big arm around her shoulder and pull her against my side. "I can try, but nothing about me is mild." I ignore her correction, but I mentally note she doesn't even like the suggestion of meanness. She's that good.

My dick twitches.

Chapter Six

Caroline

Bobby's Bar smells like sweat and lies. The music is blaring from the beaten down jukebox, and Tahoe looks right at home as he edges in at the bar to grab us a couple of drinks, his monstrous figure forcing those sitting nearby to part. I play with the hem of my shirt and try to focus on the present instead of the way he made me feel in the cab of his truck. He almost kissed me. Told me I could be his girlfriend if I wanted to, basically said I already was. Words like I like you, and more than like, did things to my proverbial armor—pierced me directly in my heart. You'd think there would be something other than stroked desire after his spoken words, I don't know, maybe something such as anger or disdain, but nothing else came. The words *yes please* nearly popped out of my mouth the second Malena banged on the window. I could have killed her for ruining that moment, but I was also grateful because I don't seem to be thinking very clearly when I'm around Tyler these days. Or ever, honestly. A man like him doesn't pursue a woman like me. If they did, I wouldn't be single without a solitary prospect. I never pictured myself with an outsider, an intruder, but it's easy to let my mind reason the magnetic draw to the massive, arrogant stranger. I can't trust myself around him. It's why I took the entire month to make a decision about the airport. Can I be around him on a regular basis and keep a level head? Do I trust myself to get closer to him than I already am? In the end, the money offered won out regardless of my feelings toward the man. Plus, my daddy didn't raise a fool. When a once in a lifetime deal comes along, you take it. Isn't that what being Tahoe's girlfriend would be, though? A once in a lifetime deal? How do I adhere to one while abolishing the other?

Casually, I watch Tahoe as every woman in the room watches him. Even old Magdalena who hasn't so much as looked at man's foot since her husband Curtis died, has her mouth open as she takes in Tahoe's physique.

Malena and a group of girlfriends, all of which I recognize, point at him. Even men narrow their eyes with contempt and jealousy as they study him. They don't know how inside the rough, rogue exterior, he's a decent guy. A smart man. A man who despite my best efforts, still hangs around after I've pushed him away. Sure, he says stupid things once in a while, but what man doesn't?

Tahoe glances over his shoulder, a lopsided smirk morphing his chiseled features into something more boyishly handsome. I grin back, even though I have no idea what he's smiling about. Surely being polar opposites never damned a relationship from the start?

The possibility of success must be buried somewhere behind our vast differences. As I smile back at him, I'm aware that everyone is looking at me, a fact that would typically send me running for the hills. He's looking at me, at no one else but me, and I'm basking in that knowledge. I make my way closer to him and grab for the foamy glass mug he's extending. "What's so funny?" I ask, sipping the white foam before it spills over the rim. "This place is kind of comical, but anything in specific?" I amend.

Tahoe takes a long swig while watching me over the rim of his beer. After he swallows, his neck working with more muscles than I have in my entire body, he lets out a long, satisfied breath. "Just how out of place you look here. Don't come here often?" He grins.

"I should have known you were making fun of me. And to think, I was thinking," I halt my words before I finish my thought.

"Thinking about what?" His laconic voice sends a shiver from the tip of my tocs all the way to my head. "What we were talking about in the truck? The g-word?" He nods his head toward the door. "Want to go back and talk…some more?"

I shake my head before he's finished speaking. "I was thinking that this whole room is staring at you right now."

He heaves a shoulder up and down quickly. "And while I'm only interested in looking at you, I'd be remiss if we didn't meet your friends." Tahoe runs his tongue over his front teeth and he catches me watching his mouth. He quirks one brow in question. "What else were you thinking?"

I chug my beer while staring down the dusty, wooden ceiling. I can't trust myself around him. Maybe that's not a bad thing. "That they're all staring at you because you're so good looking."

"Ohhhhhhh!" Tahoe yells, drawing gazes our way once again. "You actually said it out loud. It only took a month."

Before I can object to his outright vanity he snakes an arm around my waist and draws me to him. Clinking his glass to mine, he then whispers, "I've got nothing on you. Looking at you is like looking at the sun, Caroline May. Everyone looking my way is only looking because they want to know what it is about me, that made you fall." Staring wide eyed at his mouth, I'm aghast at what he's insinuating, and gutted at the same time because he's absolutely right. Not about me being the sun, no, that can't be true, that's a line, but I am falling for him. I let him hold me in this moment, staring into his mirthful eyes as some 80's pop song echoes a synthesizer chorus around the small room. "You don't have to admit it now. But I know," Tahoe drawls. "Cheers," he adds "to our first official date."

I swallow down the bitter beer taste, and let his words float around a second or two before I come back to reality. Never in my life have I wanted to kill someone and kiss them at the same time. It's a deliciously volatile feeling. Floating. Falling. Fretting. I take a sip of beer, but I don't taste anything. My body is warming—the heat from his skin melting into me. My face heats, and even though I'd love to correct him and tell him this is our only date, I know for a fact that would be a lie. At this point, I'd do anything he says. Because I want him.

I want him. The admission feels odd and right at the same time.

He releases me, leaving my stomach bereft and cold. The hand holding my beer shakes a little and I have to make a concerted effort to still it. Tahoe notices—his eyes dropping to my hand, and then skimming the rest of my body. A throaty noise lets me know his obvious appraisal is satisfactory. Desire floods between my legs from a solitary noise.

Malena and Britt bound up to us, and it takes all of my strength to muster the ability to say hello. Malena introduces Britt to Tahoe and I smile, wondering how Tahoe can turn it off and on so quickly, when I'm trying not to quake with every emotion he's invoking. The small talk seems so trivial to what's happening inside my body and mind. Like I should be sitting alone, sifting through what everything means instead of talking about the approaching hurricane season. My heart is a hurricane. My body is an unloved temple seeking refuge with a man I wouldn't know how to handle. Tahoe's laugh breaks me from my horrendous, thrilling thoughts.

It's also the same moment I see Whit approaching. "You gonna' introduce me to your friend, Caroline?" Whit asks, the hint of drunken stupor tripping up his vowels. His gaze finds Malena as she appraises Tahoe with all the reverence of Christ on a cross. My heart starts racing.

Tahoe tilts his head to the side. "Whit, right? I've heard so much about you," Tahoe croons, lips pressed together as he threatens everyone with a look. He looks at me conspiringly, and then back to the drunken has-been.

Whit runs a hand through his long red hair once, and then again. It's a tell. He's agitated. I hate that I know that fact about him. The negatives of living in a small town. Whit spits out a compliment about Malena because he assumes she's been talking about him. He has no clue Tahoe knows all about him because I told him dirty secrets. "Congratulations, Whitney," I say, breaking the awkward silence. "You too, Brittney. We all knew you guys would end up together." I smile, hoping it looks genuine. Malena rolls her eyes. Tahoe covers a laugh with a cough.

Whit narrows his eyes at Tahoe, and I drain the rest of my beer.

"Looks like congrats are in order for you too, Caroline," Britt replies, eyes flicking back to Tahoe's midsection. Her words are hollow. After a couple decades of deciphering the almost imperceptible undertones of small town gossip, I hear the empty snark for what it really is. Jealousy.

Tahoe hears it too. He wraps an arm around my shoulders. "She's pretty awesome, isn't she? Landing the biggest contract this town has ever seen. Building and finishing her loft apartment on her own. You should see that thing. It's beautiful. I'm telling you, it could be in a magazine," he explains, waving his free palm in front of him, like he's painting an invisible picture for them. I smile, because what else can I do in this moment? A moment he's saving me from so gracefully, and *mildly*, even I have to acknowledge his non-effort.

"Stop it, you're making me blush. You helped me," I quip. "Gave it that manly flair," I tease.

Tahoe brushes my compliment aside and continues on. "You should have a housewarming party," he gushes. "You guys would come, right?" The horrified look on my face must stoke their curiosity because not only do they agree, they are voracious in their agreement, Malena even offering to help me plan it.

"I don't know if that's a good idea, Tahoe," I say. "We can talk about it later."

"Nonsense. It's a great idea. Everyone wants to see what you do up there...I mean see your new house." Britt says, staring at Tahoe. "Right, Whit?" she adds on as an afterthought, grabbing his elbow.

"Yeah, I'd love to see it. Coming here and snapping up all the prime real estate," Whit mumbles, slinking back to the bar for a refill without as much as a nod.

Britt brushes him off, giggling nervously. "You'll be there?" she asks Tahoe.

Malena even looks uncomfortable, shifting from one foot and looking off to the side. Tahoe laughs, all white shark teeth and astonishment. I shrink into myself a little more. Britt is proving why a relationship with Tahoe would never work. He's out of my league and it's obvious to everyone around us. Why do I care? "I'll be there.

Caroline can't keep me away. Right, Sunny?" Tahoe asks. It takes a second for me to realize he's referring to me.

I let the nickname breeze past in lieu of ambivalence. "Sure, yeah. Why not? This is all your idea," I reply, handing my empty to Tahoe which he grabs, eyes narrowed, curious about my attitude. Social gatherings aren't my thing. Ones where I'm the sole focus are of the variety that haunt my nightmares. He has to know me enough to surmise it. Some sleuthing SEAL he's turning out to be.

Whit returns with a new beer that Britt eyes down with unmasked hatred. He ignores Tahoe in favor of looking at me. With beady eyes, Whit bops his head to the new tune. "Crick's Beach and now the airport, huh, Caroline? Didn't take you for that kind." Neither did I. Wouldn't have dreamt it up in a million years. Me, entertaining the thought of a relationship with someone who doesn't know every sordid detail of my entire life. That's not the way it works around here. Britt and Malena speak quietly to avoid Whit's accusation. "Maybe that's what it takes," Whit adds. That statement is why I dreaded walking into this place.

When I don't respond, Tahoe does. "Everyone loves fresh blood, man. Lighten up. Not like I'm stealing your girl. She's all yours. Forever," he says, his words dripping with sarcasm. The glowing smile Britt has worn since spotting Tahoe vanishes in an instant. It's probably the opposite of what you'd expect from a newly engaged woman. Whit gets to watch as she seethes in irritation so deep it's written all over her body. I could kiss him for this—for exposing their false love. Without thinking, I grab his hand and lace my fingers between his. My hand gets lost in his sheer size, and my body shudders at the immediate warmth. It takes several awkward seconds before she realizes Whit is watching her—judging her reaction, scorned in his masculinity in the presence of such a fine example.

Slowly, Tahoe leans over and grabs Whit by the shoulder. Never has he looked larger than life than in this moment. "Congrats again, man. You lucked out," he says, voice gravelly. Before he leans away he flicks his gaze to a horrified Britt. "I wish you an eternity of happiness." The wish sounds like a threat. My heart is racing because no one talks to the It's like that, no one calls them out on the lies so effectively. Tahoe even did it the southern, subtle way.

"Caroline May!" My name is screamed in a high pitched shrill. Bless that girl. Shirley. She bounds to us breaking the circle of awkward. It takes her less than two seconds to assess the atmosphere. "Don't tell me," Shirley drawls, "Whitney has his panties in a bunch because this fine ass specimen got into Caroline's panties before he did?" Shirley runs her hands, spirit fingers and all, up and down in front of Tahoe's body. I stifle a laugh. Malena, finding a comrade in her appreciation for what isn't hers nods in agreement. Britt flips her hair over one shoulder while looking annoyed.

Shirley clears her throat when no one addresses her statement. "Oh, yeah. Congrats guys. It was a slow week at the diner." She shoves a white envelope into Britt's hand, and then turns to me. "You're drinking right? Let's go grab a drink. Gaston will let you out of his grip, yeah?" Tahoe squeezes my hand and the nervous energy in my body morphs into a warmness stemming from where his skin touches mine.

Not once in my life have I been more appreciative of my best friend's insane, straight forward personality. "Beer. I'm drinking beer. Let's go to the bar." She snakes an arm around my waist and the rest of the group moves on, leaving Tahoe alone. "Thank God you showed when you did."

She skips once, pleased with herself for her social torment. "They're a mess. Notice neither denied it. Whit has wanted you since the moment you were born."

"That's disgusting, Shirley."

Shrugging she says, "He's a gross dude. I don't know what to tell you."

I lean into her ear. "He asked me to be his girlfriend. Says he's ready for something more. I don't know what to think. I told him he could rent air space and equipment, so I gave him what he wanted and he's still here." I swallow down the fear of the unknown. Somehow, I know if I agree to take on Tyler Holiday in a relationship capacity, everything will change and probably not for the good.

Shirley catcalls. "I fucking knew it. This is your reward for being a social recluse all of your life. You get to have that." She eyes Tahoe over my shoulder. "He's checking out your ass right now."

Whit grumbles under his breath as he takes another

drink off the wet bar top and retreats to his friends. Shirley orders our drinks, flirting with the bartender because that's her protocol, and passes me another foamy beer without turning around. Some of the amber liquid splashes on my neck and chest before I can sip and I wipe at it with my bare hand, managing to make more skin stink like dirty brew. It's crowded now that the sun has disappeared and folks are out of work for the weekend. I tap Shirley to thank her and make my way back to Tahoe.

A few people stop me to chat, but I can't help but seek him out in the crowd as I make small talk. Most are curious about the airport and have heard the news I was taking it over. He watches me, like he's studying me. I wonder if he regrets what he said earlier, if he's deciding I'm not worth the trouble and whether he should stick to his status quo. Malena would give him what he wants, so would a number of other girls. He knows I'm more... complicated, though. I'm giving myself a pep-talk when Shirley comes up next to me and links arms. She's not done telling me what I should think yet. I never get away that easily.

"Have you told him?" she asks. It could mean a thousand things, but without saying a word, I know which question she's asking because of how he's watching me—undressing me.

Tahoe drains his beer without taking his eyes off me. Bringing the glass down, he licks his lips. I shudder as heat overtakes my whole body. "I'm blushing right now aren't I?" I pant out. "Of course I haven't told him. It's not like that." I amend, "It hasn't been like that."

"Don't. I wouldn't. You should lie," she says, patting me on my ass as she scuttles away to tackle Caleb in a hug. It's probably sound advice, with the only problem being I cannot lie. Not for all the tea in China. My poker face looks like a scared cat after being dipped in water. Something tells me a man like Tahoe, a SEAL, will call me out on any lie I try to concoct. One watching me as closely as this one right now? Game over. It will only be a matter of time before he knows the truth about me. He'll have all of my dirty secrets in the palm of his hand, just like every other person in this bar. The beers have mellowed my mood, but my stomach is flipping wildly with the unmade decision looming in front of me. He's a breathing masterpiece of masculinity and an untouchable quality that leaves me lightheaded.

When I'm close enough to touch, he runs his knuckles down the side of my face—a feather light touch that seems impossible given the size of his hand. "Head back to your place and hang that fixture?" Tahoe says, leaning forward so he can be heard over the new, louder music blasting around us. "If you want." It feels like a loaded statement. Does agreeing to this, mean I'm agreeing to everything? I take another sip of my beer the second he brings his hand away from my face. Breathing is hard. Focusing is hard. Everything on *his* body is *hard*. Sure I've had crushes on men before, but the crackling between my body and Tahoe's feels like being squeezed to death without care of the outcome.

When I don't respond, he goes on, "What are you

thinking about right now?"

Shaking my head, I remember myself, and decide honesty is best. "How my friends want you. Even the ones that aren't supposed to want you," I say, taking another sip of beer. "How I want you and I know I'm not supposed to."

Tahoe smirks. "Go on," he prods. "You're not done yet."

Shaking my head once again, I guzzle the rest, and slide the mug onto a high top next to us. "I'm thinking it's a bad idea, wait, scratch that, a horrible idea for me to get entangled with you. You're going to be working at my airport. What happens when it doesn't work out? I have to look at you," I say, waving my hand down his body. "I've seen the muscles under those clothes. You're enormous." His grin widens—eyes dancing across my face in complete amusement. "I'm also thinking I have no idea how to be a girlfriend. Your girlfriend. I'm kind of hoping you were joking about that back in the truck. Are you asking to hang the lighting fixture, or are you asking to *hang my lighting fixture*? I need you to be upfront with me because I'm bad at this." Covering my face with both hands, I let the mortification seep in, then peek around briefly to see who is around. "I can't shut up. This is horrible."

"No one heard your tirade," Tahoe assures, narrowing his eyes. "Though, take heart. No one knows how to be my girlfriend, Caroline. I'll let you define how to do that," he says, one dimple rippling next to his smile. "If you're interested in the gig."

Looking off to the side to avoid the power of his gaze, I blow out a breath. "And the lighting fixture?" I ask, furrowing my brow.

Tahoe laughs. "Needs to be hung?" he asks.

It does. My God does it ever. "You realize how intimidating it is being in your proximity, right?" I ask. Shaking my head, I say, "I'm glad you used it earlier with Whit, but turn it down a little right now, okay?" I think about the first time I saw him. How I pegged him for a man I wouldn't approach if my Mama's life was on the line.

Tahoe rests his hands on my shoulders. "You'll get used to it," he says, lips wet and shining. I swallow hard. His hands slide from my shoulders, down my arms.

Shirley clears her throat next to me. "Don't mind me. I'm just living vicariously through you," she says, "He's touching you."

Tahoe drops his hands and pulls me to his side. "I'd like to touch more of her, but we're sitting here talking about hanging light fixtures," he says to my friend, squeezing me a little bit harder for a second or two.

"Shirley don't be so insane, please. I thought you were hanging out with Caleb tonight," I edge, trying to change the subject.

She shrugs. "He's over there talking to Malena. You know when she gets her claws out, he has no choice but to reminisce with her." Caleb and Malena have had a few passion fueled nights in the past. "Plus, everyone is talking about how Hulk was a jerk to Whit and that's way more interesting."

"He wasn't a jerk," I exclaim. "I mean, not really, anyways. Whit is incorrigible," I hiss. High school drama as adults is one of things I wouldn't miss about this place.

Shirley takes this opportunity to tell Tahoe about Whit's permanent crush on me throughout high-school and beyond. On one of his breaks from Britt, he pursued me so hard I was confident Britt was going to find out and have her posse pummel my face into pulp. I almost gave in just so Whit would leave me alone. Luckily one of the other wallflowers in our graduating class ended up fooling around with him every Wednesday behind the greenhouse and he seemed to forget about me for the moment. Anytime I had a date to a school event, Whit made it clear he wasn't happy. It was like I was choosing someone else over him and that's something he's not okay with. I saw it tonight. At his own engagement party. Shirley had it right, and everyone knew it.

"Whit wants the wrong things," Tahoe says, breaking up the lull in conversation.

Shirley harrumphs, "You got that right. Maybe once they get married they'll keep their evil contained in the confines of their marriage," Shirley muses. "Wishful thinking, though. I'm sure he's in the bathroom getting blown by Britt's best friend right now."

"This town is far more scandalous than anyone lets on," he replies, amused by my friend's musings.

I stay silent, in favor of playing back memories from the past.

"It is Bronze Bay, Tyler Holiday. We keep our tan

secrets in the Bay water. Don't swim here too long. You'll never be able to scrub the dirt off," Shirley says, winking at me. "They're not the type of secrets that wash off with soap."

"Deep insight, Shirley," I say, trying to keep my voice even. Looking up at Tahoe I say, "I'm squeaky clean. Don't worry about having to hose me off."

Shirley and Tahoe laugh, like they're in on some joke. "Fine," he says, biting his lip. "I won't hose you off… right now, but I do want to know which of the men in here are your exes." His expression grows wary as he surveys the room.

"None of them," I nearly bark out the words. A few people look our way, but pretend they're not interested in what we're talking about. "Of course none of them, I mean," I say, keeping my voice lower.

Shirley confirms my truth. "Why are they all looking at me like they want to kill me then?" Tahoe says it with a smile on his face, gaze bouncing from one BB man to the next.

I try to see what he sees, but I can't make out anything except the normal people who are in my life in some form or another, almost every day of my life. "They aren't jealous because of me," I reply. "Probably that muscle we were talking about earlier. Muscle envy."

Tahoe raises his brow and looks between me and Shirley. "She really has no clue, huh?" He asks, when his gaze lands on Shirley.

My friend cackles. "She never has and never will. It's part of her charm."

"Excuse me. I am standing right here," I say, trying and failing to pull away from Tahoe's grasp. "Just because I don't date around, doesn't mean I'm completely oblivious to…male attention."

Tahoe clears his throat. "Male attention?" Stifling a laugh, he coughs.

Shirley hits Tahoe on the shoulder. "Show her the ropes," she says to him. To me, "I expect you to be less oblivious, and not hungover at our shift in the morning." Then she disappears for what I'm sure is the last time tonight. She'll be afraid of me when I clock in at the diner in the morning. Tahoe moves us closer to the door and I can't let another second pass without telling him. "I'm not naïve. I've already told you I don't have time for a relationship."

"But you'll make time for me?" It's not really a question with the way he's smiling at me. Like he's just won the greatest victory in the history of victories.

I roll my eyes. I'm doing this. "Only because you're good looking," I say, lacing my fingers through his.

Chapter Seven

Tahoe

She changed into this little white dress as soon as we got back to her place. My mind is trying to decide exactly what to do with that fact. Every time she bends over, even just a little, I almost see her panties. I swallow hard as she leans to grab a book off the coffee table. It's a book about hurricane hunters. She's telling me something, and I can tell it's probably important because of the way her face changes as she explains things like storm reconnaissance, and the eye wall, but all I can see is everything that is mine. Caroline agreed to be mine. My girlfriend. I haven't even kissed her yet. Everything is progressing in the slow kind of way you'd expect in a small town. What does she expect of me? You can bet that lighting fixture was hung within the first fifteen minutes of me entering, but it's been a long time since I've had to deal with things like expectations. Those are tricky things because they vary wildly from one person to the next.

"They'll be flying out of here this hurricane season.

We're on the gulf and it's a perfect location for them," Caroline says. "I figured it wouldn't bother you guys much, right?" In this moment she expects an answer.

That's something that is easy to read. "Oh, yeah. That's fine. We'll stay out of their way. Got something for the hurricane hunters, huh?"

She blushes a little and puts the book down. "They fly into the center of deadly storms. It interests me. I grew up in Florida, remember? We're in a permanent state of hurricane warning."

"I do cool shit too, you know?" I say, voice like a petulant child. "Probably even cooler than a hurricane hunter." I make a note to research more. I think the Air Force reservists fly as hurricane hunters, but I'm not positive.

She offers a warm, soothing smile. "No one said you weren't cool, Tahoe. Want something to drink? I think I have a bottle of wine in my fridge." I don't need any more alcohol. Lucidity is my friend at the moment. It's a small thing that will keep me grounded so I don't make a fool of myself in this fragile moment. She could still change her mind. The window of acceptance is too new. Caroline needs a drink, though. She says things while drinking alcohol she'd never say sober—opens herself in a way that is usually off limits. I'm leaning against the wall that separates the kitchen and bedroom. "I'll get the wine. Put on some music," I order.

Caroline steps away from me slowly, keeping her face neutral. Rounding the table, I step into the kitchen, take a deep breath, and remind myself I wanted this. A girlfriend. Caroline. A new life. Something different. I need this change. I repeat these things over and over while

I open her refrigerator to get the wine. The uneasiness stems from my absolute fuck-all knowledge on how to navigate a relationship after years of shunning them—abhorring everything they represent.

Stella barely counts because that ended badly. So, am I correct to think I didn't do that right? Up until this point I've done everything to the best of my ability with regard to my career. So much so, that anything else in my life suffered. This might be the first time in my life I have the time to succeed in something other than running and gunning.

Some of my best friends are settled down and married. Smith has Carina, and Macs has Teala. Ben has Harper and those men are my brothers—SEALs I respect, and men who I look up to. Surely if they can manage to have a significant other and not accidentally shoot each other, I can manage Caroline and...sky diving with a side of boring meetings.

I grab the half-gone bottle of chardonnay from the door and find a wine glass in the cabinet above the stove. I pour the rest of the contents into it and toss the bottle into the recycling bin.

My nerves fire in every different direction. Part of my brain is reminding me of Stella, and the other half is buzzing with anticipation. The brain in my dick, is merely excited. I haven't fucked a woman in so long.

I haven't fucked a woman I've actually wanted in *forever*.

Heading back into the living room, I find Caroline staring out the wide window overlooking the airport, her long blonde hair falling in loose waves down her back. She looks picturesque. A vision of everything I've always wanted and never had—untouchable, a woman I don't deserve. She is unadulterated brilliance wrapped up in a female body so tempting, my hands shake at approach. The need to take her in my arms is strong. After a month of playing pretend friend when all I wanted was my cock inside her body, my feelings for Caroline have reached a fever pitch. I'm half burning fucking desire and half awestruck that after all this time *it has happened.*

There is a soft song playing from a speaker on a bookshelf and she turns her head to the side when she hears me. Her silhouette is outlined by the low lights in the room, and it takes my breath away. "I'm not in the business of getting my heart destroyed," Caroline says, her tone quiet, vulnerable.

Grabbing her waist, I turn her to face me full on. She takes the wine and has a sip. "Lucky for you I'm not in the business of destroying hearts. Bad men, lives, terrorist hideouts, my own life, maybe, but not hearts," I reply, watching her eyes dance across my face. She takes another sip, and sets the long stemmed glass down on the decorative sill behind her.

"Dance with me?" she says, offering one had. My heart hammering, I know I wouldn't be able to say no, even if I tried, even if it meant saving my own life. I pull her into my arms and sway to the music. Our feet are bare and as we move, they barely make a sound. It's just heartbeats and a sultry song rasping through the air.

Caroline presses her full, pink lips together. "If I'm defining what it means to be your girlfriend, I think that anytime we dance, you're not allowed to wear a shirt." I stood on the dock nearly naked in front of her only hours before, but this request shocks me—has me wavering in my overabundance of self-confidence.

"Take it off me," I return, watching for any sign of hesitation. It's there. An unsure, questioning haze clouding her decision, but timidly she grabs the bottom of my t-shirt and raises it up to my neck, as high as she can get it. With my right hand, I grab the back of the collar and take it the rest of the way off. My left hand stays firmly wrapped around her, and her fingers slide over my pecs and abs. The coolness of her hands is a jolt and my muscles tighten in response.

The song changes, but we keep sliding around the room in the waltz we've created. When we've made it back in front of the window, I dip her back, her fingers clutching my side for dear life, and her laugh cuts through the music.

Her neck is in my face and in this moment, I can't control myself. Licking my lips, because my mouth is watering, I press a kiss against the hollow of her neck. She smells like laundry detergent and tastes like sweat, and soap, and beer. One would think that wouldn't be the most intoxicating combination, but goddamn if I don't pull away right now, I'll drool on the woman.

Chill bumps rise on her skin, climbing up and down her neck and spreading across her chest. She's not wearing a bra, something I assessed the second she walked past me after she changed. The swell of her tits press against my bare skin and I work to take a long, slow breath.

"Now I have a question," I say. Her eyes are this doe eyed innocence when she meets my gaze and nods once. "Are *you* in the business of destroying hearts?"

Her tinkling laugh sounds like she inhaled fairy dust for dinner. "Weren't you paying attention earlier? I wouldn't know how to break a heart if I tried."

I believe her. How could I not? She turns to take another sip of wine, but keeps one hand on my body. My dick has been permanently hard since the second she touched me, and I'm sure she's felt it—thrilled to have this control over me. After she takes a few large sips she faces me again. "Look at us, Tahoe. If someone had to guess who would break a heart. Who would it be? You or me?"

She's unsuspecting. I'll give her that. Just like Stella was. All of my friends thought Stella was end game because of how much she loved me. Caroline has no idea how appealing she is. Not just in looks, but in hobbies and personality. Any one of the different men in Bronze Bay would give their left nut to have Caroline as their girlfriend. She sees herself as the person everyone tells her she is, not as she truly is. Stunning, intelligent, worthy of so much more than I can give her.

I rest my hand on the side of her face. "You're beautiful. Kind, smart, handy," I admit, waving my arm around the house she built. "There are things about you I don't understand quite yet, but from what I've gathered this far, you're the biggest catch in Bronze Bay. The biggest catch in my world by a long shot."

She narrows her eyes. "You're such a flatterer. Has anyone told you that?"

Tilting my head, I say, "Come on. You know the answer to that. I don't flatter anyone. What I just said was merely a compliment."

"You're going to have to meet my mama and daddy the proper way," she says, and it feels like a question.

I spin her around and her dress floats out. "I wouldn't

dream of meeting them in an improper way."

"My daddy already has a first opinion of you," she says after I pull her back to my chest. "You're not scared?" she asks.

I laugh in response. "I'm not scared of anything."

It's a boldfaced lie. I'm terrified right now. Of her. Of the things she's making me feel. Caroline May is a Cat five hurricane threatening to ravage every cell left in my heart.

"You should be," she says, referencing her father again.

"No shirts when dancing, right?" I ask, as we sway to another song.

Caroline nods. "It would be a crime," she replies.

I nod. "We take this slow," I say. "I need that in our definition."

Her forehead crinkles, and I can tell, my request has surprised her. "Okay, but that seems like something I should say. Not you."

I shake my head. "It's been a while for me and I want to do this the right way. I haven't done anything right lately and if this is my new start, I want to do right by you." And to serve my sense of self preservation, let's be honest. "Can we take it slow?" Even as I ask the question, my dick is calling her name—taunting me by revealing I'd love to do anything except take it slow right now. On the floor. Or the coffee table. Over the back of the couch? Nah, I want to look at her face the whole time. Missionary on the couch. Yes, that would work. I could sit on the coffee table and she could ride me. Goddamn, the thoughts. The desire. "Okay?" I ask.

She smiles. "Okay. But if it's on my account, it

shouldn't be. I'll be okay. I know most girlfriends do things."

That gets my thoughts off her pussy and ass. "Things?" I ask, smiling wide. "Sometimes you say things that make me question if your sexual knowledge extends to the ninth-grade health class video. Don't take that the wrong way, Caroline, but you're an adult. You can say things like…" I pause, for effect, and to watch her face change, and say, "Fucking. Blow jobs. Eating pussy. Finger fucking. Hand jobs," I say each word with emphasis and her breathing speeds. She's taking in every damn syllable like I'm speaking the gospel on Sunday morning. She steps away from me, and I'm granted a view of a blushing, hot and bothered Caroline May. "Condom," I say, biting my bottom lip. "Dick. Inside. You. Licking. Tasting. Wet. Screaming." My eyes narrowed, and my heartrate racing, I go on, stepping toward her, "Kissing." I lower my head and brush my lips on her exposed shoulder. Swallowing hard, she shudders against me. She clutches me and instead of acknowledging the sexual tension I've so graciously extended, we start swaying to a love song. She sighs as I fold her into my body. Leaning over I press a kiss under her ear. "You're allowed," I say again, reminding her of everything I said that affected her so greatly. "Remember that."

Pulling away, she swallows hard. "If we're going to take it slow, you should probably go home now."

Unsurprised, yet disappointed, I respond, "Yeah?"

"I want every single thing you just said. Right now."

It's my turn to swallow. "Good," I reply, releasing horny, and unpredictable Caroline from my arms. I dreamt of what she would look like, and like usual, she's overachieving.

"If I took this dress off right now. Would you," Caroline drawls, keeping her gaze aimed at mine. "Fuck me?"

The air leaves me body in a whoosh out of my mouth and I know I need to get the fuck out of here as soon as humanly possible. Her confidence doesn't last long, her gaze darting to the floor. With a finger, I bring her face up to look at me. "I would fuck the shit out of you," I promise. "But that wouldn't be a good idea during this moment in time. I'll go home instead."

She nods, crestfallen.

"And jack off thinking about you in that white fucking dress." She crosses one foot over the other, and pulls at the sides of the said piece of clothing. It's like all my favorite parts of a woman came together and said, "Let's make a textbook woman for Tyler Holiday. We'll make her so perfect, he can't fuck her for fear of falling, though."

A small smile appears on her face, on top of the layers of complication. "Definition accepted. Let me know when it's an appropriate time to…fuck."

The way she says *fuck* brings me to my knees. Literally. I kneel in her living room, in front of her, dragging both hands through my hair. Caroline laughs that damn, hypnotizing laugh.

Chapter Eight

Caroline

I'm literally counting down the minutes until my shift at the diner ends. I've never been this antsy before. I've never had something this big to look forward to. For the most part, my life has been a well-orchestrated symphony of scheduled and met expectations. Tahoe is the wild card. He turned last night into something that felt like a pivotal moment I couldn't go back from. I don't want to go back from it. Aside from kissing my shoulder and my ear, there was no other physically sexual touches, but his words, our words, had sex simmered in every single syllable. My body is now a lit match, waiting for the explosion.

I'm kneeling on a booth, a wet soapy rag in my hand, when Caleb comes over. He has his white, grimy apron tossed over his shoulder. By the way he's been glaring, and slamming pans around during our shift, I know whatever he's here to say isn't going to be pleasant. "Word on the street is that you're dating that dude," Caleb growls. "Whit said he's a dick." Way to blame someone else for your own thoughts. Small town tricks for 200, Alex.

I sigh, get the last of the table clean and climb out of the big pleather seat. "Does it really matter what Whit thinks, Caleb? The better question is do you think I care?"

"Everyone cares what people think of them."

I shrug, and ball up the dirty rag. "Maybe I'm done playing by these rules. You know I was never going to end up with a Bronze Bay boy." I regret my word choice the second I say it, but for once I'm speaking honestly. When you know what your city looks like from 10,000 feet in the air, you understand how much more to the world there is. Since the first time my daddy took me up in my favorite yellow plane, I wanted more—everything, anything the eye could see. It's why I became a pilot instead of going to college. I love Bronze Bay, but I know there's more out there. Leaving it has never been on my list, but neither has settling for someone who doesn't know what's out there.

Caleb scoffs. "Now your own kind ain't even good enough for you? You better be careful. These Bronze Bay Buffoons are the ones who are going to be here long after those assholes blow out of town. They never stay anywhere long. We're here always. Al-ways."

Narrowing my eyes, I reply, "How do you know that? Tahoe says this is his permanent base. The attacks changed everything, Caleb. Whatever you thought you knew about SEALs isn't true anymore. Don't worry about me," I say, softening my tone. "I'll be fine. He's not like he seems. I appreciate your concern, but I have to ask, why do you care? Because I turned you down?"

He laughs, a sadistic, mean cackle. "You think your shit don't stink now that you got some steroid filled monster tearing open that pussy every night? Get over yourself. I was only ever nice to you because I felt bad for you. And your mom. You're a fucking spinster. You'll be a spinster again when he *does* leave. Mark my words."

My blood pulses through my ears and my skin turns a shade of red reserved for true, blue fury. The last time it happened I was twenty and I'd been working on a section of airplane siding for weeks, without my father's help. On accident, I snapped off a piece that couldn't easily be replaced. Facing Caleb, I try to keep my shoulders back. To let him see what his words do to me would be criminal. "You don't have to be so rude. I was only trying to explain why I...I never really fit in. You know as well as I do, that I'm not like the rest of the women here," I say. I'm giving him grace by not tearing into him like I want to. My jaw clenched, I continue, "Not that it's your business or anyone else's, but I'm not sleeping with him. I'm not sure that's even what you meant by those nasty words."

Caleb has the good sense to look a little mortified. The high road will do that to people, you know? You can use it as a weapon if you're skilled enough—the low road seems more seedy when juxtaposed with the high road. He clears his throat and looks past me, out the window. Shaking his head, he growls, "You're pissing off a lot of people. Know your place, Caroline. That's all I'm saying."

When I don't respond, he clocks out, and lets the

back-door slam on his way out. I wince a little, mostly because the thought of people being upset with me, does affect me even if it shouldn't. Caleb's words strike a vulnerability inside me. This is my home. These are my people. Sure, everyone is upset with the SEALs for taking our beaches and changing our way of life, but am I wrong to find happiness in the midst of a bad situation?

"I saw Caleb on his way out," Mama says, locking the front door, and clicking off the open sign. The diner closes early on Sunday. Mama has always said it's important for us to be together as a family at least one day a week. Even if I think it's a bad business decision, growing up, I always loved Sundays because of it.

Swallowing hard, I ask, "Did you hear that conversation?"

Sighing, she walks toward me. "No. I assume it's a conversation you've been expecting, no?"

My mother, the kindest woman in the whole wide world has eyes that can make you feel like you're worth a billion dollars. She sees the good inside of everyone, but especially me. When she looks at people, people notice, they feel comfort, and self-worth, and it's a God given gift. I think it's why the diner has always been so successful. You can get a slice of delicious pie and validation for breathing all in one location. I don't want her to see me right now. "Caroline, look at me baby." Her soft hands catch mine.

"Mama, why do people care what I do so much? I'm an adult. I've never done anything bad to anyone. I'm kind. I work hard and stay to myself."

Her face, creased with worry, softens a touch. "It's

your light, honey. Everyone else sees something they don't have. It's because you're all of those things that people care. People are always going to talk. It's just the way it is here. You only give them good things to talk about. Perhaps they're waiting for you to make a misstep—watching like hawks to see a stumble."

Her eyes crinkle and I have to close mine. "Do you have a problem with me dating Tyler Holiday?"

"The only problem I have is that you haven't brought that boy up the hill for dinner yet," she replies. "Daddy had to hear from the man who mows the property lawns, that you had a guest last night."

I drop her hands. "Dear Lord, daddy knows he was at my house last night?"

"Caroline. You just said moments ago, you're an adult. He doesn't, we don't, mind that you have a man at your house. Heck, for a long time we were worried you didn't like men that way, and that my sweet daughter, would have really given these people something to talk about."

I run a palm across my sweating forehead. There truly are no secrets in this place. "It just became official last night. It wasn't something I was keeping from you, okay?"

"You're allowed to keep things from me, honey." She swipes back my hair on each side of my head with a sweet smile on her thin lips. "I'm happy if you're happy, and the rest of the lot can stick it where the sun don't shine."

I laugh. "I'm going to take him up tonight," I say, grinning. "I can't wait to take him over the bay. It's so beautiful at dusk." I get caught up in thoughts of watching Tahoe's face as I show him my favorite place in the world. I turn back to face her.

From the corner of her eyes I see a hint of glistening tears. Shaking her head, "Mamas wait for this their whole lives. I get to watch you fall in love. I'm gonna give you some advice. I know it's usually your daddy who gives you all the tidbits and facts about the stuff you both love, but I want you to hear this."

With her eyes, piercing that soft, soul section of my body, I can't say no. I nod. She pulls me into the booth, takes my hands in hers across the table. Her thumbs rub my knuckles in circles. "You know how you throw yourself into projects? It's 100% or nothing?"

I smile and nod. It's something that's infuriating when you're living with me. I remind her of the time I didn't sleep for days when I was studying for my pilot's license. Logically, I knew the book would still be there in the morning, but I wanted the information to soak into me as quickly as possible. After all the hours I'd already logged in an aircraft, the test was child's play, but I couldn't chance failing at something that meant so much to me. "Are you telling me I shouldn't give 100% in a relationship?" I ask, guessing at the avenue of this talk.

She shakes her head. "The opposite. Give it your all. Every last molecule you can spare without crumbling and dying." She furrows her brow. "I know this is really new and you'll be figuring things out for yourself, but give it your all, I promise you'll never have any regrets."

"But…the heartbreak. It happens to everyone around me. Everyone."

Her concern turns to happiness. "Heartbreak tells you the love was real. You can't be afraid of the end at the beginning. Go full throttle and see what happens."

"That sounds like advice daddy would give."

She shrugs one shoulder. "He must have rubbed off on me after all these years." Her eyes go a little far off and I know she's thinking of my daddy and all the years between their beginning and right now. "You go and have fun tonight. Be careful in the air, Caroline May." "I'm always careful," I reply. "It's takeoff and landing that hold the most risk," I quote straight from Daddy when she says the same thing to him.

She smiles. "In the air is the fun part."

I nod, kiss her cheek and bound outside to my bicycle, Caleb and his ugly words all but forgotten.

Tahoe looks absolutely horrified about my plan for us. There's a crease on his forehead that hasn't disappeared since I uttered the words, *sunset flight*. I checked the schedule and radioed in to air traffic control, and we are set to go.

"You seem so young to have so many hours under your belt," he says, sweating, as he buckles himself into the seat next to me. "It's small," he adds, swallowing hard. "Are you sure we shouldn't throw on a pack to be on the safe side?" he asks. I already told him three times we can't wear parachutes on our backs.

"It's a safe airplane. I learned to fly in the Cessna 152, Tahoe. You're in good hands. I picked this one because I knew you were…frightened," I add, grinning, adjusting my earphones.

"I am not frightened," he barks back. "It's about control. I like control. Fun fact, I hate riding in airplanes on the way up to jumping altitude. I don't feel in control until I jump out of the airplane. My body and life are in my own hands at that point…not the pilots." He rubs his hand across his lip to brush more sweat away.

I laugh, looking to my right. "You are terrified and I'm sorry, but it's absolutely darling," I say, taking a jagged breath around my laugh. He looks at me while I giggle, and a small smile appears. It's small and crooked at first, but as I continue to laugh, it widens to a large white grin.

Shaking his head, he blinks slowly twice. "You can fix anything with that Tinkerbell laugh, you know that?"

"Tinkerbell," I gasp. "Should I be offended?" I take this opportunity, while he's distracted to hit a few buttons and switches. The engine rumbles to life. I wasn't lying. I could fly this plane, in almost any condition, in my sleep. I'm confident in this seat. In my knowledge. In all of the ways that matter. Autopilot clicks, and I confirm all my gauges match with specifications, and look back to my nervous passenger.

Tahoe licks his lips. "It's a compliment, pilot. We getting this show on the road? Before I change my mind and grab a chute." His gaze wanders down to the straps on my chest. "Or before I decide I'd rather join the mile high club without being a mile high," he says. His hand sneaks over and clutches mine.

I squeeze his big fingers once. "That's a horrible pick-up line," I reply.

"I know," he says. "I'm under duress."

"It makes a pretty good racket during takeoff." Releasing his hand, I hand him earphones. "You can talk to me if you need to by pushing this button."

He grins. "This is just like my comm. I'll just go ahead and pretend I'm on a mission. Okay, boss?" he asks. "Although I'm not typically this sweaty when I'm on a mission."

"Beggars can't be choosers. Once we're at cruising we can take them off. It's not so noisy," I reply. He puts on the set and I pull away from the hangar and roll toward the runway.

This does feel like a mission. I've never taken a guy up before. My friends will ask for a ride every once in a while, but somehow this feels more intimate. I'm sharing my whole self with Tahoe and I wonder if he realizes it. I glance at him to find him clutching the seat. I laugh, but he can't hear me. The plane roars down the runway and I make adjustments for a slight wind, and in a short time we're airborne. I check measurements and when I'm sure we're at a safe altitude and speed I sneak a hand over to nudge him.

His eyes are slammed shut, face contorted as if he's in pure agony—awaiting his meeting with the devil himself. "I'm not going to kill you," I tell him, clicking the button so he can hear me. "You can take the set off. Look around." He does, and his face morphs into something more recognizable—beautiful. He's so large next to me, taking up space that is usually empty.

It's clear and beautiful outside. The view never fails to take my breath away. The ocean glitters, and the lush greenery of a landscape blessed by a near continuous stream of spring rain lays in front of us as far as the eye can see. "This is why I had to be a pilot," I admit. "The peace up here. Away from everything down there."

"I've jumped out of hundreds of planes and I have to admit, I've never actually appreciated the view until I was a part of it, falling toward earth," he says, joking. "I understand," he says, turning his head to look directly at me. "You look beautiful up here," he says.

"Now, that's a compliment," I tell him. "Thank you." It reminds me of my conversation with Caleb earlier, and then my mama.

Tahoe pulls at the harness holding him in, still not at ease by this point in flight. The breeze isn't as strong now, and I'm able to cruise and really enjoy the view. "Do you think you'll be leaving Bronze Bay?" I ask, insecurity eating at me. "I know you told me this is your permanent base, but I was wondering how long permanent is in your world."

He bites his lip. "As permanent as it is in yours, Caroline. I might leave to do a mission here or there, maybe I'll have to do training in another state for a week or two, but this is it."

"Was that always the plan?" I ask. My heart knocks against my chest. "Or, did something change?"

He grins a lopsided smirk, and it does things to my insides that should be illegal. "I'm a SEAL, I pretty much can do whatever I want. This isn't Big Navy," he says, keeping his grip on the straps crossing down his chest. "I told Leif today that this was a permanent change. After the entire squadron hazed me for having a girlfriend."

I must look disgusted or horrified, because he adds, "I'm joking, Sunny. We don't haze people. They make jokes on a group message thread and draw penises on sticky notes and put them on my locker. Nothing that will seriously hurt me. I mean, maybe they hurt my pride, but I'll take it if it means you're mine. I'm here. This is it." The confession is as surprising as it is terrifying.

I swallow hard. "You know just what to say. It's quite unnerving."

"Wait! You're flying a plane in an open sky, and my words are what are unnerving? You need to check your priorities." Granted, maybe for a second or two, I did forget I was flying a plane even though my hands are firmly placed on the control column.

"You're still mine today, then?" Tahoe asks, raising his voice to make sure he's heard.

"Depends," I say, flicking my gaze back to my instruments. "Are you all in?" I ask, remembering my mother's suggestion. "I have it on good authority that all or nothing is the way to go about anything in life. Especially in relationships." Not that I know a hill of beans about relationships, but if Mama said it, it has to be.

"I have it on the authority that all or nothing is the *only* way to go about *everything* in life," he replies, tilting his chin to the view in front of us. "I'm all in, pilot."

I'm giddy. In my happy place with an infuriating, misunderstood man that has transformed into a sweet, interesting man. Or maybe he was only infuriating because I didn't know him, or wasn't open to viewing him in any other light except the one I assigned him by looks and first impression alone. How many people have I done that to in the past? Smiling, I point to his base and he cranes his neck forward to look at it.

Instead of looking at the black buildings and fence like an eyesore that stole my memories, I see it as something that gave me something new and exciting. Tahoe. I tell him several stories about Crick's beach. They span from when I was a kid and broke my arm jumping off a sand pile, trying to touch the sky, to when I was in high-school and the bon fires we had that would send the fire department out here every single time.

The blue water is clear. It's one of the few places around that isn't polluted…yet. Tahoe's smile vanishes and his brows pull inward. "I'm sorry about the beach. The Navy does what they want, and everything is far more complicated than I could explain. The plus side is you can come visit me there anytime you want." It's not a consolation prize, I can tell he knows it's not the same just by his grimace. I make a few adjustments and edge over the water a bit more. Tahoe points. "I'm thinking of building a house over there," he says. Tahoe has told me before how he built his house in San Diego from the ground up. He sold it when he came to Bronze Bay and I can't imagine how sad that must have been for him. When you pour your blood sweat and tears into something—try to make it as perfect as you can, and then you're told you can't have that or see that anymore, it changes you inside. Well, it would be like someone telling me I had to move out of my apartment and there's no way I'd ever want to. "I'm not sure if I should tear down the building or build something new."

"The Homer Property? Did you buy it? It's been in their family for years!" I exclaim when I see what he's pointing out, and telling me about his potential plans.

It's the first time he's relaxed in the cockpit. "It's close to work, and now that you don't need my help anymore, I need something to do." He waggles his hands in front of him. "I have to keep these busy. If I'm not working or," he says, trailing off, "hanging out with you, I'll need something to call my own." It's time to turn around, the sun is setting, giving everything around us a sweet golden hue. The sky is free of clouds except for a clump to our right that look like a fluffy cotton candy. Tahoe talks about several different plans. "Maybe you can help me?" he says, trying to lure me back into the conversation.

The Homer property is an enormous chunk of land on the water. The Bed and Breakfast that was there for years, since I was a child, closed after the attacks and never reopened. The land sat with a for sale sign for some time and I assumed the city would buy it to regain waterfront property back after the base gobbled up a chunk. I don't even want to think of the consequences when the Bronze Bay gossip gets ahold of this information. "Why didn't you tell me?" It comes out a bit catty, but that's not my intent. I'm mostly confused as to why something like this would strike his fancy.

He pauses, silence, but for the wind, rustling around us. "The deal began right when I moved here. I wasn't sure how long it would take to be official. Is it a big deal? You're upset?"

Shrugging off his question I explain, "It's a big

commitment, that's all. It also gives permanent a new definition. Owning a house." I swallow down the lump in my throat. "In Bronze Bay."

I don't dare look at him. "Just because I own a house doesn't mean anything. I've built houses before, remember? Old ladies like jigsaw puzzles, grandpas like rummy or backgammon, I like fixing shit. Houses. It's not a big deal." It's a reminder I needed.

"I guess so. You can't tear down that bed and breakfast though. The town will crucify you more than they already are."

He laughs. "I wasn't aware I was being nailed." The innuendo is so strong I have to squeeze my legs together. "I'll do what I want, but I will take your considerations to heart," he amends, folding his hand over mine. "Investing in property is practical." If he asked Leif to make Bronze Bay his permanent home just today, then this really is an investment purchase started well before he knew me.

Sighing, I mess with the rudder pedal and the wind causes a batch of turbulence. Tahoe grabs the straps of his seatbelt again—panicked. I grin, ignoring it as best I can. "You're not being nailed. I am. Well, in the figurative sense. It's not a big deal. I'll help you. We're going to land soon. Takeoff and landing, Tahoe."

His eyes widen. Even he knows the threat in those two things. He looks at me, and his gaze is so strong, I chance a look. It's a mistake. "All or nothing, right?" he asks.

He's right. All would be celebrating his property purchase, and making immediate plans to select upgrades and paint colors. My immediate reaction was what everyone else is going to think about it. What it means for the relationship. What it means if it fails. Before it's really even begun. There will be a constant reminder of the first man I've ever wanted. The Homer Property will no longer be the Bed and Breakfast that my Uncle Stan used to stay at when he came to visit us. It will be the place where I fall in love with the beast of a man sitting next to me. I feel it happening even now—the connection, that unquantifiable quality used to describe falling for a person. It's a textbook case.

I point the nose down a touch and my hangar comes into view. "You're right. I'm sorry. All."

"And Caroline?" Tahoe asks, voice loud and unsteady. "Don't fucking kill me today."

Laughing, I shake my head. "Not today, Tyler Holiday. Maybe tomorrow."

"I look forward to that. On the ground."

He doesn't close his eyes this time. His eyes are focused like lasers on my house, the side that has the large window.

For once, I know we're both thinking about the same exact thing.

Chapter Nine

Tahoe

"Good job at the range today," Leif says. "With all the razzing, too. I still can't believe you're taking yourself off the market, dude." I've tried to explain that I actually like Caroline, but my friends just don't understand, won't even try to understand why I would throw away my old ways for a solitary woman. Maybe if my buddies got to know the women they spend their time with, they might find a match. Might find something to ease the loneliness of our existence.

I clear my throat as I push open the metal gate of my brand spanking new property. It looks a little like a jungle—in an overgrown state from lack of attention. The gravel driveway is lined with green trees that desperately need a trim. This is exactly what I need to keep my head in check. Lately, all I can think about is Caroline. Her laugh. Her smile. How perfect she is for me. It's a dangerous slope, and this will be a good decompression when I'm trying to find the old me in this new place, with a new outlook. Tilting my head, I survey the three story Victorian house in front of me. "Don't you ever get bored fucking random hoes? It's not even a challenge anymore," I exclaim, taking mental snapshots of the windows and doors. Almost all of them will need replacing if I keep it. "Honestly, Leif. An actual relationship is more of a challenge." That's quite an understatement.

He trails behind me as we head toward the house. I pull the key ring from my pocket. It contains about twenty keys, but the front door key is marked with a red piece of tape. The rest I'll have to figure out on my own time. The owners were basically giving it away and didn't even negotiate when I offered fifty thousand under the asking price. Some things didn't change after the attacks. The real estate in Florida is still a fraction of the price of what San Diego places go for.

Leif rattles on about the woman he had sex with the night before, and I try to blur out the names. If I've learned anything, it's that Caroline knows everyone and I don't want to have to defend my friend against his whore allegations when it goes south. Like it always does. "This place is a shit hole, Tahoe," he says as we step through the front door. "You're crazy. What's wrong with your apartment by the base?" Nothing except it's not mine, and doesn't need any type of work. It's boring.

"No one got anywhere being sane. You know that," I reply. I've seen houses in worse shape, but I've seen better. The grand foyer is beautiful, with two dark wooden staircases on each side of a round marble table in the center of the room. The ceiling is a brilliant stained glass bent into an oblong shape. "Fuck, she's right. I can't tear it down." Shaking my head, I run my hands through my hair. It changes my plans.

"You were going to tear it down?" Leif asks, raising one brow. While he's aware of my handy man capabilities, he's been a SEAL on the east coast all of the years I was on the west coast. He never saw my house, or my work first hand.

"Weren't gonna' help me with demo, then?" I ask, smirking in his direction.

"You need a bulldozer, not a SEAL Team," he replies, brusquely.

Sighing, I take out my cell phone and start jotting down notes. "I was buying it for the property, I only saw the few photos they posted online. It looked like a piece of shit. My realtor said it was a project," I explain, shrugging. "Caroline is going to be here soon," I tell Leif.

"And you want me to leave?" he jokes.

My boots are noisy as I walk into the grand room to the left that overlooks the drive. "The last time you saw her you offended her so gravely I had to make her my girlfriend to make up for it." I'm half joking, but Leif laughs like I've just said the funniest thing in the world.

"Have you really not fucked her?" We've gone over it a thousand times. Twice this morning when he was spotting me on bench, again when I asked him to pass me a bottle of shampoo in the locker room shower, and about seven times during today's meeting when all the guys were there.

I glare in his direction. He puts up his palms in front of his body. "Okay, okay. I just don't understand it. You spent every day with her for a month and you didn't play hotdog ham pocket. It's unreasonable." We will always come back to this, I realize. I don't fault him, I can't, when I've been him. "You don't even claim big swole pucker hole either. Does she not put out? Give me something."

Rolling my eyes, I try to think of what I could say to shut him up. "Stella."

Leif swallows hard. He knows about that disaster. You respect heartbreak. No questions asked. "If that happens again, I don't know what I'll do," I say. "Go ahead and make fun of me for having feelings," I edge. "I'm a giant pussy, but that's my right. I haven't fucked her yet because I want to make sure it's not a mistake. She's not a mistake. The expectations come after you've slept with a woman. I'm trying to do this the right way. Instead of swinging my dick, I'm handing her flowers. This is my new start." I turn towards the bay window in the great room to find Caroline pushing her bike up the driveway. The basket on the handlebars holds a large paper bag. "That's why they sent me here," I add. "Because I needed something different. And as fucked as I thought it was, I think they were right." Leif's boots are loud as he marches up next to me, looking at her, eyes narrowed, as if he's trying to solve a puzzle.

She's wearing a tank top and a pair of cropped overalls,

hair falling over each shoulder in thick braids. Caroline looks like a fucking Playboy centerfold, country girl edition. "I see it. I do. I even understand what you're saying about making sure you don't blow your shit up again, but how the fuck do you know if it's a mistake?"

I shake my head. "I have no fucking clue." Risk assessment is something SEALs are good with. When you can't assess something, like a relationship, it is confusing. It's wild, and carefree, and stunning. It takes my breath away and jolts my entire being with a foreign rush of adrenaline.

Caroline props the bike up on the kickstand and grabs the bag. She doesn't see us, not yet. Caroline is taking deep breaths. After a few seconds of that, she shields her eyes with one hand and glances up all three stories of the large house—taking stock. She licks her lips and smiles when she's happy with her assessment.

Leif swallows hard, and I meet his gaze. "Good luck with that, then," he says, voice cracking.

To this, I smile. "There's no luck involved."

"What then?" he asks, backing away.

"Intuition? Practice? Skill? A little bit of elbow grease?" Those things are required for any relationship, surely. I flex my biceps and wink at him. Leif winks back, keen to my joke.

Caroline walks right into the open front door. "Tahoe?" Her small voice echoes in the large space causing a riot of emotions I'm not sure I want my buddy to see.

I shrug at my friend, and call out, "In here."

Caroline stops short, startling when she sees Leif. We came together in my truck, so she wasn't expecting to see anyone else here. "Oh, hi," she says, not meeting Leif's eyes. "How are you doing?" I know it's not a question I'm supposed to answer.

I smile at her manners at any cost. Even when she's pissed. "How was your day?" I ask, walking up to kiss her on the cheek. She sighs a dreamy little sigh, and her breath tickles the side of my neck.

"It was good. Just getting ready for some military men to take over my airport tomorrow. What about you? How was your day?" She meets my gaze first, and then Leif's. "This place hasn't changed a bit," she adds looking around the foyer. "I love it. I wish you saw it back in its heyday."

My friend has the good sense to look a little embarrassed and I know whatever he says next will be either an apology or something completely inappropriate. "Listen, Caroline. I want to apologize to you for the last time we spoke. My friends and I were out of line, and uh, everything is cleared up now. Obviously," he warbles out, looking at me and then her again. "I didn't mean to offend you in any way. I-I," Leif trails off.

"My friend assumed wrong," I helpfully explain, because watching Leif make amends is about as painful as you'd expect from a man who doesn't care about anyone except himself.

Caroline taps her converse sneaker on the floor, and chews her bottom lip. "I want to get along with all of you guys," she replies, voice light. "I have to be around you now, and we're in a working relationship regardless of the things you say. Your forwardness was a shock, I admit, but I forgive you." She goes on to tell him a story about the Bed and Breakfast to take the sting away from his embarrassing moment—erasing the awkwardness in mere seconds. It's a trait that only some people have. It should be considered more of a skill than a trait—a finesse if you will.

When she's finished speaking, Leif asks a few questions, makes a joke about me and vanishes out the door. I call out to him to take my bicycle out of the truck bed before he drives home. Clearing my throat, I turn to my beautiful guest. "You're ready for us tomorrow then?" I ask, trying to keep the conversation on anything except the crackling flame that sizzles between our bodies every moment we are together. We're alone and as always, she's this delicious mix of understated grace, dripping sex appeal, and tinged with that shroud of innocence that frightens me to my bones. One bone in particular, isn't quite as scared as it is blustering hard. I readjust as slyly as possible, which isn't very.

Caroline blushes as she sets the bag down on the table in the center of the room, averting her gaze. "As ready as I'll ever be. Your pilot came in today and was checking everything out. Also, the jump master was there checking chutes and unloading a ton of gear." Aidan. I'd forgotten he was going to be there today or I would have tried to come, too. We all have different responsibilities dependent upon our skill set. Aidan has the qualifications with regard to skydiving. And keeping his dick wet at all costs. Out of the band of merry assholes, he's the one I trust the least with regard to anything female and mine.

I take Caroline's hand in mine and bring it up to examine it closer before kissing her warm palm. "How was that? He give you any issues?"

Her gaze is like fire as she looks at my lips on her hand. "Fine. He apologized. It was just as awkward as you'd expect. The pilot was nice."

"How nice?" I ask, grabbing her other hand and repeating the gesture. "Not too nice?"

She narrows her eyes. "Tyler Holiday. Are you jealous?" Her smile is beatific, and it accompanies my favorite laugh.

"Maybe. Does that turn you on?" I fire back. "My sexy pilot who rides a bicycle."

She steps closer, but folds her arms across her chest. "Are you teasing a pilot who rides a bicycle?" she whispers. Her tongue sweeps across her lower lip, an unintentional nudge reminding me to take her lips and make her mine.

I circle my hands around her arms, my fingers brushing her chest. "I would never," I reply, grinning. "It doesn't make any sense, but that's status quo for you."

"If I can't travel 130 miles per hour, or more, in some of our other planes, cutting through the clouds, I'd rather stop and smell the roses. On a bicycle," she explains. "A man who is used to a fast and furious life wouldn't understand that." It's easy for her to lump me into a category other than the one she's in.

Caroline's cheeks flush crimson and she crosses one foot over the other. Narrowing my eyes, I run my hand up to brush the side of her face, and then finger one of her golden braids in between my fingers. "Fast and furious is behind me now. I'm turning over a new leaf." Even super heroes need a break. Doesn't Superman hide in his fortress of solitude for a while? Batman bunker down in his cave while the world falls apart around him? This is my equivalent, my serenity. So long as she's with me. "How about I'm turning over a new seashell?" Grabbing her hand, I guide her to the back room, past the stairways into a dark paneled sitting room that overlooks the ocean. If you squint hard enough you can see Crick's Beach and our base fence in the distance. Caroline turns around, neck turned up as she examines the walls, dragging a finger that leaves a trail in the dust. I don't let go of her hand. I tell her about my plans for the house now that I'm positive it's worth restoring.

"You like Bronze Bay that much?" she fires back, quirking one brow, trying her best to not look affected by my touch.

Craning my neck, I look around the grand foyer. The dusty wood and the haunting glow from the stained glass makes this place look more like a castle from the 18th century. I didn't intend to like this old house. Didn't intend to keep it standing. Didn't think I'd want to stay here in this small town for longer than my punishment allotted. Caroline clears her throat, bringing my gaze back to hers. My heart skips a beat. You get this feeling when you want to keep something. It's scary and vulnerable. It makes you feel like your skin is flipped inside out. It changes everything. Keeping that quality, keeping it, has to be protected at all costs. You become obsessed with keeping that which you can't sacrifice. Because the feelings you have right now never existed before. They will never exist again. "I like you that much," I admit.

She pretends she didn't hear me—turns her face toward a portrait of someone's old relative painted in dark burgundy and white.

"You know when you have the same dream over and over again?" she asks.

I grunt, upset she won't reply to my sentiment. "Yeah."

"Well I feel like you're a dream I'm going to wake up from. But you're here every single day. It's like I'm dreaming. I'm waiting for the goblin to show up and suck out my brains."

Raising one brow, that garners a smile. "A brain sucking goblin? I'd like to think I'm a good guy, but I'm probably the proverbial goblin that will turn your dream into a nightmare. I'm learning as I go."

Her cheeks— are a dusty rose that match the shade of her lips. Tucking her thumbs into the pockets of the overalls, she looks to her feet, but then directly into my eyes. "Will you tell me about Stella?" That name spilling from Caroline's lips seems so wrong, but on a second assessment might prove to be okay. She'll be the one to erase her from my heart forever. "I brought dinner from the diner. Well, mama sent it with me. I figured you wouldn't have anything to eat here. I brought you that burger you like. The one with the onion rings inside it." She's babbling to detract me from her ask.

I pull her to my chest, one hand wrapping around her back underneath her overalls. My hands are against the warm, bare skin of her lower back. I swallow hard once. "While I will always take food from you, even my favorite food, don't feel like you have to bribe me for information. I'll tell you about her."

She blinks hard. "Well, it's just, you didn't seem to want to talk about the relationship before and now that we're…official, I was just wondering if that was fair game." It's not the first time I've wondered why Caroline is so meek and mild mannered. "I'll tell you anything you want to know," she adds. "If you want."

I want to kiss away her fear. I want my lips to be the ones that erase every bad thing in the world. It's the wrong time to be obsessed with kissing, while she's asking about Stella, but I'm not sure how to stop it without acting on the desire. "I want to know everything about you Caroline May. Everything." I lick my lips and trade my grasp for the side of her waist instead of her back. My thumbs skim the top edge of her panties. She sucks in a surprised breath and every inch of her skin prickles. "Everything," I say one more time leaning in close to brush my bottom lip around the curve of her ear. I grab the sides of her ribcage and feel every breath she takes, my hands spanning the whole side of her small body. "Can I kiss you? Just a little?" I ask.

"Just a little?" she asks, breathing out, her words tickling the side of my face. Inhaling her scent is a mistake I know I won't come back from. Not right now, at least. I need to devour her.

"Yeah," I reply, rubbing her skin, letting my fingertips memorize every pore they touch. "Just a little. A lot would be too fast," I explain. "Your skin," I hiss. "I want to see it. Touch it. All of it." Leaning my head down to place my forehead on her shoulder, I close my eyes. "So, just a little kiss. Then we can eat and talk about remodeling and all of the other shit we should be doing right now."

"Just a little, then," she says, brazenly pressing her lips against my neck. A goddamn shiver slides down my spine and I feel it in the tip of my toes. When I pull back to look at her, she's smiling. "Follow me," she says, grabbing my forearm because my hands are still inside the overalls. I let her guide me through the house out onto a terrace that overlooks an expansive lawn and the ocean. "Even if it's a little kiss, it is our first," she explains, eyes twinkling. "Bronze Bay should be here for it, too." Her words warble and I know she's nervous—her innocence so strong even a manners-pro like Caroline is unable to change the dynamic of this moment with her conversation.

"Caroline," I croon, letting my chest puff out. I know how to save her right now. Smiling, I crook her closer with my pointer finger. She smiles, presses her lips together, and shuffles her feet so her toes are pointed at mine. Her chest lined up to my stomach, the breeze passing between us like an infidel, and my heart racing like a fucking steam roller. Gently I grab her chin with my thumb and forefinger.

Her huge blue eyes widen as she sucks in a breath. I bite my bottom lip as I survey hers. "It doesn't matter where the kiss happens. You're always going to remember it."

"Yeah?" The word is almost inaudible as she squeaks out a response.

I could explain that the chemistry between us isn't normal—that most people don't have this unsung passion in every moment, the visible pull our bodies have to each other when we don't have control over it, but proving it with a kiss seems like a better idea.

"Are you making me feel like this because you don't want to talk about her?" she says, air rushing out in a breathless plea.

Dropping her chin, I place my hands on each side of her neck. "I'm trying to kiss you because I want to taste you, even for a moment. Want to know what it feels like when my lips are on yours," I say, letting my gaze drop to her heaving chest and the swell of her pert tits. "I'll tell you anything you want to know about her." Hopefully she doesn't ask anything right now, because this moment is magic. The seawater sifts through the air mingling with the honeysuckle vines that have taken over this terrace. "Can I kiss you because I want to?"

She nods, rubbing her lips together. In this moment

I've never wanted something more. Never held myself back for the sake of anyone or anything else. This right here is the reward. Caroline's blue eyes, soft skin, waiting lips, and open heart begging me to give her what I want just as much. Sliding my hands from her neck down the side of her body to land on her hips, I lean down slowly, calculating how long I'll be able to hold myself back before the kiss has even begun. Caroline's eyes are closed, and her full lips part moments before mine come in for the proverbial kill. The longing is so strong when we connect that I slam my eyes closed and wince as the feelings of...everything course through my body—an unfamiliar onslaught of emotions. Moving my lips against hers softly, I tentatively let my tongue slip against hers and moan when her sweetness tinges my tongue. Caroline makes a small noise of pleasure and I think my dick might break through its jean cage to attack, and destroy, but I'm careful to keep a distance, because this is a little kiss. The kind when you give a shit. The one that snowballs into a million memories that stain your soul for the rest of time. The kiss that starts and never really ends because hearts are proven correct.

I won't get over Caroline, or this kiss. Not ever.

She pulls into my body, her hands fisting my shirt. The excitement inside my pants only makes her more ferocious—her kiss deepening, as I try my best to separate what's happening inside my head with what's happening on this terrace, in the warm ocean breeze. I bite her bottom lip, and she opens her eyes to meet mine. What I find there takes my breath away. It's like I've unlocked something that's been stowed away for all of time. I grab the braids that fall over her tits and pull lightly on one so her head tilts to the side. I kiss her from that angle, sliding my lips against hers while she stares on, mesmerized.

I repeat the gesture on the other side, yanking her braid just enough to get her right where I want her—in my control. In my arms. I'm calculating everything about this kiss and she's eating it up. We separate our lips, forehead to forehead, and catch our breath when she slides her hands under my shirt and sneaks her fingertips into the top of my jeans.

Her breathing is jagged, and her lips are red and glistening. I kiss them again, just once. Deep and controlled, until she slides her tongue into my mouth, begging for more. Against her mouth I remind her, "Just a little."

"A lot. More," she replies, trying to get her hands back where they were before. I shift my body back to juke her intent. I pin her by the wrists against the white wood of the terrace guardrail and kiss her as a consolation prize. If she touches my dick, I'll end up inside her. Right here. I might have strong intentions and valiant decisions about taking it slow to preserve the both of us, but I'm still a man who is wildly attracted to the woman grabbing at my package.

"Touch me," she says, in between kisses, sliding her lips across my jaw, and then down my neck.

I groan, at the feel of her on my neck. It's one of my spots. The ones that drive me absolutely crazy. I'd probably come right now if I wasn't so focused on controlling myself with Caroline. It's been that long since I've been with a woman.

"Keep your hands where I can see them," I breathe out. "I'll touch you, but you can't touch me." I shake my head, trying to shake off some of the lust. There's no ocean air, or honeysuckle anymore. It's all sweet perfume, saliva, and desire. The gulls have been drowned out by the thunder of my pulse.

She looks crestfallen, but she nods her head up and down. "Okay," she says, leaning back on the railing, putting her hands on the wood, almost exactly where I just had them. "Touch me," she says again, like it can't happen quickly enough.

I make a snap decision, because when a woman like Caroline is asking to be touched, you touch her. In a way that you know you can come back from. Slow, I remind myself. I need to take this slow. Nothing about Caroline and I feels slow. She infiltrated my being—weaving her way inside like a virus that affects my whole system. I meet her eyes, and nod once, and let my gaze flit to a few parts of her body. "Can I unfasten these?" I ask, fingering the metal buckles that are holding on her overalls.

"Yes," she replies, licking her lips, gaze like molten lava. "Yes."

Nodding, I flick them open and let the straps fall over her back. I kneel in front of her. Almost like the night we danced at her house. A little more. I can give her a little more and keep my heart intact. With the buckles undone, the pants slide down and expose the lower part of her stomach and the top of her panties.

Above the waist, Tyler Holiday. I tell myself as I envision licking her pussy until her knees buckle. What will her face look like when she's coming around my cock? Will her eyes roll back in her head? Will her thighs tingle? Will she call out my fucking name? "I'm going to slide your shirt up," I say, glancing up to meet her gaze. Her eyes are warm, curious, fully trusting. She gives me an imperceptible nod, so I slide my hands under her shirt and up her stomach. I watch my hands, like they're painting a masterpiece instead of touching a woman. She has one of those perfect kinds of belly buttons, so I lean over and kiss the skin next to it on all sides, while stroking the side of her body where her waist nips in.

She sighs, and her fingers clutch the wood tighter— knuckles white, and body tense. How easily I could make her come. I bet she's soaking wet for me. Do I dare take this any further? I know she'd be accepting, gladly willing to let me play with her body any way I saw fit. I shouldn't. I drag my lips across the top of her panties and listen to the tiny, hot breaths she takes in between whimpers. "You like that? Me touching you with my lips?" I ask, watching her beautiful fucking face.

"Yes," she says, a plea for more. "My whole body feels like it's been...plugged in. I don't know how to explain it."

"I feel the same way."

"How?" she squeaks out. "You won't let me touch you!"

"Touching you does everything to me," I explain. "Trust me."

A lock of wild hair brushes her collar bone when she hangs her head to study me. "How can I trust you when I can't even trust myself? I'd tell you to pinch me, but I feel so good right now I don't care if it's real or not."

Biting my lip, I grin up at her before kissing under her belly button once more—my cock dripping with envy. "When you touch me, it will be game over." This is the chemistry I've been seeking without realizing it. Why I offered to help her with projects for a month before telling her how I felt. When lightning strikes it's hard to believe it's real, that things like this exist in the real world. Especially for horrible men like me. Men who don't deserve this kind of out of body experience with women like Caroline May, a hidden diamond in this tiny, perfect town. This is where my life has been hiding all of this time. I've endured so much to get to this point. *Don't fuck it up*, my mind whispers.

The surreal floating sensation extends to her awareness, too. "I won't pinch you but," I say, dragging my lips across her stomach to end under her ribcage, and bite the tender skin hard enough to make it red. Caroline squeals in delight, taking my head into her hands in tight fists. There's three freckles on her lower stomach that I connect with my pointer finger. One strays desperately close to her panties and I snap the elastic. The slapping sound against her skin sends a shock to my dick.

I stand, keeping my hands on her skin because I know she wants more. Things I can't give her yet, but I want to please her, fuck do I want to please her, make her happy in any way I can. When I'm upright she pulls me by the collar in for another kiss. Mouth to mouth, chest to chest. I swallow, and a taste of her slides down my throat hitting my system like a drug. Is this chick even real?

I don't need intuition, practice, or even skill. I only need her.

I am so fucked.

Chapter ten

Caroline

His dimples haven't disappeared since he kissed me. The sight of them makes me deliriously happy—my stomach tipping with excitement, my hands shaking with anticipation. When I first arrived here, I was unsure how I'd feel being inside this house that now belongs to him. The news traveled around town quicker than lice in a kindergarten classroom. Everyone has an opinion on the matter, and they're mostly not favorable. I'd be lying if I said their reactions didn't cloud my own opinion. It's an uphill battle, the pack mentality is seeded so deep it's a fight I wish I didn't have to wage. It means I'm like them. But, the second he kissed me, any sort of hesitation I had about him or this huge whopper of a purchase vanished into the salt filled air. He's shown me, unmasked, how much he wants me. His touch sends fire through my veins, the heat of his gaze ricochets to parts of my body in ways I didn't know existed. I want Tahoe in every single way a woman can possibly want a man. His kindness bleeds into his masculinity in a way that makes his whole package something close to perfection.

We're sitting at a broken table in the dining room of the Bed and Breakfast. He's cobbled a fix to steady the wooden legs. The orange of the sunset is slanting in the large curtain-less window casting a dim glow on everything it touches. The place came with a lot of furniture and it's a little creepy. The Homer's locked up and fled town after the attacks. They never returned. Several members of their family were killed or harmed on that fateful day, and I don't think Mr. Homer recovered from the loss. There are family photos still hanging next to the old olive green fridge, left behind in an attempt to make a quick exit.

After I swallow a bite of the Reuben sandwich my mama packed for me, I say, "Maybe you should rebuild instead of renovating." The image of the kids' smiling faces that would be around my age, force the statement even if it's not true.

Tahoe notices where I'm looking. "It has good bones. Even if it's haunted," he says, grinning wide when he catches my attention. "You can't tell me it doesn't."

I can't. Most of the community believes this place should have been a town landmark, or a city building, hence the uproar caused by an outsider buying it. I bite my cheek, sip my water bottle, and turn a discerning eye to kitchen. "It needs a lot of work."

"What would you do in here?" he asks, extending his arm to the space around him. The tone of his voice sounds like he's asking a question of a different caliber, one that makes my whole body feel hot and wiry, my mouth bone dry. I'd do anything he wanted in here, that's what I'd do in here.

Renovations, I remind myself. "I'd probably gut the kitchen entirely. Everything needs to be updated. You know that already though. I like the floors. They're original," I reply, standing, my gaze focused on the light hard wood, instead of on the man that is making feel completely insane. Pacing toward the window I catch sight of an airplane in the distance. "What if I want to skydive?" The question bubbles out before I have time to tamp it back, make it something more hesitant and unsure. "Could you take me?" I pivot to face him.

His face darkens as his eyes rake my body. "I can't take you, but I can go up with you. You'd have to go tandem with a jump master. I don't have that qual."

I laugh. "You say it like it's a crime. I was just wondering. Taking an interest in the new ventures of my airport, that's all."

"I wish I could take you," he replies, snaking an arm out to pull me close. "I'll work on getting that qualification now that we'll be jumping on a regular basis, okay? Then I can take you."

His arms are enormous, swallowing every inch of skin they touch.

"You don't trust Aiden?" I ask. Tahoe's arms stiffen, his whole body rigid with tension. It's confusing. "You'd jump tandem with him, right? Aren't you guys sort of like, the best in the world at what you do? Skydiving included?"

He softens a little. "I don't trust *you* with anyone except me."

"Why?" That womanly tact begins crawling out,

hoping for praise and compliments. It's an uncontrollable urge because of him. "You think he might crash land?" I tease.

He shivers. An honest to God shiver. "No," he growls. "He would never."

"What are we talking about here? I was joking."

Tahoe grits his teeth as his hands clamp tighter on my waist. "I trust in his ability to do his job. I don't trust him with a woman. Especially not with you," he says.

Jealousy. It feels so good. The ultimate in compliments, really. "I'll wait for you to get the qualification then. So, if we crash land it can be all your fault. Not your friends." Twining my hands around his neck, I see his stress ease at my touch.

He pushes me back so he can look me square on, a mischievous twinkle in his eye. "Please, Caroline. Now it's a challenge. I'm going to have to scare the life out of you to prove a point. It's going to be one step before crash landing."

"That's rude." Releasing him, I fold my arms across my chest.

He quirks one brow. "You question my skill. That's rude."

"It's not even a skill you have...yet," I fire back, smiling. "You're not a jump master."

Tahoe's hands slip down my waist and around to my ass. "Right now I want to show you a few of my other skills."

"Kitchen demo? I hate to burst your bubble but I have that skill, too," I tease. His gaze is fire as he watches my mouth while I speak. Wetting his lips, he swallows hard, his grip firm against my backside. "Not impressed with that," I add, egging him on. "What else do you have for me? What skill?"

His eyes spark open wide, then he nods slowly. "Something you'll never forget, Sunny."

It's a threat. One I willingly accept without offense. The sunlight has all but vanished since our conversation began and now there's just the low light from a chandelier with two working bulbs. It's easy to have more confidence than I should, in the dark, with his hands owning me the way they are right now, so I press my mouth to his. The response is immediate and real—the lighting of a fire that has never been here before. He pulls me into his lap and the bulge between his legs is so mountainous I inhale sharply.

"You're feeling one of my skills right now," Tahoe says, nuzzling his face into my neck.

The scruff on his cheeks and chin scrape against my neck.

"Isn't that more of a gift than a skill?" I ask, my voice breaking. Caroline May doesn't play games like this—she doesn't play games at all. Against his lips, I steer away, "Why do you call me Sunny? You think I'm the sun? My sunny disposition?"

I feel his grin against my skin. "A touch more morbid than that," he admits, bringing his hands up to hold my face in place as he works his mouth against mine for a beat or two. "The earth would die without the sun," he growls, then looks me directly in the eye. "Sunny."

I do die a little inside, right at this moment. At least the little girl with dreams of a man sweeping her off her feet swooned.

Tahoe groans, and pushes me out of his lap, with that look in his eye that turns my stomach upside down. Now that I understand what it means, I know I've seen it many times in the past month. Dozens of times, when I mistook it for irritation, or annoyance. It seems I'm as delusional and blind as my friends say I am.

A loud bang on the front door sends both of us across the room. Instinctively, he pushes me behind him with a straight arm before he opens the door with the other. "I saw your bikes when I was driving by. Just wanted to stop in," Shirley says, peeking at me around Tahoe's body. "What are you guys up to? Congratulations by the way," Shirley says, focusing on him instead of me. "You have some big balls. Buying this place. Man!"

"Shirley," I cry. "Stop it!"

Tahoe chuckles and opens the door wide enough for my friend to slip through. Shrugging, she says, "He does! Whether he knows it or not. Don't be such a prude, Caroline," she says, and then licks her lips. "I was congratulating him on purchasing another piece of Bronze Bay."

He raises one brow. "*Another* piece?" he asks, a half smirk pulling the corner of his mouth.

Shirley cranes her neck to look at me and lets her gaze float back to Tahoe. "Yeah," she replies.

"Oh, my God! I'm right here!" Suddenly, I don't want Shirley meddling in my love life, or lack thereof. "Humans can't be purchased!" I shout, throwing my hands up.

Tahoe's smile fades to something more somber. "They

are, though." He runs a hand through his hair, the tattoos under his biceps peek from his shirt.

Shirley and I both look at him, with what I'm sure is the standard, horrified expression. I'm reminded of what he is. What he's capable of.

"I closed with your mama tonight. She mentioned you two are having dinner up on the hill tomorrow," Shirley says, doing her best impression of me, trying to wield the power of the southern topic change.

I'm still thinking about what it is Tahoe does when he's working—the things he's been exposed to that I have no clue about. He responds to Shirley's statement by making a joke about the house on the hill, and confirms the plans. I wasn't nervous about the dinner. Not until now. What if they ask him what he does? Will he answer in generic code words to hide the truth?

They continue to talk and I don't chime in until I hear a lull in conversation. "You going to the spot tonight?" Sometimes they have parties on weekday nights if the weather is nice.

"Yeah," Shirley replies, picking at her fingernail polish. "Caleb was pretty pissed tonight so I asked if he wanted to go with." She meets my eyes, and I understand why he's pissed.

"Oh," I reply, swallowing hard. "I was just about to head home. We were finishing up," I explain, motioning to the kitchen. "Deciding what should happen in there."

"They still got the ugly olive appliances?" Shirley asks.

Tahoe sighs, nodding. "Yep. Pepto Bismal tile in the bathroom, too."

"Caroline can give you the heads up with all of the local stores. The appliance store downtown doesn't have much of a selection, but he can order most anything you want. Everyone ordering stuff online these days really is a buzzkill for stores like that," she explains. "Making peace after buying a portion of town history is a good choice." Holding a hand out with a takeout bag. "Dessert." Shirley thrusts the bag into my hand.

Narrowing my eyes, I examine the bag. "Oh, I saw your bike and decided to stop in," I mock. "You're such a liar. I knew better, Shirley."

She laughs. "Fine, you caught me, but I did come bearing gifts." I peek in the bag to find two slices of my mama's famous peach pie. "I'll see you later, Care." She glances at Tahoe, and instead of bidding him farewell, she growls like a tiger, a throaty, embarrassing noise.

Closing the door behind her, I spin on Tahoe. He's ready for me, hands on his hips. "Don't beat around the bush," he says, tilting his head to one side. "Give it to me."

"What do you do when you're not training? You've told me bits and pieces here and there," I say, trying to keep the panic out of my voice. "This is a simple town filled with people who up until now, haven't been exposed to," I say, swallowing and waving an arm to his beastly, prominent frame, "your kind. Don't get me wrong, I know we need you and I appreciate what you do for our country, but you can't tell my parents the truth."

He stalks forward, his smile slipping into something more comfortable. "What are you asking, Caroline?" He licks his lips, and my confidence falters.

Looking left and right I avoid his piercing gaze. "You've killed people? Like, what happens in the movies?"

He laughs, a short burst. "Yes. Are you asking if I'll go into gory detail about the details of my job with your parents? You're worried about dinner?"

"Sort of, I guess. So, you have killed people?" It's like a swift punch. You expect it, so you flex your stomach, but it will still take your breath away regardless.

Closing his eyes, he folds his arms across his chest. "Bad people are killed. Yes. I have killed bad people. I'll never lie to you. If you ask me something I'll tell you the truth, but sometimes you won't want to hear it."

"Right, yes. I can see that. Bad people. Yes. That makes sense. And you're okay with that?" I'm rambling. Even if my ears hear it, my brain isn't doing anything to fix it. "I assumed that, do you kill a lot of people?" I throw my hands to the side and weigh them up and down like I'm an awkward human scale.

Tahoe heaves a sigh. "I'm not a paid assassin. It's not my whole job. The fact of the matter is SEALs have a lot of skills that are useful when you are trying to kill a bad person, so by proxy, killing happens. People who purchase humans," he says, a knowing look on his face. "Evil men who want to hurt those you love. Terrorists. "

I nod violently, slipping my hands into the oversized pockets of my overalls. "Of course."

Tahoe reaches a hand out and grabs my chin. "Look at me," he orders.

I focus on his beautiful blue eyes and breathe. He's different. That's not a bad thing. Is it? I knew this from the start. Even the village idiot knows Navy SEALs kill people. He grins when he sees me fitting the pieces together. "I'll never hurt you. Is that what you're worried about?" he asks.

I think about his hand. The fingers touching my face. How many lives has he taken with the same body parts caressing me right now? He didn't answer the question purposely. I don't want to know. Not really, anyways. The bubble I've resided in my entire life has been popped. Not just a pinprick either, with a warhead missile.

The dimple on his cheek deepens and I focus on that. A smile he surely doesn't wear when he's taking lives. "I know you won't hurt me," I whisper. "You are something entirely different and that is a little scary."

Everything about his demeanor softens with my reply. "I won't tell your parents anything that would be construed as gory or detailed," he says, laying a hand on his chest. "My parents don't know any of that either, and my dad is military. Caroline, it's not like I keep lines in my bedpost to mark each occasion."

"Of course not. That would be weird," I retort, swallowing hard. "Do you keep notches in your bedpost to keep track of...anything else?" I can't help how quickly my mind flits back to sex.

My question garners a full-blown smile accompanying a laugh. "Are you asking how many women I've had sex with?" He's completely amused, cheeks pink and grin calculating.

Embarrassed, I turn away. "I guess," I reply. He's already caught on to so much. Because of things my friends told me in the past, I always assumed men would be clueless—oblivious to the ways a woman is capable of asking for information. Tahoe destroyed almost every single pre-conceived notion I've ever had about expectations. He knows everything.

When he doesn't reply straight away, I ask, "Or is that something I don't want to know either?"

Clearing his throat, I can see indecision light his eyes. "I'm not sure of the number. That's an honest answer."

Accepting his answer is easy. It's truth. Tough because how does a person lose count? "You're not staying here tonight, right?"

He shakes his head. "Want me to ride you home?" A corner of his mouth pulls up.

"It's the opposite direction of your apartment," I say. "I'll be fine riding home by myself."

"There's no way I'm letting my girlfriend ride home by herself in the dark. If we were back in San Diego I'd drive you home in my truck. The nice one you didn't get a chance to see. The one I had to sell to come here."

I back toward the door. "We're in Bronze Bay. Or did you forget?" I ask. Tahoe moves around the room hitting light switches and grabs the ring of keys off the center table. After he locks up the front door and the gate we set off on our bicycles toward the airport.

The crickets chirp out their night song, and the stars shine brightly in the vast sky above us as the light on my bike illuminates the road in front of us.

He tells me stories about his travels as we ride. I'll ask questions when something comes up I don't understand. The stars look a little smaller by the time I'm parking my bike in the rack next to my airplane hangar—the sky, once the only freedom I've ever known, a little more suffocating. "Here's the thing," Tahoe says, parking his bike next to mine. My stomach flips when I think about him walking me inside. "I've been trying to come up with a proper explanation that isn't...offending. Kissing you was sort of like playing just the tip," he says, smirking.

"What's just the tip?" I ask, narrowing my eyes at him through the dark.

"Caroline," he growls, moving closer, until the flood light shines on his face. "Please tell me you're joking."

Familiar territory now. "Yeah. Of course. Joking," I say, rolling my eyes, hoping he can see it.

His neck works as he swallows. "You understand why I can't kiss you goodnight for more than a second then. Not while we're this close to your house. With a door that can lock. Your bed."

Instead of waiting, I close the distance between our bodies and kiss him. If I wait any longer, he'll see the hesitation and the innocence I'm trying so desperately to hide. His fingers twine around me and I shudder in pleasure. He moves his mouth against mine, his tongue dancing with mine, his hardness pressing into my stomach. "We could go upstairs," I utter against his lips.

His lips brush mine as he shakes his head no. "I got you something," he says, clearing his throat. "Well I snagged it from the dermo bin at work when I couldn't get ahold of you. It's where we toss gear and electronics when we're finished using them, or when new stuff arrives and we upgrade."

"Oh," I ask, leaning away. Sliding one hand into his pocket, he produces a small, older model cell phone. "It will work no matter where you are. I know you don't want to be tethered to a cell phone, but this can send and receive text messages. It will be helpful while we're working on the house," he explains, stepping away from me. When I make a move to approach, he puts a hand out. "Just the tip, Caroline. I have to leave," he says. "Right. Now."

"I don't really need this," I tell him, holding up the weird square phone. Everyone has one so I recognize what it is, and technology isn't foreign to me, but it's odd being reachable at any given point. "We could use the home phone."

"My house won't have a home phone. Most people's homes don't have home phones," he says, mounting his bike.

I laugh. "It looks like you're going to break that bike," I say.

His response is a wide grin, and then, "Better than breaking you."

"Text me," he says. "Have a good night, Sunny." He rides off into the dark after he watches me go inside and lock the door.

I look at the device laying in my palm and squeal like a little girl.

Chapter Eleven

Tahoe

"I have to do it," I say, a sheen of sweat cropping up across my hairline. Leif is on the other end of the phone. "Can I leave next week?" I have dinner with Caroline's parents tonight and I really, really don't want to miss it. We've jumped out of the airplane about eight times today. It was the stress relief I've needed. It's the adrenaline I've craved. My muscles are coiled hard and my mindset is intense.

"Yeah, next week shouldn't be a problem," Leif says, rattling off details about the mission I'm needed on. One of my brother's in San Diego has business to attend to and I'm needed to go fill in for him. It should be a quick mission—one that is in and out, and has me back to Bronze Bay in a few weeks. They're confident I've had enough time away to jump back into the game if only for a bit. My shooting is still top notch, and if anything, my mind is clearer now than it's ever been. As Leif tells me about the terrorist quad we're hunting in N.Y.C., I let my gaze trace the vast landscape of the airport until I see her. She's been ghosting around all day—staying out of our way almost completely. She's wearing that fucking white dress and a pair of Converse sneakers, her hair up in a massive bun on top of her head, arms full of some sort of metal piece that looks half the size of her body. Aidan rushes to help her carry the part the rest of the way into a hangar. She lets him.

"Three weeks, you said?" I ask, when there's a lull on the other end of the line.

He grunts. "Yeah, maybe longer, but you saw the intel last week. They can't have moved very far." When Leif called today, I knew exactly who they were going after. We may be on the opposite coast, living in small town, U.S.A. but they do a good job of keeping us up to speed. "It will be a quick flight from Bronze Bay, so you can leave any time of the day, really, especially now that we have our planes and pilot there," Leif explains. After a beat or two he adds, "You're going to miss your puppy. Awww."

"Shut the fuck up, Leif," I retort. "I can't wait to get back in it. I've been out of the game so long."

"Don't pretend you aren't having the time of your fucking life here. With her," he throws back. "You are constantly smiling like a lunatic and your testosterone levels are at an all-time low. Don't fuck up again. Before, it was because you were overworked. Now, it would be because you're underworked *and* underfucked," he says, changing our conversation completely. *Not for long*, I muse. Readjusting the parachute harness caging my chest, I look back at the hangar. Aidan and Caroline are laughing about something. Her white smile visible from here, and Aidan's body language says everything. He touches her arm before bending over to touch a part on whatever the fuck thing Caroline is working on. "Fuck you, Leif," I mutter, then click off the call.

With deadly purpose, I march toward the hangar. Mentally flipping through all the jealous insults I can't say for fear of being judged by my friend, and they would offend Caroline in a way I'd never dream of.

Their backs are toward me when I stop at the wide opening. "You didn't reply to my text," I growl. A greeting would be too easy, too simple.

Aidan spins first, his eyes wide, and fists clenched and ready. Caroline merely turns her head, a wide, lovesick smile on her face when she sees me. Guilt washes away any trace of envy.

Her cheeks pink as she stands and covers her mouth with a dainty, grease covered hand. "The phone," she exclaims. "It's in my bed. I'm not used to carrying something like that around with me. I'm so sorry. You messaged me?" Her blue eyes are clear and hopeful. If Aidan didn't realize I had her so completely before, he does now—his narrowed eyes and pinched mouth a clear indicator of defeat. "What does it say?" she says, lowering her hand to show black streaks now on her face.

I tilt my head toward my friend. "We're in mixed company right now," I say as an explanation. "Read it later."

"Aidan knows a lot about airplanes. I didn't realize that jumping out of them and working on them went hand in hand," she explains looking between us.

"Not all of us have that kind of interest," Aidan replies, a small smirk appearing as he looks at Caroline. "I've always loved aircrafts."

"Why didn't you become a Navy Pilot then?" she asks, genuinely curious. We both scoff. This is common ground. "SEALs have more fun," Aidan says, relaying both of our sentiments, exactly. "It's the hardest thing you can do in the Navy."

She shuffles one foot forward and backward. "It's not like you guys are having that much fun here," she says, but it's more of a question. "I had the news on last night and there's a lot going on over on the West Coast. SEALs are always handling something it seems."

She looks up at me. "Not that I watch the news very often, but I was curious."

Aidan says something about how he's glad he's in Florida because of the operation tempo. "There's plenty of stuff going on that's not on the news, Caroline. We're all happy to be here for more than one reason."

Aidan clears his throat. "I'll see you next Friday," he says, gaze lingering on her face longer than I'm comfortable with. She responds with her sweet smile. "I'll have this part taken apart by then. You can take a look when you have down time," she says, gazing at the huge metal piece like a mad scientist. Aidan says goodbye, lets his eyes slide to me briefly, and exits into the sunshine.

"You forgave him awful quickly," I growl.

She spins, a screw driver in one hand and the other perched on her hip. "Well, he does know a lot about airplanes. That sped things up a touch. Women never forget, Tyler," she says, using my given name, sending a shock of lust to my dick.

Swallowing, I let my eyes skirt down her midsection down her tan, bare legs. "Why are you wearing a dress to do work? It's almost as if you're showing off for someone."

Her lips form a thin line. "Just because I'm a woman who can turn a wrench doesn't mean I'm not a woman. It is too hot for pants. Shorts are restricting. Plus, I was in the office going through accounting stuff for most of the morning."

"Don't make excuses on my behalf," I reply, grinning. "Unless you say you wore it for me. Because you know how much I want to fuck you when you have it on."

Her blue eyes widen the moment her mouth pops open. "Is that what the text message said?" she says, voice a small whisper.

I move in, and use my thumb to try to smear the black grease spot off her face. "In some form or another. Yes," I reply. Caroline licks her lips. Sighing, I say, "What time is dinner? I have a dumpster arriving at the B and B in a couple hours," I say, looking at my watch. Now that I have the mission, I have a lot of planning to do and not a second to waste. "I'll pick you up after and we can ride up the hill together?"

She grins. "You're catching on."

I shrug. "What kind of boyfriend would I be if I didn't?"

"The kind that kisses his girlfriend even though she's covered in grease?" she replies. My heart does that melty thing it tends to do anytime she says something so sweet. Leif is right, my fucking testosterone is being demolished a little day by day.

Leaning over, I press my lips against hers. She tastes like fresh air, and the indescribable scent that is… Caroline. She pulls closer, but I don't let her, breaking the kiss before it truly begins. It gets harder and harder to remember why I wanted to wait to fuck her. Quite literally. "Tonight after dinner, how about we go a little faster? Your place?" I say, tone low. "I need more of you." Does she know what it costs to ask? That it causes me physical pain to not have her in all ways?

"A little faster?" she asks, breathless, dropping the screwdriver on the cement floor to place both hands on my chest. "What does that mean exactly?"

My breaths come quicker as her question sparks a million ideas of what I want to do to her and with her. "It means you trust me not to fuck you tonight."

She nods, complete compliance, utter infatuation with the idea of fucking me. It's so obvious anyone can see it. I wish Aidan was here right now. "Careful with Aidan," I say.

She smirks. "I only want you."

"Doesn't mean he won't try." He's a solid player—weaseling in at any sign of interest. I'd pat him on the back on a normal day. Now, I'll sleep with both eyes open.

"Stake your claim," she retorts.

I raise my eyebrows. "Okay then."

She swallows hard, and backs away. "You're finished jumping for the day?"

I nod. "See you in a bit."

"I'm going to clean up," she replies.

"Not too much," I say, biting my bottom lip as my eyes drop to the hem of her dress. "I like you dirty."

Turning, I adjust my uncomfortable hard on, and head back to my troop. Tonight. Tonight. Tonight. The beast, the old Tahoe can come out to play, just a little. Enough to give her pleasure and enough to tamp down the lust coursing through my veins.

Just the tip.

May cracks another joke about the military. He doesn't mean to be offensive, it's just that jokes are the only things these people know about the military. With the closest large base four hours away, little trickles down this far. Caroline, wearing another goddamn sundress, sits next to me at the long table in a fine dining room. Her mom buzzes around the room clearing dishes and refilling glasses that are perfectly full.

"Mama," Caroline croons. "Sit down. You're not working right now, remember?" It's a reminder her mom responds to. She takes her seat opposite me, and settles in to take a bite of pasta that's probably cold.

"How was the air today, Tyler?" May asks, sipping his Budweiser from a tall, iced glass. "Looked mighty fine from the ground."

I nod. "It was good flying today. We got in almost a dozen jumps. I think once a week will be perfect. Thank you again for letting us use the airport. The space is perfect." Caroline's hand snakes over to squeeze my upper thigh. Either she's worried about me talking about work or she can't keep her hands off me. "Our pilot was pleased with the set up and everyone was happy."

"How could we possibly say no to the generous offer?" he chortles. Caroline looks down. I knew it was a foregone conclusion when we made the monetary offer, but leave it to her to string me along for a glorious month. The month she made me fall for her due to sheer stubbornness.

Leaning back in my seat, I wrap one arm around Caroline's wooden chair back. "I'm not sure you could have refused," I reply, glancing from May to Caroline. "We wanted it pretty badly."

"You sure did, son. And because of it we don't have to worry about the bills anymore!" he exclaims loudly, one hand slapping the table.

Caroline shakes her head, laying a hand across her forehead. "Daddy. Subtlety has never been your strong suit. He's a business partner now. Try to be professional."

In that moment, the switch is thrown. Dad mode. "A business partner is he? That why your hand is on his leg, is it? Why we're eating dinner together as a family, huh? That why he looks at you like you hung the moon? He's a business partner then? Nothing more than that?" May dares her to challenge him, a narrowed grimace on his face. When Caroline takes a small bite of food he says, "That's what I thought."

"Tell us about yourself Tyler. Other than the glowing praise Caroline has given you, we don't know who you are," Mrs. May says, taking this as a prime opportunity to ask the hard questions. Clearing my throat, I set down my fork. "Well, ma'am, I grew up all over the world. My father is a Navy man himself. We never lived in any one place longer than a couple of years. They've settled in Chico, California." I lift and lower one shoulder. "I don't have any brothers or sisters by blood, but the Teams have given me a slew of brothers." Mrs. May is smiling when I finish my explanation, and I hope that's as much as I'll have to talk about my career path.

"Taking up after your Daddy. I like that," Mr. May says, glancing to his daughter with a fond look. "You're liking Bronze Bay then? Going to hang around for a while?"

Caroline snakes her hand away, and clasps her hands in her lap. "It's hard for some to fathom why someone like me would like to stay in a small town in Florida, but when you've lived the life I've lived, sir, you begin to appreciate the small, important things in life. You know when you have a good thing. A perfect thing. A beautiful thing. Something you want to keep," I explain, reaching under the table to take her hand in mine. "Bronze Bay opened my eyes to a whole new way of life. I love it here."

"Love is a pretty strong word," Mrs. May declares, her mouth quirking up in one corner. "It is a lovely place, though. We do know that Caroline loves Bronze Bay as much as we do."

Caroline tucks a strand of blonde, wild hair behind her ear. "Though I'm thinking I'd like to see other places."

"Oh," May asks. "You always said no sense flying anywhere when you couldn't get back the same day. This man got you thinking about branching out a bit?"

She swallows hard. "His stories are pretty amazing," Caroline says meekly. "Things I'd like to see for myself, that's all. Not on a screen, but with my own eyes."

It's the first she's mentioned it, not that I'm surprised. She has the flying bug. I'm sure it's only a small nudge to create a traveling bug, too. "We could start in New York?" I say.

"Really?" she says, eyes lighting.

"That's not safe. It's not safe at all in them, there big cities," Mr. May remarks.

Mrs. May lays a hand on his arm. "She'll be with Tyler, honey. How much safer could she possibly be?" At least mama bear catches on quickly.

I put one hand on my chest. "I'd never let anything

happen to Caroline, Sir. Trust that. I'd protect her with my own life."

You could hear a pin drop in that living room. The crickets chirping outside make their presence known in our acute silence. Caroline is staring at me, bottom lip pouting out. I'd kiss her if we weren't sitting at her parents table, and by the way she licks her lips, she knows it. "I haven't told you about the trip I have to take next week. How about we fly up there a little early and check it out?"

Her eyes slant down in the corner. "Oh, you're leaving?" Her mom and dad are talking to each other, ostensibly about Caroline going to New York and my credentials of caring for her safety.

I squeeze her hand. "For a few weeks. A quick trip. It will be like I'm not even gone."

Her eyes widen. "Three weeks is a quick trip?"

A rumble of a laugh shakes my body, I touch her arm lightly. "I won't have to do this a lot. I'm kind of, ah, filling in for someone. Don't worry," I coax. "Hey, what do you say? Do you want to go paint the town red with me? It will be a quick flight. You can even fly us if you want to scare me again."

She smiles. "How can I say no to that?" I release her when I realize every single word and move are being scrutinized by her parents. "Why didn't you tell me?" Caroline is still caught up in us, so she isn't aware.

"I found out today," I say loudly, including everyone in the conversation. "We have a block of rooms at a very nice, very safe hotel in Manhattan. I assure you despite our presence there, that city is one of the most protected in the country. The problems we'll be dealing with are on the outskirts." Lie. Lie. Lie. "You've never been there, right?" I ask Caroline.

Shaking her head, she says, "Of course not! Shirley is going to die when I tell her. She's always wanted to go! Oh my gosh." A woman who flies airplanes, but hasn't visited a bustling city mere hours away boggles my mind, but I'm learning. Caroline has quirks and hang-ups like any other woman. Hers are just, not as…normal. Or, at least not what I'm used to.

"She can come if she wants," I offer, hoping she declines. The prospect of having her all to myself in a different atmosphere fills me with anticipation. "I can show you both around. I've been there quite a lot over the years. There's so much to see," I explain.

"He goes from business partner to showing our baby around one of the biggest cities in the world," May says, tone droll.

"Now, now, dear. Remember the time we went to the city? How much fun we had? I think it will be an amazing experience for her."

Caroline interrupts. "I'm not a baby, daddy. Not even close. I'm a full-grown woman capable of touring a big city all by myself if I wanted to." She wouldn't do that, we all know that. May nods his head, because even he knows when not to push a woman. "I'd love to go with you, Tahoe," Caroline says, sliding her head to meet my gaze, and then bounces back to look at her mom. "As long as mama can live without me at the diner."

Her mom squints, like Caroline's words sting her on soul level. "Of course, the diner can live without you. Never feel like the restaurant is holding you back, honey."

Mr. May clears his throat. "You should know better. Your mama can replace you anytime you want. We both know you're going to want to spend more time at the airport as I ease my way out. We were expecting you to call it quits before now to be honest. You've been so busy working on that apartment, and with hurricane season approachin' you're about to get even busier I'd reckon."

Caroline looks down at her lap and our entwined hands. "If you say so," she replies softly.

"Whatever you want, darlin'," Mrs. May says. "You definitely need to go on that trip. Shirley can cover for you when I can't."

Mr. May swigs back the rest of his beer. "You'll take care of her then?" he asks.

I hold up my hand, palm facing outwards. "On my honor, sir."

He nods. I nod back. Mrs. May laughs, and claps her hands together. "This is such exciting news. I knew you were going to be a good thing for her, I didn't imagine you'd be the one to open up the world."

"Her world is already open. I'm excited to show her another piece of it," I reply, using caution with my words. When I dated Stella, I was constantly reminded that words matter. As infuriating and frustrating it was to get my language just so, I suppose the usefulness carried over. Words are, quite literally, forever.

Caroline sulks, arms folded, bottom lip inside her mouth. "You approve then?" she says. A beat or two passes before I realize she's asking her parents if they approve of me.

"We know he's capable of making you happy," May says, looking at me. "Maybe he doesn't fly planes, but he jumps out of them so I guess that counts for something."

"He commits," Mrs. May announces, interrupting her husband. My palms sweat at her proclamation, but isn't that exactly what I did from the moment I decided to befriend Caroline? First, I committed to infiltrating her life—getting the airport. Next came the complicated part, deciding she was worth the risk. The ultimate commitment.

"Mom, please. That's presumptuous," Caroline whispers.

She tsks in response. "You are a gem. A prize in this world. We spoke about this already. I think you two make a terrific couple and we're happy for you. Commitment is important, honey. It's what separates the men from the boys." Mrs. May glances at me, winking slyly.

I'm sure the gesture is her rendition of a threat and that's all well and good, but I don't need her threats. The threat looming inside my chest is enough to propel me into this relationship full steam ahead.

When I was growing up, I was aware I was an all

or nothing type of boy. That quality carried over to my teens, and then my carousing in adulthood. Merely joining the Navy like my Dad wasn't good enough. I needed to work my way into the most elite tier of the military. I was all in. When I was hunting pussy, I was all in. When any goal presented itself, I crushed it. It's a strong character trait on a good day and a debilitating disease the next. Right now, I've committed to making sure Caroline's heart is cared for properly. Fucking her too soon and I'm doing a disservice to her and to my own intentions. Waiting too long, and I'm asking for trouble from every other swinging dick in this town that wants a piece of her. Middle ground is what I'm searching for and hoping to land on. Tonight. After this dinner.

"She's right," I say to Caroline. "You are a gem." Her cheeks flush and she looks down to her lap again.

Mrs. May, laughs, pleased I'm siding with her. "You are such a flatterer," Caroline mutters. Then she asks me for details about the NYC trip. I tell her and the rest of the table as much as I know, and can. "Can we go to Central Park?" she asks

I nod. "There's a deli next to the park that I go to anytime I'm in town. You'll love it," I say.

"When you get back hurricane season starts," Mr. May says, reminding her of her airport duties. That peaks her interest and it isn't long before she's lost in conversation about storms and airplanes and weather. Sort of like my grandparents who like to banter about the chance of rain on a Wednesday afternoon. While they talk, I help Mrs.

May clear the table, stacking as many dishes as possible before entering the kitchen behind her.

"You're a natural," she jokes, taking the top plate that has a glass balancing on it. "If you need a waiting job. I know where you can find one."

I grin, and I see her face change, and I know whatever she has to say next isn't something she relishes talking about. "I'm afraid I can't be employed outside of the Navy, ma'am."

"That's a shame," she says, eyes downcast into the sink filled with soapy water. "What are your plans for the bed and breakfast?" she asks, moving a sponge against a plate.

There it is. The foreigner encroaching upon local land. "That's an awful big house for just...you," she adds, looking at me square on.

Telling her I had plans to tear it down and build a single-family home seems like a bad idea, so I go with the truth. "Well I'm just going to fix it up first, Ma'am. It needs a lot of work. I haven't really thought much past that. The time I spend with it will give me some indication of what I want to do with it."

"That's a big purchase to not have firm plans," she exclaims.

I swallow hard. "It was a shame it was sitting there empty, don't you agree? Someone had to buy it. Why not me?"

"Are you going to flip it? Fix it up and sell it?" Now her question makes even more sense.

Clearing my throat, I say, "I'm sticking around here," I say. I tell her that I put the offer on the property when I first arrived—that I knew I could make it brighter and more beautiful than it has been in the past. "The house is just a house. Bronze Bay is my home now. This is just my second hand slice of paradise."

Her smile seems genuine. "She's plum crazy about you, son. I hope that you will stick around. The men around here don't understand her. I've always been a little proud about that. Thinking maybe she would move away one day and find her match elsewhere. Being tied to a small town has both its ups and downs." She places the plate into the drying rack and starts washing another. "I don't want to frighten you off or anything. Don't think that."

I run my hands through my hair. "It takes a lot to scare me off," I reply. "Have any photo albums of Caroline as a teenager?" I joke.

She laughs, and Caroline clears her throat from behind me. I spin to meet her harried gaze. "What are you guys talking about? Only good things hopefully," she says, grabbing me around the waist. "Daddy thinks it's going to be a bad season this year," she adds.

"Don't change the subject. We were talking about scaring me off," I tell her, setting my big hands over hers.

Caroline's mother looks on fondly and I try to keep my dick in check. It has no clue we're in her parent's house. "I wasn't awful looking as a teenager," she cries. "Let me show you something cooler." She pulls on my arm and I follow her to a window next to a smaller table inside the kitchen.

"The hill," I say, nodding toward the steep decline.

"The famous hill," Caroline chimes in, releasing me a touch.

She points down the hill and through a copse of trees. "My hangar," she says. You can't see her parents' house from her hangar, but you can definitely see her house from here. It's the angle. The distance between the two is more than you'd guess.

"Because the property is close to the airfield with planes taking off and landing they got an amazing deal on the house and all of this land." It looks like they own half of this tiny city from where I'm standing.

"While this is a nice view and all," I whisper into her ear. "I'd really like to be looking out of your window right now." I have one arm wrapped around her waist—a heavy weight showing her how much I want to be on her in every way possible. "Except without clothes on," I add, so softly I wonder if she's heard me. Telltale pink cheeks tell me her truth.

"Dessert first?" she squeaks, turning to glance at her parents. Mr. May is drying dishes and Mrs. May is prattling on about the NYC trip while she tops a pie with whipped cream. The fact that they have a dishwasher, but wash dishes together tells me something about them as people.

If you pay attention you can know someone without speaking a word. Part of my training as a SEAL is reading people's body language and expressions. The phrase *actions speak louder than words* was never more true than when I discovered how easily people can be deciphered. It's when my heart gets mixed in that my radar is fucked. Caroline confounds me constantly and profusely, yet I want to unravel her one thread at a time.

Swallowing hard, I reply, "As long as you're on the menu for second dessert." My chest squeezes a little, knowing I'm finally going to be having a piece of her I've never had before.

"Don't mind my mom about that commitment stuff. She doesn't know that we're going slow," she says, facing the window once again, trying her best to brush off my come on. "Don't let her scare you. Even if you say you aren't, I don't see how it wouldn't." Licking her bottom lip, she chances a quick glance up at my face.

"Caroline," I say her name like a curse word and a scold at the same time. Both of her parents turn to look.

"Pie?" Mrs. May says, a chipper, hopeful smile on her face.

"Yes, of course, mama. We'll be right in."

May grabs a newspaper and vanishes into the dining room after his wife. Taking her by her elbows, I spin her toward me. "Do you honestly think I'm afraid of committing to you?" I ask, eyes narrowed.

She shrugs, both shoulders. "It wouldn't surprise me. Isn't that what men typically do these days? Have problems with staying with one girl. With the exception of the few good ones, most of the guys I know are like

Whit."

"Whit is an idiot," I return. "He's also an asshole."

She grins, pulling her bottom lip with her thumb and forefinger. "Sort of," she replies.

"Are you defending him," I ask, rumbling with mock outrage.

She smiles wider. "What if I am?"

"Then I'll have to kill him."

She drops her lip and looks at me, eyes wide, a horrified grimace transforming her beautiful face. "I'm joking, Caroline. I'm not going to kill him."

I have to give her credit for making a valiant attempt at masking her terror.

"I knew that," she says, rolling her eyes.

Glancing at the door to make sure we're truly alone, I settle my hands on either side of her ribcage and look her straight in her piercing blue eyes. "There's always a point in life, a moment that stands out as the one. The moment that changes things—forces you to realize that despite what you want, the world is giving you something else. I wanted the airport. Yes," I admit, pulling her closer. Lowering my voice even further, I say, "Then I danced with you in front of your window. The moonlight. Your voice when you asked what I would do if you took off your dress. The way I walked away. That was a moment when I realized I could thrive within the parameters of restraint. Because I want you. All of you. For as long as you're willing to offer yourself to me."

She breathes out deeply, alternating her gaze between

my eyes and lips.

"We can define the word commitment if you want, but to me? That's fucking commitment." I shake my head. "I don't want anyone else. There isn't anyone else for me."

"Pie is getting cold," May bellows from the other room. Caroline looks like she's about to reply, but then thinks better of it.

Taking me by the arm, she holds my hand. "Thank you for saying that," Caroline says as we take our seat and dig into the pie. Part of me wonders if she thinks I'm saying it to say it, that I don't truly mean what I've said. The fact I want in her pants so badly can't lend to my advantage. What would I say at this point if it meant I could fuck her in to next week? The answer comes quickly: *anything*.

Escaping work conversation was easy before, but now they're asking more specific questions about the attacks and it's hard to share stories without getting too graphic or striking a nerve. Everyone has a story about what they were doing when the terror attacks rocked our world, and fundamentally changed America. I was already a SEAL and if I'm being honest, we pray for work, action, a place to showcase our skills. That being said, no one wanted something so severe and life altering to happen. Caroline tells the story about how she was in the diner, serving at the counter when the television in the corner started replaying scenes of explosions and destruction in different cities across America and around the world. In her initial confusion, she dropped a steak knife and was cut. She moves the hem of her dress up more than I am comfortable with at the moment and shows the thin, red scar from the cut.

Mr. May was at the airport when he got a call from his wife who was having lunch with a friend two towns over. It helps that the attack connects us all even if it's in a terrifying way. It happened. We can't undo it so we move forward. Together. More unified as a country than we've ever been.

Caroline cuts off the conversation when Mr. May asks about what type of missions I've been on. She looks at me curiously, as if she really wants to know the answer, but in the end isn't ready to hear it. The only people I talk about this stuff with are my brothers and my father after he's had a few too many beers. Our relationship was strengthened through our patriotism, and the bond reinforced by our commitment to serve our nation in good times and in bad.

Instead of waxing poetic about war, I tell them a story from my father's glory days and that appeases them.

"We have to get down the hill," Caroline blurts during a lull in conversation. Standing, she clears our pie plates and hugs her mother.

May stands, wobbles a little because he's downed another Budweiser, and goes to shake my hand. "I'm proud to have you dating my daughter," he says. "The airport and the skydiving aside, I'm glad you're going to take care of my sweet Caroline." His jaw ticks.

Swallowing hard, I made my departure with the

weight of expectation weighing on my mind. We rode here on our bikes, and now that the sun has set, Caroline leads because she has one of those weird lights beaming on the front of her bicycle.

I'm left pedaling behind her on a well-worn path leading down to the airport. You can see the road off to the side. The absence of cars doesn't surprise me anymore, but it does remind me how different my life is now. The trip to N.Y.C. to use my God-given skills is probably a well needed dose of reality—it will remind me of who I am at the very least. Caroline calls back to tell me to watch out for a tree root protruding from the ground, but it's too late and I hit the damn thing at full speed and tumble off the bike.

I only stop rolling, because my body slams against a small tree. By that time, Caroline has stopped and is walking her bike back up to me.

"I told you!" she cries, looking me up and down. "Are you hurt? Your arm is bleeding!" Her voice echoes off the trees. "I knew we should have ridden the road instead," she muses to herself. "Let me see the cut," she orders, taking my arm into her hands.

"Only my pride is wounded," I sigh. "It's a scratch."

She shakes her head. "This bike is too small for you. You need to look into a bike for a giant or something. It was only a matter of time before this happened. Anytime I see you on the thing it looks like you're teetering on the edge of disaster." It's cute how she's fawning all over me, so I let her. "Tahoe, you could have killed yourself!"

"Sunny, you called out the warning about ten seconds too late," I say, smiling. "You'd be a horrible SEAL." I lean up to a sitting position and eye my bike. The front wheel is bent. "I might need a new bike though."

She laughs. "I called out the warning in plenty of time," she argues. "You were probably looking at my ass or something instead of paying attention to the trail."

Now it's my turn to cackle. I make a big production of standing and then fake limping over to my bike. "What hurts?" she asks, practically yelling. "You need x-rays, don't you? It's because my parents approved of you, isn't it? You're sabotaging everything!" It's one of the few times I've seen Caroline joke around.

My bike leans to one side. "Well, you're the one that didn't believe I was committed." Taking off my shirt, I press it against my bicep to catch the blood before it drips down onto my jeans. Jeans don't get washed but once a month. I'd hate for a little blood to move that date up. I have standards to uphold.

Caroline's gaze drops to my bare midsection. Clearing her throat, she says, "Here's the thing, I know we are supposed to mess around tonight, but I think we should have a discussion about expectations first." I pull the shirt off my arm and examine the cut. The bleeding has stopped for the moment.

"Oh," I ask, raising one brow. "What with my injury and all?" I joke. "I can assure you this arm is fully functional. I've been through worse." Tossing my shirt over one shoulder, I start rolling my mangled bike down the path.

She looks away and then down to the ground. "We need to get it cleaned up as soon as we get home." I like how she says home. Like I belong there as much as she does. I've lived in a lot of places, but no place has ever embedded itself deep enough to be considered home; not even the one I built. My friends who have wives and long term girlfriends say it happens when a person becomes home. I didn't know what they meant until now. Caroline feels like home.

The outside hangar lights hit our bodies like spotlights and it's a short distance to park our bikes before we head inside. The first thing she does when she closes the apartment door behind us is go into her bathroom to grab her first aid kit. I sit on the sofa because I know what comes next, and I know not to argue about anything she feels the need to do.

She clears her throat and dabs the cut with a piece of gauze. The scent of the medical grade cloth makes my heart pound. My mouth waters and I close my eyes, trying to inhale her scent, any scent, other than the cloth. I'm not in another country. I am not in a hospital bed. I am not getting bullet holes tended. No. I'm sitting in Caroline's house. Deep breaths. Then one more.

"Are you sure you didn't hit your head," Caroline asks, putting a hand on the top of my pec muscle.

Opening my eyes, I'm met with blatant concern pooling in her clear, see-through soul eyes. This is another of those moments. The urge to lie is there, but if

I don't, it means something. "I didn't hit my head," I say, leaning over to peck her lips quickly.

Caroline nods softly, almost as if she doesn't believe me. "The scent of the gauze," I mutter, swallowing down the terror. "It reminds me of other times I've been hurt."

She takes it away from my body, and puts it behind her back. "You don't have to hide it," I say, smiling widely. "I'm okay. You're the one holding it. You could be stabbing me with a knife right now and I'd be okay."

Tentatively, she brings the gauze back up to my arm. "If you're sure. I'm almost finished cleaning it. Do a lot of things trigger bad memories?" she asks, not meeting my eyes.

"I don't know until I stumble upon something that reminds me of something else. The scent of a hospital is pretty awful. Fireworks and sewage, too."

Caroline crinkles her nose, leaning away from me. "We travel in the sewage lines to find targets. One time it took far longer than it should have and evidently my body revolts now," I explain. She opens a bandage and applies it with the softest touch. "I can't pump cesspool on a build. That's a messy job anyways."

"You're all fixed," Caroline declares. "I'm sorry about the gauze. I wouldn't have used it if I'd known."

"It's fine. I meant it. I'm not a woman. I don't say it's fine when really I'm a bomb of emotional destruction. I'm really fine. Now you know one of my weaknesses."

She sighs. "If only that were the case," she says, wadding up the used medical supplies in her fist. "You are pretty perfect in every single way. So you don't like the smell of gauze. A lot of people don't like the scent of hospitals. Tell me something awful, Tyler Holiday. What is your greatest flaw?"

"Deep questions tonight, huh?"

She shakes her head. "I'll go first. I live inside my head too much. It keeps me from truly living. I mask it by piloting planes and throwing myself into projects full speed ahead. Because really, how can a woman who flies planes, be scared of everything else?" Caroline says, standing from the sofa. I watch her through narrowed eyes. Her chest rises and falls as she confesses her truths, eyes brimming with tears. "A man like you isn't scared of anything so it's hard for me to rationalize what you see in me. My fear is that I'm your project. You'll fix me and then leave me." Taking a few steps away from me, she lets her gaze flit to every part of my body.

I stand, towering over her. "My greatest flaw? That's what you want?"

She shakes her head. "It's what I need," she amends.

I look out the large window, setting my hands on my hips. "In a job interview you'd have to say something like, I'm too ambitious, or I am a workaholic. In this instance, I think my flaw is simple," I say, my voice cracking on the last word. Shrugging, I slip my hands into my pockets, my arm stinging from whatever ointment Caroline smeared on me. She's rapt, waiting for me to confide in her. "I'm mediocrity's greatest opponent."

"Explain," she whispers, folding her arms across her

chest.

I cross to her, until I'm close enough to see the freckles sprinkled across her small, perfect nose. "I have to be perfect. Or whatever my mind deems as perfection. I don't do halfway. My moral compass is set to one standard. Perfection," I growl, shaking my head. "If I can't do something flawlessly, I won't do it."

Under her thick lashes, her eyes search my face for reason. She won't find it, though. I know this flaw is something no one will understand unless they are like me. "That's a little…intimidating," Caroline croaks.

I brush her hair back so I can study the planes of her face, the high cheekbones, the bow of her top lip, an errant scar that marks the spot on top of her eyebrow. I lose my breath. "No, you're intimidating," I growl, bringing my lips to the tip of her nose. She slides her hands up to rest on my stomach and my body jolts from her touch—everything springing alive with ferocious desire.

"I'm not flawless," she says.

"You're my definition of flawless." I let my hands skirt the small part of her waist. "I'm going to take you into the bedroom now," I say, my heart hammering out a goddamn symphony.

Biting her bottom lip, she grins. "Can you do that perfectly?"

The feral look in her eyes calls to me, tells to me eat her alive. "Fuck yes, I can." I scoop her up—her light weight in my arms a reminder how delicate and precious this human is to me.

I lay her down on the light pink bed and take in the sight.

"Come kiss me," she says.

With one hand on either side of her body, I hold all of my weight up for fear of destroying this crystalized moment. Lowering my head, I rub my lips across hers back and forth a few times before taking her mouth in a kiss. I close my eyes and bask in the feelings. When I open them as I pull away from the kiss, she opens her eyes—a hazy, longing urging to give her more.

The words come before I can stop them. "I'm falling for you, Caroline May."

Her smile is beatific, something that simultaneously takes my breath away and gives me life. "I'm flying for you, Tahoe Holiday."

Chapter twelve

Caroline

The heat seeping from his body warms me to my soul. The way he's looking at me like I'm some long-lost treasure solidifies everything I've been trying to prove to myself. Inside this huge beast of a man is a fragile, hesitant heart. I'm in love with Tahoe so endlessly and deeply, I already know no one else in my entire life will compare. The tenderness in moments he has no control over is intoxicating, his subtlety lacks therefore, it's all on display. He sets my every nerve ending ablaze. From the roots of my hair to my baby toe on each foot, everything is vibrating with uncontrollable excitement. My stomach tilts and turns merely looking at his chest, his coiled, tight stomach, the mouthwatering square jaw line. This is the first time I've felt anything even remotely similar to what everyone tells me love is. Confusing it with lust was a concern, until I realized I was holding myself back   standing in my own way. I perceived him as a jerk in the beginning because that's what I labeled him. My self-doubt wouldn't let me believe a man like

Tahoe would choose a woman like me. Here we are, though. His body inches away from mine, my pulse echoing inside my ears, and my hands reaching up to his shoulders to pull his body against mine.

I want him. I choose him. "I need to see you naked," he says, breaking the kiss to push up on his arms, his eyes telling me it truly is a *need*. Naked. Naked. Naked. The word ricochets around my mind as the realness of this hits. He senses the panic, shaking his head. "I can hold myself back. I'm not a complete caveman, Caroline. We're not having sex tonight. Not yet."

Biting my lip, the fear slips out. "Why not tonight?" I ask, admiring the veins pulsing on his biceps, and then focus my gaze on his.

"We defined this," he says, sitting back on his knees, pulling me to sit in front of him, "As something we wanted to take slow. Raise your arms," he says. Lifting them above my head feels strange, but the feral smile on his face tells me this is going to be fun. He slides my dress over my head in one fluid movement. He tosses it on the chair in the corner of the room without taking his eyes off my body. I planned for this, knowing something like this was going to take place tonight. The bra and panties are matching—a cotton candy pink set.

"You're perfect," Tahoe rasps, trailing his fingers over my shoulders and down my arms, his gaze following in their wake.

"But not perfect enough to have sex with?"

He sucks in a noisy breath. "That's what you think?

That I don't want to rip off those tiny panties and fuck you until you can't walk straight for a week?" He shakes his head, a wide smile on his face. "That's why I can't have sex with you tonight, Caroline. I need to ease myself into you. Us. Literally. I want you terribly."

"Oh," I say, swallowing hard. "I just assumed you were used to having sex whenever you wanted."

He slides the bra straps down my arms until my breasts spring free. "I'm not used to having sex with you," he replies. "Can I kiss you?" His gaze darts up to meet mine. It's a plea.

I grin, but then his blue eyes dip down to my panties and I understand his meaning. "Yes," I squeak out. Talk about rounding the bases at warp speed. Tahoe leans over and kisses one nipple and then another. My whole body shudders in pleasure, even my lips tingle. The way he reaches behind my body and unclasps my bra with one hand sends a flood of wetness between my legs. He knows exactly what he's doing. This is a trait I want in a man. Need in a man. His confidence will rub off on me and I'll feed off it.

The bulge in the front of his jeans is protruding large and in charge. He's adjusted it at least half a dozen times since we've been in my bedroom. The curiosity is almost too much to bear. "Lay back," he orders, putting a huge palm on my chest to ease me down.

As he edges nearer, I let my fingers trace the dark blue tattoos etched on his chest and arms. He watches the movement with interest, but I see the goosebumps rise on his skin. "You're a magician," he whispers, leaning down to kiss a freckle on my stomach, and then the other two close by. "You do things to me I can't explain."

I try to keep my head in the conversation, but with his lips searing against my skin it's hard to think about anything except what I want. More. More of him. All of him. All over me. Inside me. However I can get him. His kisses make me greedy. "That feels so good," I say, letting my eyes close.

"Keep them shut. It will feel even better," he orders.

"Can I touch you?" I ask on a sigh, imagining what he looks like without pants. "I want to touch you too."

He groans, and my core clenches with need. "Not now."

When he sucks my nipple the intense feeling of floating hits me in dreamy waves. His tongue flicks the other nipple before closing over it in a lavish kiss. I arch my back and spread my legs further—begging for his attentions elsewhere. "Your skin tastes so good," Tahoe growls, and then trails his fiery kisses up the side of my neck to my ear. "I'll never get enough of it." His tone is a low raspy promise of pleasure.

A tiny noise escapes my mouth and I have to open my eyes, I need to see him right now. His face is close to mine so I take it with both of my hands and bring his lips to mine, pulling him on top of me and in between my legs.

His smile against my lips encourages me more. Raising my hips, I press myself against his steely shaft.

It's hard and although I'm still wearing panties, in this moment, it feels like I'm bare, exposed in every way. "I haven't kissed you yet," he says, taking his skin away from mine. The calculating gaze he wears as he touches my legs ties my stomach in knots. Leaning back on his knees, he hooks two fingers into the side of my panties.

I swallow hard and lift my hips as the perfectly selected underwear skim down my legs and land on the floor next to my bed.

I hold my breath as he exhales for what seems like eternity. "When you wear those tiny shorts I think about what this might look like," he says, touching me lightly, causing me to shiver. He goes on, "Because they leave so little to the imagination," he admits, shaking his head. "Somehow seeing you right now, just for me, has exceeded all of my wildest dreams." The dimples next to his smile pop. "Caroline, I'm not sure what I did to deserve you, but I'm glad you think I'm worthy."

Even through my embarrassment of being naked when he's not, I smile. "How could you possibly think you're not worthy?" The question is simple, but my body has so many sensations sliding around, I've never been more confused or turned on in my life.

One hand splayed on my upper thigh, the other hand teases me between my legs, small, faint strokes against my clit. "Because I'm not," he says, flicking his gaze up to meet mine. "As long as you know that."

I'd tell him anything to keep his fingers moving against me. "I know," I say, letting out a held breath.

Tahoe places a wet kiss on my lower stomach and then down further. His tongue darts out and I watch in awe as his face moves. "Ahhh," I yell, as the sensation of his mouth on me settles in. My thighs quake with pleasure and the warmth of his presence heats my entire body. The noises of him licking, and his grunts of primal exhalation send my body into overdrive. I grab my hair and close my eyes. This isn't what I thought it would feel like, it feels so much better. My belly warms as his mouth works, and the tingles start enveloping me as a whole. The muscles in my stomach tighten and coil as the orgasm approaches quicker than I ever thought possible. It's like he caught the scent of the impending waves, because he licks more furiously, and my toes curl, and everything below my waist explodes—ebbing and flowing in ecstasy. The fireworks behind my eyelids fade to black, and my quickened breathing slows. Leaning up I look at Tahoe's face, smiling, in between my legs, his lips shining.

"Perfect?" he asks.

I nod. "Brilliantly perfect," I respond. He wipes his lips on the inside of my thigh before moving up my body.

"These lips. I want to kiss them and your pussy at the same time." He growls, and then closes the gap between us with a kiss. Clutching around his neck, I ride the waves back down to reality.

"So, how many times can you do that in a row?" I ask, grinning. He kisses me savagely and we bump smiles. "I mean, an average."

Tahoe chuckles, a throaty, turned-on baritone. "Is that a challenge Caroline May? Cause I'd eat that pussy all night long if it is." I wrap my legs around his body and raise my hips to press my wet core against his jeans. "You wouldn't survive coming that many times."

"Let me return the favor," I say, leaving my words at the edge of his ear. I kiss his ear and he shudders—his whole body shaking with need.

His whole neck works as he exerts self-control—holding himself at a distance, but his need eats at my awareness, I can taste it in the air. "You know what goes well with an orgasm?" he asks.

"I don't smoke. You know that," I counter, pressing my mouth against the rapid pulse on his neck.

He shakes his head, causing my lips and tongue to rub across his neck, back and forth. "Another orgasm," he deadpans, dragging his fingers up the side of my body.

"That's witty," I reply.

"It's truth," he deadpans, slipping the hand on my thigh around to between my legs, as he edges his body down. "You're so wet." Opening my legs, I give him better access.

And a better view. "My God, your pussy is perfect." I watch as he looks between my legs with narrowed eyes. "Literally perfect," he says, confused. "Have you been told that before?"

I open my mouth to respond, but he shakes his head. "Never mind, I don't want to know." He licks his lips, which causes me to fist my comforter. Instead of using his tongue, one finger traces the lips, gliding around with ease. "I feel like I would destroy you," he admits.

I know it's a joke, but he has no clue that is a real possibility. "Let me see you," I order again.

He leans his head to one side. "I don't know if I'm strong enough to be naked with you while I still have the taste of you on my tongue and that masterpiece in my presence," he says, nodding between my legs.

"Come on. Fair is fair. Ladies choice," I say, trying and failing to wiggle out of his grasp.

He raises one brow. "If you insist. But you don't have to return the favor, Caroline. That's not what tonight is about."

"What if that's what I want?"

He leans up, and then stands at the foot of my bed. He towers over me and takes up the majority of the space in my bedroom. Leaning up on my elbows, I recognize the blood is rushing around my body in a manic manor, all concentrating at my core. Tahoe kissed a girl and awakened a woman. One that lusts after his sculpted body and whatever he has below the belt. His jeans slide off and pool around his feet. No underwear. That answers my question about boxers or briefs. I've seen him in a speedo so I'm not violently shocked by the size of his package, but I admit it's still stunning, cutting the air in between our bodies, standing straight out in front of him.

Before I can check my emotions, one of my hands flies to cover my mouth as I wide-eyed gape at his manhood. "Oh," I say around my hand. "That's big."

Tahoe laughs. "Big, huh? You know how to stroke a man's ego."

I swallow once and let my hand fall. Shaking my head, I say, "I am not stroking your ego, Holiday. It's enormous," I exclaim. Then the horrific truth about my virtue flashes in my mine. "Is, is, that a normal size?"

Stepping out of his jeans, he walks toward me, chuckling. "I like this game. Keep going," he remarks. "Tell me what you want to do with my huge dick." I'm not sure if it's possible, but it looks like every single muscle on his body is flexed. The dropped pendant lights in my room shine from above, highlighting every ripple and vein on his body. He's magnificent.

I scoot closer to the edge of the bed and look up at him. "Tell me what you want me to do with it."

He flashes a half grin. "You wanted to touch it," Tahoe says.

Tentatively, I reach out a hand and palm it in my hand. "I can't even touch my fingers," I say, surprising even myself.

"Maybe you have small hands," he replies, holding up one of his palms. With my free hand, I press it against his big one. Mine is small compared to his, but that doesn't say much given his size.

I stroke his shaft in front of me as he watches every move I make, though he does alternate his gaze to my naked body, and my face every so often. "That feels good," he says, closing his eyes for a beat or two.

Thank God, I think. "Should I put my mouth on it

now?"

A gentle smile appears, but he keeps his eyes closed. "You never have to ask permission to put my dick in your mouth. That's a firm rule. Consider it in the definition," he says, sighing.

I let my hand do most of the work, and use my tongue to graze the head, the tiny hole with clear liquid spilling out. It tastes salty, but not really a describable flavor. I hide a grimace.

Tahoe sways on his feet. "Lay down on the bed," I tell him, pausing my sucking.

"I want to come standing," he replies. "It feels good this way."

Is this something I should know? I start to panic and immediately throw myself back in to the act. With my pace steady, it can't possibly take that long. He made me orgasm in minutes. And easily. *But he's perfect, Caroline.* I'm not. So I work harder, letting his hand on my head guide me.

When I feel like my mouth is about to fall off of my face he announces he's about to come. "Just like that. Keep doing that," he says, the words broken in gasps.

Then, when I should be expecting it, he comes in my mouth. The strange salty flavor at the start stings my tongue in a mass flood I'm not sure what to do with. My gag reflex won't let me swallow, but my pride won't let me spit, so I hold him in my mouth, with the come.

His hands stroke my hair softly, and he pulls my head away. I'd tell him not to if I didn't have a wad of hot garbage in my mouth, so I suck it all in to avoid dripping anything anywhere.

Sighing, he tilts my head up to look at him. He's wearing a sleepy, satisfied grin. "Swallow or spit?" he asks, confused. God, is there an option? Shit. A story Shirley once told me erodes my brain, and I do what she did. I push the gelatinous load to the back of my throat and swallow it down. It's warm sliding down my throat and maybe I keep a disgusted look off my face, but I can't help the shudder.

Tahoe falls on the bed, pulling me with him. "I never would have pegged you as a swallow girl," he remarks, kissing me on the forehead.

"I'm, ah, usually not," I tell him. "Guess I was in the moment."

"You don't like giving blow jobs?" he says, it's less of a question and more of an observation. Maybe I wasn't as subtle as I thought I was.

I clear my throat and get a taste of the remnants. "It tastes weird. I like it."

He laughs. "Liar. It's fine. I'd rather eat you out anyways. Can I do it again?"

Maybe that will take my mind off the most embarrassing blow job of all time. "I'll never say no to that," I quote him.

Then, he's on me.

When I wake in the morning, Tahoe is gone—the other side of the bed faintly warm. He left a note on my pillow using male chicken scratch. It says three, reassuring words. *You are perfect.* I smile like a lunatic and hug the crumbled paper to my chest, and then see words written on the back, *because I know you won't check your phone.* Back in the real world, I have a job, and friends counting on me. I grab the cell phone from my night stand drawer and fly into the bathroom to crank on the hot water in the shower.

We slept naked last night, which was a test of my self-control, because even after the last orgasm had been rung from my body, I wanted to mount him like a stallion and claim him completely. It was an out of body experience. I didn't feel like me. I feel new. He gave me a piece of myself I didn't know I was missing. The phone lights to life and his text message pops up on the screen. *Last night was the best night of my life.* Another message chimes a second later. *In case you didn't see my note… you are perfect.* My heart skips a beat. I hear I love you, inside those three words and I wonder if that's his intent. It's scary and exciting, and everything in my life is being tilted all at once in another direction. *I'm at the B&B this morning before I head in to work. I hired a contractor to get some of the demo finished while I'm we're NYC. Is that cheating?* The message pops on my screen moments before I step into the steaming shower.

I type back. *Hiring demo help isn't cheating. I guess… because you are busy saving the world and stuff. I'll* be splitting my time between the office and the garage today. Call me if you need help. I hit send.

I had to borrow your bicycle. Well, I guess he would have to.

I tap back. Don't break it, beast.

I'm getting into the shower. I tell him. Because it's a fact. The secondary meaning to that statement rushes ahead and I wish I could take it back. I'm not a forward woman. Southern women are raised to be mild mannered and well behaved. Telling a man I'm naked and about to wash myself is bad form. Last night I broke about seventy-five rules for the southern lady, so I shouldn't get red cheeked now. I make a mental reminder to talk to Shirley about the art of blow jobs, and get into the shower.

Memories from the night before trickle in and the warmth spreads across my body so quickly, I'm hot before my hair is even wet. He said it was perfect, but my stomach knots when I think about his huge shaft in my mouth. How is that supposed to fit inside me?

Taking the bottle of honeysuckle scented body wash from the shelf I pour some into my hands and lather them together before working them over my legs, arms, my neck—washing away his kisses. Then I let my fingers gently glide between my legs. I'm still sore from his fingers working me over and over. I'm still wet, more than ready, and it is doubtful that desire is going anywhere until he's satiated me. Tentatively, I slip one fingertip into my slick entrance. "There's no way it's going to fit. No way," I say out loud. Water and soapy bubbles cascade down my body as I try to perform fuzzy math. His dick is too big. Shaking my head I resolve to talk to Shirley about that, too. While one of my other friends, Malena perhaps, might have more delicate sex advice, Shirley is the only person I want knowing about my extracurricular activities. It's my only fair chance of keeping my business off the town radar while still getting the knowledge I need.

Once I'm downstairs in the office sorting through paperwork and returning emails, the land line rings. I recognize her number right away.

"What took you so long to call me back," I ask. "What if I was in trouble?"

"Whoa, whoa, whoa. Ease off the volume button, girl. I, ah, just got my phone back. I left it somewhere last night."

Rolling my eyes, I wind the coiled cord around my finger. "Whose house was it last night, Shirl?"

"Caleb," she says, sighing.

"Again? That's the third time in one week. What's going on between you two? I thought you weren't interested in him in that way?"

"What way?"

"More than sex," I reply.

She grunts. "Its good sex so it's nice when I forget my phone. I can wake up and get a little action. Speaking of," she says, her sentence trailing off. "You mentioned in the voicemail, you needed some advice. The only reason you'd want my advice is if it was something you don't know about. Let's face it. You know everything. Except for one area of inexperience. Did. You. Fuck. That. Beautiful. Man?"

Cringing, I debate talking to someone else, but she is right. She knows things I don't. Things I need to know. "No!" I exclaim, cradling the phone between my ear and neck so I can pick up my chiming cell phone. "Maybe we should talk about this in person. We had dinner with my parents last night."

"And what happened after?" She goes straight for the jugular. It's exhausting.

"He invited me to go to New York City with him before his mission."

"You bitch. I hate you," Shirley crows. "When?"

I tell her the details I'm sure of and explain how my parents now approve of him. It kind of spills out and I know this is how rumors start, how the amazing things in one's life turn into something awful and callous because it doesn't exist in someone else's, but I can't help myself. Shirley eats up every single word. She asks about the Homer property and I tell her about the plans he has finalized and the work that's being done as we speak.

"It seems everything is perfect for you, Caroline." She emphasizes the word perfect because I told her what he said about me. For the most part she does seem happy for me, though I know what will happen next even if she is my best friend. Whatever Tahoe and I have won't be ours anymore. It will belong to Bronze Bay.

I clear my throat. "Please don't tell anyone, Shirl. We are taking things slow."

Her eye roll can be heard through the phone line. "What did you have to ask me?"

Tahoe texts me again and I thumb a button to clear the screen. "Tell me how to give a proper blow job, Shirley. Don't leave out any details. I mean, I think I did it right because he…came, but what are the rules? Are there rules? Swallow, spit? Standing, sitting, laying down? These are the things I need you to tell me and so help me, God, Shirley you better not make fun of me. I called you because I knew you would give it to me straight. No bullshit."

Shirley's laughter overshadows another small ping on my cell phone. I hit another button to try to clear the screen but it seems to have sent a message instead.

"Shirley," I croak, reality setting in.

She pauses long enough to ask what else I want to know. "I just sent him a voice message."

Her laughter rings out again, louder this time. "Everything I just said. Can I delete it before he opens it?" As I say it I notice the message says, *Read* underneath it. "Oh my gosh! This is worse than me asking for blow job advice to begin with. Now he knows I don't know what I'm doing."

"Honey, chances are last night he knew you didn't know what you were doing," she replies. "Are you ready? I'm going to give you the rundown. Get a notepad and some paper, I have a shift in an hour."

My cheeks redden and my stomach flips as I wait for his reply. "Ha-Ha. Don't make jokes. Just tell me," I say. No reply comes.

I'd never admit it to Shirley, but I do jot down notes as she rambles on about the finer nuances of sucking the male cock.

I don't want to forget.

Chapter thirteen

Tahoe

I'm jittery. Not from the pot of coffee I drank this morning while tearing out cabinets either. Caroline. Her laugh, her face, a snapshot of her body is on repeat in my mind. I can't escape the memory from last night. Her body is indeed a fucking wonderland. A candy coated, sugar infused, soft, tight, morsel of sheer delight. I've never wanted anything or anybody more in my life. She accidentally sent me a voice message that I'm sure was meant for a friend. It confused me at first, because she gave good head. Then after I dissected the blow job and the things she said, I realized she may not have given many blow jobs in her past. Poor, sad, sorry ex-boyfriends of Caroline. I didn't text her back for fear of embarrassing her, but my chest is puffed out a little more than it usually is today.

Last night truly was the best night of my life. If I close my eyes I can smell her arousal and that makes my cock stand like a goddamn soldier ready for battle. Right now, I'm wearing a shortie wetsuit and flippers, standing on a boat full of testosterone filled men waiting to drop in the water for a dive and that is not where I want him. It's off the clock, we're out here to have fun, spear fish, and bullshit. "I need to tell everyone something," I call out, my voice loud. There are a few grunts and groans in acknowledgement, so I continue. "I'm in fucking love," I yell.

There's more groaning, and someone tells me to go fuck myself, but they aren't going to wipe this smile off my face. Not by a long shot. "I need everyone to know this!"

"We know. We know. Your balls are in the vice. Got it," Aidan barks. "Let's get on with it now that it's off your chest."

I shake my head. "My balls are in the very soft hands of one, Caroline May," I reply.

"Someone slice his air hoses the next time he dives. He doesn't deserve oxygen," someone says to my back.

Chuckling, I throw my hands out wide. "All you assholes don't know what you're missing. I'm telling you."

Aidan sighs. "Tell us then. What are we missing? As far as I can tell, you're stuck with one pussy and you become a slave to a schedule. Neither of those things sound appealing, bro. Neither."

For a moment or two I stay silent, trying to concoct a reason they'd accept, or not shut down immediately, but I realize nothing I say will sway them. You have to live inside of this feeling to understand how it exists. Stella never gave me this feeling. She was a comfortable safety net capable of making me think she was irreplaceable. To think people confuse that for love on a daily basis is terrifying.

"You're missing *everything*," I say, turning to face my friend. The companionship. The trust. The conversation. The way you view a person after you've fallen.

Leif clears his throat, and pats me on the shoulder. "You're delusional. When you fall from grace, again, I'll be here for you, man."

"She's it for me."

His eyes narrow. "What does that mean exactly?"

"Yeah, man. We gonna' be suiting up for a wedding then?"

I gulp. That word takes me aback. Like it always does and probably always will. I'm married to the Navy. That's the first priority, it has to be. *I don't know any other way.* How can I do both things perfectly? It's an impossibility. Isn't it? The scales will always be tipped in one direction.

They pick up on my silence and go in for the kill. "That's what we thought."

"She's different," I explain. "More."

Leif crosses his arms across his chest. "Not different enough, though. We are your family," he says. "Women come and go, but we've always been here for you. Go ahead and get hard-dicked over her, just don't be crazy. Bros before hoes, Tahoe. Teams before seams." Aidan grins at the crude joke. A phrase I used to live by and accept. With Caroline, it seems offensive and dirty to associate her as that. I wave them off, playing at nonchalance. I should have kept my mouth shut, shouldn't have given them anything to hound me over, but I can't shake her. It's the truth. I am in love with Caroline May. Irreparably so.

Clearing my throat, I step up to the edge of the boat with an image of Caroline circling inside my mind. It took a lot of praying and internal pep talks with myself to keep from fucking her last night when she all but begged me for it. At this point, I know we are going to. It is just the matter of keeping it on my terms. Making it special for her. Forcing perfection in the one area of my life I have full control over. Few understand my wild quirks, but those that do, don't question them. New York City. That's when it's going to happen. I'll take her to a nice dinner, get my hands on tickets to see a show, and then a romance infused, passionate night at the luxury hotel I have booked. I've rehearsed it in my head since the second my eyes popped open this morning. A solid plan was never made without preparation.

Leif nods at me, still grinning from besting me, or assuming he bested me. Instead of replying, I set my mask in place and drop into the deep ocean waters.

They think they know me so well. They don't know everything. Sure, some of these guys know my parents and have seen me through the ups and downs of my life, but for others it's a surface understanding, an assumption of character based on those around me. The bad part about all of this is that I care what they think.

I kick in the water, following the guy in front of me, checking my surroundings to make sure everything is copasetic, and I get even more irritated. I might be in love with Caroline, but these guys are my brothers and they're important to me. Respecting their thoughts, or at least giving them more than quick consideration is the very least I can do.

I branch off and swim in the opposite direction. Usually when we're doing a legit dive it's under the cover of night, only the phosphorescence lighting the pitch black waters. I dive down deeper, deeper than I know I should without equipment, because why the fuck not? I watch the bottom of the boat to gauge my depth and kick faster toward the bottom of the ocean. I look at my watch and the boat and I know I've cracked my depth record, or at least tied it. The second I get to that point—my lungs screaming out in protest, I kick toward the surface, my flippers speeding me along. I'm about halfway up when I realize my mistake.

I'm huffing and puffing when I rise out of the water, tearing the mask off as quickly as possible. I stroke over to the boat with my mask in one hand, slowing me down. Hoisting myself into the boat, I shake my hair like a dog. "Have a nice swim?" Aidan croons.

"Dude, look at my eyes," I say, rubbing at them.

He starts laughing and I know I'm fucked. With a capital, hellraising F. "Fuck," I mutter, grabbing a towel to dry off. "Mask squeeze. So stupid."

"You didn't equalize pressure before you decided to be a cocky idiot," he says. "In a few days you'll look like Satan himself. Just in time for the mission. The bad guys will think the devil came to kill them in person." He's grabbing his stomach in hysterics. Others have joined in now that my stupid mistake is on display. We don't fuck up often, but when we do, it goes down in a book for recollection at any given point, for the rest of time.

By not clearing my mask pressure, I gave myself a hickey, on the whites of my eyes. It will turn a dark red shade and be noticeable for weeks, sometimes even months. My friend Ben did it during a dive once, and the whites of his eyes were fucked up for a family reunion. His Grandma wouldn't hug him.

Leif rises out of the water with a fish spear in one hand. He looks like Triton. "Did I hear Tahoe got a mask squeeze? That can't be right. Love hasn't made him *that* stupid."

It's mild right now, but I can feel it. I know the blood will rush to the surface over the next few days, getting worse and worse until I look like a Berserker. It wouldn't be so bad if the rest of my body didn't match that description. Too bad it's not Halloween.

"Does anyone have a mirror? A cell phone? Let me see it."

Someone rustles up a cell from a dry bag and hands it to me. I turn on the camera and face it toward me. "Goddammit," I mutter. "This isn't good. Anyone remember how long Ben's was?"

Everyone is telling stories about friends they know who have gotten mask squeezes and it makes me feel a little better, but then a thought hits me.

"Caroline." Leif cackles. "I bet she likes fucking a demon."

They still don't know I haven't had sex with her. I'd catch a rash of shit if they knew I was professing my love before I've sampled the goods.

"Role play," Aidan chimes in.

"She could be an angel. A white little nightie. Think of the possibilities," he explains, holding one hand over his heart.

"Stop thinking about Caroline," I mutter. "How long?" I ask, pulling up Google on the cell phone, and tapping my question into the search bar. "Maybe it's just a little one," I pep talk myself. A barrage of horrible, scary images glare back after my search all I can do is shake my head. With my light blue eyes, it might look a little less atrocious than if I had brown, because then the whole eyeball would look black, the iris blending with the blood shot white.

Leif stops laughing long enough to call my name. When I look up, he snaps a photo with his phone. "This is your right after it happened photo. We'll take one every day until your whole eye looks like a hickey."

I make a grab for his phone, but he's too quick. "You guys are the worst friends ever," I say.

"She's going to be scared of this. Any normal person would be."

Leif claps back. "Okay, Ben just texted back and said the one he got off the coast of Catalina Island lasted seven weeks. He also said to call him. He hasn't heard from you in a while."

Scrubbing my palms into my eye sockets I try to remember how many pairs of sunglasses I have.

keeping it

Aidan walks over and puts a hand on my shoulder. "No one will notice."

Such a fucking bullshit artist. "Fuck you, Aidan."

Aidan's eyes light up as he remembers something. "Oh, while I have everyone's attention, or while Tahoe has everyone's attention I'd like announce that we will be attending the local party at the spot tomorrow night. This will serve as the before mission celebration so tie on your mother fucking drinking shoes." Everyone lets out a cheer in agreement. There's always a shit-show of a party before a mission. The last hurrah. The importance of comraderie and brotherhood wrapped into a liquor festooned vomit session. It started when the war did because the unknowns are larger than the knowns these days.

"How did you manage that? Did they invite us?" Even I don't believe that. Aidan probably threatened someone. The animosity aimed our way from the locals isn't a secret. It's not supposed to be. They honestly thought they could get the town hall to stop us from moving forward with plans for our base. While it was laughable, we've learned that a little respect goes a long way.

Aidan tells us he made friends with someone who was helping at the airport and he invited him, and that is basically the same thing as inviting all of us. Everyone agrees it's a good idea merely from the standpoint of checking out the party place heralded as the most fun in Bronze Bay. I get a little excited at the prospect of letting loose. It's been a long, concentrated month with all of my efforts zoned in on one thing.

"You can even invite Caroline," Leif says. "I want her to bring her friend."

"Which friend?" I'm almost positive he means Shirley. That one is down to fuck, one-hundred percent.

Leif describes her and I'm surprised he's describing her other friend. "Malena," I deadpan. "Why her?"

He tilts his head and starts listing things he likes about her using one finger at a time. The list is all physical, of course, but he's remembered features about her that I didn't, so he's really into her. "Sure. I'll ask," I offer. Caroline might not be down with the idea at all. The last time we were all together at the bar those people ate her alive in that twisted frenemy way.

"They're already darker, dude. I bet by tonight you'll be a right fine monster," Leif says, admiring my face.

Groaning, I tell them to take me back to land. "I need to work out or something," I say. "So she'll look at other parts of me instead of my face." No one ever questions their vanity until something happens to their fucking face. I went and cock-blocked myself.

"Sound logic," Leif replies, coughing. Once everyone is onboard he starts the engine and we head back to base. I debate going to visit Caroline at the airport office before my eyes get worse, before I'm more monster than human, but I actually have a bit of work to get done before I leave work for the day.

And I do need to work out.

Chapter Fourteen

Caroline

He looks like a female wet dream as he walks toward me. He has on a pair of cut off khaki shorts, flip flops, and a black tee that shows off every rippled muscle. I didn't see him yesterday after work because he was busy, nor earlier today because we both had a busy schedule. I expected him to pop into the diner for lunch with a friend like he would do from time to time, but he didn't. Tahoe did text me almost every waking second all night long. When I broached, as delicately as I could, the voice message I accidentally sent, he said he had no idea what I was talking about. I was relieved, yet suspicious. He called me three times today to make sure we were still on for the party at the spot tonight. While it's not my typical choice for spending my free time, the fact that we'll be together changes everything. I'm pretty confident he could lead me up to the gates of hell with ease. It's not something I'm proud of.

Holding my door open, I lick my lips when he gets close enough to see my face. I want more of what he gives before we leave. It is part of my reasoning for having him come over so early. Tahoe is wearing a pair of dark, aviator sunglasses. That's not something I've ever seen him in before, but we are in Florida where most of the inhabitants wear sunglasses 99 percent of their lives.

He grabs me in a bear hug, lifting me off the ground as he brings me in closer. "I've missed you so much," he whispers into my ear. He inhales deeply and I can actually feel the relief wash over him.

"Don't be so busy at work then. I missed you, too. Did you get those tickets?" He was trying to get tickets to see *Wicked* while we're in N.Y.C when he called earlier today.

Pulling away, he grins. "I did. I can't wait to see it with you," he says. "How was your day?" He carries me through the entrance and sets my feet down on the stairs leading up to my house.

We walk up together as I tell him first about my boring shift at the diner, and then working on an engine when I got to the airport this afternoon. He closes the door behind us, still keeping the sunglasses on his face. When he notices me studying, he tells me about the work he's getting done on his house, and the contact I gave him for the appliance man worked out great. He was able to snag top of the line kitchen appliances for next to nothing. He's using distraction. "Hey, uh, you wear your sunglasses at night?" I sing, moving my shoulders.

"It's afternoon," he counters. "I have something to tell you," he explains, moving his hands by his sides. "Or show you rather." He clenches and unclenches his fists.

My heart starts hammering because this disposition is something I've never seen portrayed before. Not on him, anyways. His shoulders slump and his chin tucks into his chest. He's sad. He has the sunglasses on because he's been crying. That must be it. Which probably means something horrible happened. Someone died. And here I am asking about Broadway tickets like some jerk.

"Oh, God. Just tell me now. Spit it out," I say.

"Sit down."

I follow his directions, and put my hands on top of my knees. He sits next to me, but leans his back against the arm of the sofa so he's facing me front on. "You're scaring me," I tell him, voice wavering. "Are you okay? Is everyone else okay?"

He clears his throat. "I'm fine. Everyone is fine. There's, ah, nothing to be scared about," he says. "I had a little bit of a diving accident when we went out on the boat. Fishing, remember?"

I look over his body up and down, at all of the exposed skin, looking for some kind of wound.

"I remember. And?" My voice quavers with unease.

"And I didn't clear my mask while diving deep. Essentially, the best way to put it is I got a hickey on my eyeballs," he says, taking off the sunglasses, keeping his eyes closed. "It's called a mask squeeze and it will take a long time to go away," he explains, and then his thick lashes flutter up.

I'm not sure what I was expecting, but it wasn't this.

I jump back, and cover my mouth. "Have you seen a doctor?" I wail behind my hand. It's that bad. His blue eyes are in stark contrast next to the deep maroon color that used to be the whites of his eyes. "Doctor," I say one more time, trying to swallow down my fear. He said he was okay. Said that it would go away on its own.

Tahoe winces. "That bad, huh?"

"You knew it was that bad!" I reply. Leaning in, I get a better look and then wish I didn't. He closes his eyes.

"I'm an idiot. It happens to inexperienced divers a lot. I did see the doc, and the only tincture for my stupidity is time."

I nod. "Okay. Okay," I say again. "I can get used to it."

"You can date a character from Dungeons and Dragons?" he asks. I make the mistake of looking at his eyes a touch longer than I should, so he shuts them.

"You're not my boyfriend because of the scleral sections of your eyeballs, Tyler Holiday."

My statement garners a laugh, but he slides his sunglasses back over his eyes. "You don't have to wear those. Don't be silly." Even as I say it, I'm relieved I don't have to look or not look. It's awkward either way.

"Why were you diving deep anyways? Weren't you fishing? I didn't realize spear fishing involves depth diving."

He swallows. "I was trying to see how far down I could get. Beat my best depth," he explains, using his hands to talk.

I quirk one brow and look off to the side. "Sometimes you're so predictable and then other times it's like you're a wild card. You probably almost die on a regular basis doing your job, and then do stupid stuff like that during your off hours? Seems ludicrous."

Sighing, he takes my hands in his. "I'd take it back if I could. I'll never hear the end of it. Leif and Aidan will bust my balls all night long."

Having all of his teammates mingling with the Bronze Bay crowd is going to be weird. They're trying to integrate themselves into the community and it must be working on some level. I had to call Malena to ask her if she was coming to the spot tonight. Of course, like always, she is, but she also wanted to cash in the housewarming party planning chip. I nailed down a date a few months away. She whined, but I stood firm—said I was busy until then, and if she wanted to help me she would have to wait. I don't relish having anyone in my world. Except Tahoe.

He's the exception. The scary-at-the-moment-exception.

Tahoe runs his rough, calloused palm over my bare thigh, and up to the hem of my dress. A dress I chose very carefully after standing in front of my closet longer than I ever have before. In the Florida heat it's shorts and a tank or a sundress. Worrying about impressing anyone else with my clothing wasn't even on the radar. I want him to want me like I want him. The black dress is cut high on hem and low on bust, breaking one of the cardinal rules of dress wearing. Typically you can only have one. Your boobs hanging out, or your ass. Both? Dig your societal grave.

He leans forward, intent on kissing me, but stops halfway. "I can take the sunglasses off if you want," he says. I try to pick out his eyes behind the black lenses and can barely make them out.

"Whatever you want." I place my hand on his, the one on my leg, and drag it up further.

His low, gruff chuckle floods me with desire. His fingers take over now that he knows exactly what I want, what I've been thinking about since the last time his fingers were on me. My skin heats, and butterflies flutter in my stomach.

"You don't have any clue how beautiful you are, do you? Rewind. How fucking captivating you are on every level."

The heat from my body rises to my cheeks in what I'm sure is a full on telltale blush. I should check my reflection in his sunglasses, but I won't. "Stop it," I say. "You'd say anything right now." Leaning up, I kneel in front of him on the couch, but his hand stays put, on the edge of my panties, teasing the elastic band. I've never hated elastic more, or wished I was brave enough to go commando. The thought didn't cross my mind until right now. I'll learn. I'll be better at this seduction thing if it's the last thing I do. Or have Shirley teach me when my phone is nowhere in my vicinity.

His fingers pull aside the fabric. He kisses my lips,

long and leisurely. Tahoe halts the kiss abruptly. "Don't ever say I'd say *anything*," he says. "I always say what I mean."Raising my chin, I reply, "Say what you mean then."

His neck works and I can't help but watch as it affects the muscles of his chest, too. "You are the single most perfect human being. For me. I want to fuck you. Own you. Keep you. I'm crazy about you." He works one finger against me.

"Anything else?" I say, moaning a little as I writhe in pleasure. Biting my lip, to stifle a cry, I circle my hips to increase the friction.

"Yeah," he growls. "When I fuck you I want to pull out and play connect the dots with the freckles on your lower stomach." I raise my dress up to expose the offending marks. His head tilts down, but that's the only tell that he's admiring me, and his finger gliding over me, because the sunglasses hide all expression.

"When are you going to fuck me?"

His hand pauses for a beat, but then he moves it again in a pace he knows drives me wild. "When I can look you in the eye," he says, sadly.

I'm almost to orgasm—the feeling building like a volcano of pressure. My hands drop the hem of my dress, and clasp around his neck to steady my body. "Take off the sunglasses Tahoe," I order, leaning my cheek on his shoulder and kissing his neck. My plan is to look him in the eye as I come, but it hits me fast and hard, and he probably did it intentionally because he is so good at this, like most things.

I cling to him as I ride the waves of pleasure, feeling the pressure of his finger smoothing against me. I'm still breathing heavy when he slides his hand out from underneath my dress and puts the finger in his mouth.

"Saying it like I mean it?" he asks, I smile. "You taste and smell so incredible I could live off you alone for months."

I grin. "You'd shrivel away to nothing without nourishment."

"And die a happy man. Don't take that away from me," he teases, rolling his tongue around the finger coated in my desire.

My chest is red and my breaths are still short and wild. "Well if I'm going to say it like I mean it. I wish I could keep you in my bedside drawer. You're so good at that it's disturbing. I thought about asking how you got so good at playing the woman's orgasm after you spent the night, but then realized I probably didn't want to know the answer to that."

The knowing smirk on his face is beautiful. "I'm good with my hands, Caroline. That applies to everything I do in life. Sometimes it's not a practice makes perfect thing. You can make up for lack of practice with…fury."

Something about the way he says that last word creates that low, burning in my lower stomach. "So you're out of practice?"

"Define out of practice," he counters, good at the avoiding game.

He folds me into his arms, and I snuggle against his chest, the side of my head bumping his aviators. "Who was the last girl?"

He swallows and I feel it. "I don't recall anything before two nights ago."

"You're so smooth."

"Momma didn't raise a fool, Sunny."

He must know by now. Must be intuitive enough with his sexual prowess to have ticked all of the virgin boxes, but every time I broach a conversation that could lead to my verbal confession, he shuts it down just like he's doing right now.

"We don't really have to wait until your eyes get better, right?" I ask, honestly fearful that if he sticks by that resolution, I might die of anticipation. While every sexual encounter we've had this far has been explosive and full of depth, I crave the connection as much as I fear it.

Tahoe shifts under me, and I can feel his hard dick through his jeans, butting up against my ass cheek. "Want to drive my truck tonight?" he asks instead.

I go to open my mouth to ask my question again, but he's kissing me instead, the sweet taste of his mouth making me forget anything I previously wanted to know. This is all the education I need.

He lifts his sunglasses with a free hand and sets them on the arm of the sofa, but his eyes remain closed as our lips lock. He lays me down on the couch, positioning himself between my legs, just how I wish we were, but naked, and starts jutting his hips forward. He groans a little each time, as he rubs himself against my wet panties.

The friction against my clit is immediate and every nerve ending focuses between my legs. He releases my lips and kisses my neck, and ear, and breathes in the scent of my hair. Wrapping my arms around his back, I find the bottom of his shirt and work it up until I get it over his shoulders. He pulls it the rest of the way off by grabbing the collar behind his neck. When I can see his skin, touch his muscles with my fingertips. It's over. My pussy tightens in what seems like a death vice grip and then explodes, contracting around nothing, yet the sensations are full and amazing. Again.

I'm still lightheaded and lust filled, but I know I need to take care of him. His arms are shaking and his body is coiled—ready for release. If he'll let me. "Let me give you a blow job." The words don't make me gag this time. Shirley said I needed to get used to it. That it wouldn't be so bad once I had a few dozen under my belt. Told me if I could coerce him into eating pineapple that the come would taste sweeter than normal. The thought made me dry heave, but then I checked myself. I'm an adult woman. This is part of doing business.

"You make me dry hump you like a teenaged boy. You realize how wrapped you have me, right?" Tahoe says, his tone light. "Only if you want to. About the blow job," he adds, licking the edge of my ear, sending goose bumps down one entire side of my body.

Pushing him up with one hand, I wait for him to situate

himself. "Of course I want to," I say, grinning in what I hope looks like a reassuring manner. I took notes. I have this. He sits down on the couch, and I kneel between his legs, trying my best to keep my hands on any part of skin I can in the process.

Licking my lips, I watch intently as he slides his shorts down. His erection, loud and proud, springs free.

"I love everything about this right now. How you look. How you're making me feel. So out of control. I have no idea what to expect next and for once, I don't care. It's just you and me. I'm so happy," he says, putting a hand on the side of my face as I take him into my right hand to stroke him up and down. The skin is so smooth, like silk, and his pleasure in my touch is obvious. "I'm not, ah, saying that because you're about to put my dick in your mouth either."

"You're saying it because you mean it," I finish for him.

He nods, his eyes still closed, a sleepy turned-on smile on his face. If I asked him to open them, I wonder if he would. Remembering Shirley's words about tempo, mouth to hand ratio, spit, and zeal, I move in to wet it with my tongue.

Tahoe guides me with his hands on my shoulders, the back of my neck, and with gentle words. It doesn't take as long this time. Because I want to be legit more than anything else, I even swallow

We would both be happy staying in. Cooking a nice dinner, having a glass of wine or three, and then heading to my bedroom to explore each other's bodies for seven hours, but tonight Tahoe is the one urging us to go to the spot. We already discussed that I would drive his truck tonight, because his plans don't involve staying sober. I'm okay with it, if anything, that's what I'm used to. It's always more fun to see everyone act like idiots with a clear focus.

I don't drive often, and his truck is a big, old thing that probably shouldn't be trusted, but he coached me all the way there, telling me how third gear sticks and what I should do to unstick it.

There's a lot across the street where everyone parks relatively uniform, in lines spanning about ten cars deep. I make sure to back into the next spot for an easy exit. I recognize a few people parking and heading across the deserted street. "You don't like coming here?" Tahoe says, pulling me against his side.

I quirk up one side of my mouth. "It's not that I don't like coming, it's just that everyone else does." Sliding my arm around his back, I hold on to him tightly. I'm still floating in that orgasm induced good mood when I see Britt and Whit. Whit is holding one of those tall metal cups that keeps drinks cold for a long time and Britt is wearing RBF like she's the one who coined the term.

"It's our friends," Tahoe says, noticing them, too. He chuckles and shakes his head.

Swallowing down the nerves, I say, "You're going to

see everyone here." We cross the street and head onto the property owned by a distant relative of Malena. It remains open to everyone just because it always has been and no one complains. It has access to a canal, which opens to the bay, and then the river that feeds to the ocean. There are picnic tables and someone is setting up the kegs on the concrete slab that was poured for this occasion exactly. "Watch out for the mud," I tell him, during the walk over. "I meant to ask you. Leif have a thing for Malena? She was planning on coming tonight anyways. So don't let your friend think she's here especially for him. She is a bit feisty." Tahoe stretches his neck, his sunglasses still in place. "Leif likes feisty. Are you sure you don't want to drink? We can produce a DD if need be."

"I'm sure. You have fun. Is this some sort of tradition?" I ask. He didn't give me specifics, not unlike anytime I ask about his job. He merely said it was something they did before a mission, and an opportunity like this is too hard to pass up.

Tahoe explains that the one time they didn't go out boozing before a mission a SEAL was killed. Sort of like a good luck charm. He likens it to basketball players not cutting their hair, or hockey players not shaving until the end of the season, but that seems so trivial in comparison. We're talking about life and death.

Britt and Whit are making their way over and I see Tahoe's jaw tick. "Hey guys. A great night for it, huh?" I ask.

Britt agrees, looking only at me, and tells me about

the boutonnieres she selected for the groomsmen today. I pretend to be overly interested, because Whit and Tahoe are talking about something completely unrelated, but they aren't fighting. That's what I want. For him to just be himself, not the outsider. A part of Bronze Bay.

"Shirley told me about NYC. You must be excited. Do you have plans?" Britt asks. I should be skeptical because she rarely takes this much of an interest in me, but I tell her the truth anyways. And I can't help it, my excitement bleeds into my words. She's smiling when I finish telling her about the reservation Tahoe made at a restaurant I saw on *Sex in the City*.

"You're lucky, Caroline. I'm so happy for you," she says, her eyes downcast for a moment, then on her fiancé next to her. All traces of happiness vanish as she looks at Whit and my stomach flips with unease.

"Want to grab a drink?" I ask, making a grab for her arm. She smiles politely and comes with me toward the kegs. When we're enough distance away. I just come right out and ask what's on my mind. "Is everything okay? You seem really sad."

Her smile is wistful. "I'm always such a bitch to you, and yet you're the only person who has noticed I'm not the bubbly bride I'm supposed to be. Why is that?" she asks. I can't tell if it's rhetoric.

I glance back over my shoulder and meet Tahoe's gaze. He winks once. To Britt I say, "Because it's Bronze Bay and everyone in it ignores things that might rock the boat. All I do these days is rock the boat. Are you okay?

You don't have to give me details," I say, shaking my head. "But if you need anything, let me know." It's the neighborly thing to say, and I think she'll respond better to that than if I pry into her life.

"You're so sweet, Caroline May. That's why this place didn't take you down. Why you're getting out of here with a man like that. I'm not sure how you managed to remain unscathed, but thank your lucky stars, okay?" she grabs me by both shoulders. "Nothing is as it seems around here." If she's just realizing this, I gave her too much credit all of these years.

"I know that," I deadpan. "It doesn't mean you can't change if something isn't sitting well with you, though. You don't have to do something because that's what everyone else expects you to do." I learned that the hard way. No one thought I'd get my pilot's license. Not one of these people, aside from Shirley and maybe Malena, thought I'd eventually take over the airport. They saw my future as the uneducated daughter of really good people. The diner was where I was relinquished.

She gives me that look. The one that says I don't have a clue how the world works, and I bite my tongue.

"He's cheating on me with Milly," she says, and then heaves an exasperated sigh. "He was drunk. Because how could he not be." I mask my face the same way I do when someone at the diner mentions something scandalous and I want to be trusted. She's not done. Not by a long shot. She wants to spill it all, and she thinks I'm lapping it up. "I mean, he's always cheating on me,

I thought maybe once we were engaged, and then when that didn't happen. I figured maybe when it gets closer to the wedding he would stop, but now I realize it's a life sentence if I don't break up with him now."

Swallowing hard, I try to straighten my face into something sympathetic. "I'm so sorry, Britt. You deserve better than that." I always assumed she knew, but I guess I didn't realize the extent to which Whit was digging himself down. I can't help but glance back, but Whit is nowhere to be found, and Tahoe is with a group of his friends surrounding the keg. He's laughing, and his smile makes my heart skip a beat. He would never be a Whit. He couldn't.

"So what do you think?" she asks, drawing my attention back to her.

"You want my opinion? I'm hardly the person to give opinions about relationships. Mine is so new I'm still peeling off the purchase sticker," I reply. We slide onto a picnic bench because I can tell this conversation is far from over and she's latched on to me.

"If it were you what would you do?"

"Are you asking for permission to break up with your cheating fiancé?"

"Of course I don't need permission," she says, letting her gaze wander. Probably looking for her manwhore. "Everyone would freak, Caroline. Everyone. I'm basically finished planning. I've got wedding gifts lining our hallway. All the gossip aside, we'd lose so much money. God, he'd never forgive me."

I narrow my eyes. "Do you really want his forgiveness?"

She shakes her head. "You're right. It's so hard when you've been with someone for so long. You wouldn't understand."

Burn. Typical. "I think you should do whatever you want, Britt. I think you can handle whatever happens, but I also know you're a beautiful girl with a ton of prospects. Maybe one that wouldn't cheat."

"All men cheat, Caroline. It's a fact of life," she breathes, tossing her hair back. "A man like yours is the worst kind." I guess my non-opinion on her love life made me the punching bag.

"A man like mine?"

"One everyone wants."

My stomach roils. "I'm going to get a drink. Want one?"

She nods and I rise and make my way toward the keg opposite to the one where someone wearing boots and shorts is doing a keg stand. The raucous cheers and sloshy voices ricochet off the trees lining the sides of the property.

Once I fill two beers with mostly foam, I head back for Britt and find her talking to Malena, poor old Caroline all but forgotten. I can tell Malena is getting the same earful, and I can't help but be a little relieved. Maybe Malena will have advice for her. Maybe Malena will have the balls to tell her Whit is a disgusting asshole who should rot at the bottom of the bay. I take a small sip of the light beer and wince. I hate boat beer. It's what we call all light beer. It goes down like water though and that's what you want in the hot, hot sun.

Tahoe sneaks up next to me, and grabs one of my cups. "What is my DD doing with two beers? This place is awesome," he exclaims.

Smiling, I nod. "It is. Looks like you guys are having a good time so far. Anyone giving you a hard time?"

He laughs, the beer already gone. "Who is going to give us a hard time and live to tell about it?"

He kisses me. It's all beer and foam and the light scent of his face soap. I go into his arms willingly. He pulls back and looks me from the top of my head down to my breasts and back again. "What were you and the bitch talking about?"

I sigh, the mood broken. "Her cheating fiancé. She's thinking about leaving him. I guess he's just as bad as he's always been. She thought he'd change."

Tahoe throws his head back and laughs. "That's the oldest, dumbest trick in the book. No one changes. What the other person is willing to accept changes."

Biting my lip for a moment, I ask. "You don't think cheating is okay though, right?"

His eyes widen. "You think I would cheat?"

"Of course not," I say, looking down to the water where several canoes wait for their drunken captains. That won't happen until later.

"You do think that. Why?"

I shrug, look down, and kick the sandy grass. "I

don't have much experience with relationships and Britt mentioned that all men cheat. I know she probably only said that to make herself feel better, but I have to wonder about you guys. Always traveling. Never settling down. Your reputation precedes you in that regard. You admitted you were only in a committed relationship with Stella."

I'm glad his sunglasses are on. I hate how sad his eyes get when I mention her name. Like he's a failure because he couldn't make it work. He leaves his hands on the small of my waist. "You aren't Stella. I never felt an ounce of what I feel for you for her. Do you understand? I would never jeopardize what we have. You mean more to me than some one night stand in whatever city I'm staying in. That's saying it like I mean it, Caroline." He shakes his head. "Never, and I mean never, doubt my affection for you."

It's nice to hear and it does comfort me, but he does still look like a man that every woman wants. "You look so...handsome. Don't you get hit on constantly?"

He chuckles. "You're worried about other women hitting on me? I like a bit of jealousy, but now you're going overboard." Tahoe brushes my bottom lip with both of his thumbs. "I don't get hit on because I'm rarely in that kind of situation. I won't be any more especially. Remember this mission is a one off for me. I'll be home in no time.

I hop up, throw my hands around his neck and accidentally knock his sunglasses off his face. The sun is setting, but I can still see his monster eyes.

Instead of picking up his sunglasses, he's watching my face for a reaction. "Keep them off. It gives you an edge."

He closes his eyes and shakes his head. "You're scared of me. I saw it."

Putting my hands on his stomach, I coax him with a few rubs. "I need to get used to your red eyes if you don't want to wear the sunglasses constantly, Tahoe. Leave them off and let me get used to it." I stoop to pick them up for him. He examines them and slides them into his t-shirt.

"Fine. I've had just enough to drink to not give a shit, but Caroline?"

"Yes?"

He shakes his head. "Never compare me to other men. That's not fair."

My face heats with guilt. "I'm sorry," I say, interlacing my hands. "Britt said something and I should have just brushed it off. You've never done anything to indicate anything but perfection."

He lowers his voice. "All these people are jealous of you. All of them. Not because of me, either. Because of you." He aims one finger at my chest. "I'm not perfect," he says, backing away from me. "Not even close. I've told you there's no one else for me and I meant it."

I'm standing there thinking about various different things. Mostly about how much I love him and how much losing him would hurt. The cheating scenario is there because she said it, but is that how Britt actually feels? I can't blame her for acting the way she does. It's unapologetically heinous.

I hand over my piss beer. "Here. Get back to your friends," I say.

He swallows the solo cup full down in one deep swig. "I'll find you in a bit. I want you to show me around here. Don't be talking to any naysayers while I'm gone." He grins, starts backing away from me, but then lunges forward and pulls me in for a world halting kiss.

I hear manly cheering and I know catty, quiet stares are abound, too.

But for once, I truly don't care.

Comraderie

Tahoe

Only a couple dudes from Bronze Bay are brave enough to approach us. It was curiosity, but we were nice enough that they stayed and started drinking keg beer with us. I like that they are comfortable with us enough to hang out because it means we are making progress in being considered locals, and they tell us shit about the town we don't know. They're like clueless informants we can be friends with. Last I saw Caroline, she was with a group of girls and her face wasn't completely miserable looking, so she must be having an okay time. She's steered clear of Britt and Whit, though I haven't seen the latter since we spoke earlier. There's that many people here right now. It's impressive.

I'm pissed Caroline doubts my feelings for her, even if the doubt came from a woman scorned, but at this point in my evening I'm so drunk that it's hard to decipher any of my emotions. Leif went off to try to woo Malena back into his car like some horny high schooler, and Aidan is next to me shooting the shit with a few of our other teammates. We're telling stories, getting caught up in the past. This is what I need. The atmosphere is intoxicating—the salty ocean air breezes in every once in a while, and now that I'm getting used to the heat, I can appreciate the warmth in the air. We're sitting around a bonfire, and one of the guys switched us to bourbon about an hour ago. I considered not drinking my share, but didn't turn it down either. Now, the world around me is a nice shade of fuzzy fuck all.

My eyes are fucked all to shit. The doc says I should be happy I still have my vision, but they look like hell. Literally. The drunker I get, the more I forget about the injury until someone talks to me and their eyes widen as they notice it.

"What the fuck are you on, dude?" a guy asks, slinking down on a wide tree stump next to me. He works at the home improvement store in town. I recognize the scar on his face.

Swallowing the last sip in my own cup, I toss it to the ground and reply with the truth. He listens intently, but he's just as drunk as I am so I'm sure the story sounds like an elaborate cover for drug addiction or the likes. To change the subject I ask him about the brass drawer pulls I ordered last week and he just stares at me. Granted, I slurred through a couple of words, but he knows I'm done explaining.

Leaning in closer to my face, he repeats, "Your eyes are so fucked up."

One time in a bar in Texas I knocked out a guy for

breathing in my space. He was also fucking up my game with the brunette of the night. The chick ended up getting wet because she dug assholes, and what is more of an asshole move than knocking out another dude for smiling too wide? Not much. "Get out of my face," I say, making sure my smile is equal parts threat as it is gleeful.

He shakes his head and leans back. "Want to go canoeing?" he says, hiking his thumb over his shoulder. "They keep a bunch of canoes over there. You can paddle out to the river from here if you're strong enough to make it." The challenge makes me laugh. "Some of us race at the end of the night." I look to my right to see if my buddies have heard.

"Something I can't resist," I coo. "Sloppy drunk I will crush you." I nod to his face. "That what happened to your face? Get a little too drunk and crash your baby boat?"

He stands, shaking his head. "Nah, car accident," he replies. "I'd gladly scar the other side of my face if it means beating you assholes."

My teammates are in the conversation now—the spark of a challenge lighting them like a strand of Christmas lights. One by one, they decide it's the best idea they've heard all month. Others join my hardware employee friend on their side and we swagger and sway down to the inlet. Our proverbial guns loaded. Solar powered lights line a seashell path on the ground, but I stumble into one, crushing it into shards. Leif calls out from behind and I turn toward his voice.

Malena and Caroline are standing on either side of him. "Get your ass up here!" he hollers. I break another of the lights by barely stepping on it. The crunching sound of glass echoes as I pick up my flip flop and head back up the embankment toward Caroline.

"You're not really going to race canoes with them are you?" Caroline says, lunging forward when I'm close enough to touch. She sees my eyes, and probably the way I'm swaying like the wind. "Come," she pulls on my arm. "Talk to me."

Leif cackles. "He's been challenged, darling. He'll be racing itty bitty boats and win if it kills him," he chortles.

"But you're so drunk," Caroline says, blinking her big, beautiful eyes. Her face is moonlit perfection. "People have drowned before. It's so…stupid."

"It's a celebration of life," I reply. "Are you underestimating my skills? Please."

Leif laughs, Malena takes a large swallow of her drink, and Caroline folds her arms across her chest. "Just go, Leif," Malena says. "They'll crown you king of Bronze Bay in no time. Plus, if you guys win, your street cred will go up." I think we've found the only place on earth where our career doesn't endow us with street cred on its own. We kind of like it. A level playing field is where we stand out the most.

"A title I will cherish forever, madam," Leif replies, snaking an arm around the petite brunette.

Caroline watches them with a scowl on her face. "You're being unreasonable," she says, swiveling to face me. "We could head back to my place and…hang out."

I stumble backwards a touch. "This will be quick and then we can go back to your place," I reply.

Her face settles into stoic annoyance. "Guess there had to be something," Caroline snaps, eyeing me and then Leif. "Idiot when drunk. Check."

Idiot? Idiot? Idiot? If I wasn't so obsessed with the package of Caroline May I would throttle her. I'm a lot of things, but in this unfettered moment of weakness, she's calling me an idiot. I swallow hard and try to reign in the anger.

Leif ambles away shaking his head and laughing. Malena almost falls and he catches her, his hands like bear paws all over her body. Dog. "This was a bad idea. I'm glad I got a chance to see it," Caroline says.

"I'm having a good time with my friends, Caroline. I'm not saying I can canoe drunk because I'm drunk, I'm saying I can kick their asses in a canoe race because I *can*."

Biting her lip, she crosses one leg over the other at the ankle. "Whatever. Go have a fun time treading water completely annihilated. If that doesn't sound like a fun time, I don't know what does."

"You have a better idea for a fun time?" I crow back, stepping toward her. I can smell her shampoo, and the soft hint of laundry detergent. "Let's go back to the truck and talk. That's what you want to do? Talk?"

Under the blue hue of the moon I see her flesh prick with goose bumps. Caroline's chest rises and falls, and her pouty lips separate. She's weighing the cost of her answer. Her eyes flash with the decision. "Fine. Let's go talk."

I step in the exact place she does as I follow her back across the street to the parking lot. There's no need to lock my hunk of junk, so she cranks open the door slides in and then waits for me to climb in after her. I grasp the oh shit handle and use it more than I should so it breaks off in my hand. I toss it to the floor board and she watches it with wide eyes.

"I'm not an idiot, Caroline. I'm still going to race canoes regardless of what you want. My brothers are down there. They'll wait for me. So, what did you want to talk about here? In the private seclusion of my grand truck cab?" My words slur together and I realize how it affects my case. I lean over and kiss her shoulder. Her face remains straight ahead, but even drunk Tahoe affects this woman. The pout of her lips, the way her eyes blink slower when she's turned on. Scooting closer I place my lips against her neck and drag them side to side.

She pulls away, trying to keep her composure. "You're angry," I say.

The tilt of her chin tips up a touch. "You're being irrational. Pardon me for not wanting to delve into the drunk tank with you, Tyler."

"Oh, Tyler? Burn," I say, grinning. My dick hardens. "Tell me something."

"What?" She looks at me. A mistake she'll pay for.

"I'm finished waiting. I want you right now." The

words slip—my true feelings blaring louder than any rational decisions.

"That's not a question," she replies, folding her hands in her lap. She plays with the material of her dress, twisting it between two fingers.

I swallow hard. Remembering what she looks like under that dress gives me all the ammo I'll ever need to get hard. Caroline was made for me in every conceivable way. "In this truck. In this parking lot. Across the street from all of those people."

"Are you sure?" She narrows her eyes, and her mouth turns down in the corner. "After all of this time, and all of *your* rules? When you're being a complete drunk asshole? You pick now?" Something about the way she insults me and swears flips the goddamn switch. The one usually reserved for when I need to be a monster. Maybe because she's right and subconsciously I know that. Maybe it's because I'm the best person I know at ruining a good thing. Perhaps it's a mixture of the two sparked with bourbon, but I grab her wrists and pin her back against the seat, trying and probably failing at keeping my weight off her. Between her legs, I settle my hips. My head spins and my stomach flips, because for as drunk as I am, I still know exactly what is about to happen. Leaning down, I chase her lips.

Caroline swallows hard, turns her head away, the pulse at her neck hammering against my lips. "Stop being a cunt," I rasp into her ear. "I am not a drunk asshole. I fucking love you." I reach between our bodies and unbutton and unzip my pants. "I love you so fucking much that you're making me insane."

She whimpers, and the noise breaks my fiery haze of desire. Pushing up on my arms I stare down at her and see the stray tear lingering on her cheek. The moon provides the right amount of light to reveal the travesty. "Are you crying?" I blurt out.

"Will you at least kiss me?" she says, words jagged, wiping under her eyes.

My heart starts pounding out of my chest. The adrenaline and realization mixing in that horrific kind of way. "Kiss you?"

She nods her head furiously. "Tahoe," she whispers. "I'm a virgin."

If there were words that could have sent me running, those are the words. "What the fuck?"

Caroline sits up and scoots away from me, wrapping her body with her arms. "I thought you knew," she says, sniffling once.

I run a hand through my hair as her words sober me faster than anything in the history of time. I basically just mounted her. A woman I'm in love with, a virgin on top of that, in a dirty parking lot. "Why didn't you tell me before? You know what they say about assumptions?"

She cries and my heart breaks. "You wanted to wait. I figured it was because you knew. It was too quick tonight. And you're so drunk. I'm sorry. I panicked. I should have just gone with it."

"You're sorry? You're sorry? I just tried to fuck you in

this disgusting truck!" I roar. "I knew you were innocent, but fuck, Caroline. I thought it was an act or something." I shake my head. All of the encounters come to mind as I'm reminded that it should have been obvious, but my judgement is always clouded when it comes to her. "I didn't know virgins your age existed." Especially beautiful fucking ones. Her wide gaze flicks over me, judging me. If I could disappear right now and never come back, I would.

"Everyone told me not to tell you. That it was a non-issue. At first it *was* a non-issue. We were friends. Then when things changed, too much time had passed and I thought maybe you might think of me differently if you knew I hadn't slept with a man before." She's right. I would have. I probably would have run as far and as fast as possible if she was honest about that up front. I'm the type of man you fuck before you find Mr. Right. I'm okay with that. I'm the man that you tell your friends about because he does a cool trick with his tongue in bed. I'm not the fucking man to take your virginity. That impression lasts too long. Being embedded in anyone's mind longer than a little while is scary. Impressionable. As I look at Caroline, I realize what I need to do regardless of how I feel. Because it's the right thing to do.

My stomach is a steel trap, I never vomit. Right now? It flips so fucking hard I barely get the door open before spilling the alcoholic contents all over the ground. I open the glove compartment and hunt for napkins to wipe my mouth. This would be a tough conversation to have sober. Drunk? Implausible. I realize it now, that her pure innocence is what made her different, kept me interested, and I open the door to heave once more. At least I won't have a hangover tomorrow. Not from alcohol at least.

"You called me a cunt," she says.

I nod. "I'm sorry." That's the least of my offenses at this point, right? Still, my stomach flips at the reminder of my cruelty. There are moments in your life where you can't see the future because it hangs in the balance of whatever you say or do next. That moment for Caroline and me is right now. It's a real shame because it's not just her and me. There's also fuckers named bourbon, and keg beer here too.

Several seconds pass as I stare out into the moonlit field. "Say something," she whispers.

"What the fuck am I supposed to say? That I almost stole your innocence with angry drunk fucking? That I never thought for one moment to make love to you? That I'm sorry? Nothing I could say would take that back or make it seem genuine. Not right now, when the world is spinning and you're sitting over there afraid of me." She is afraid, too. The combination of my messed up eyes and my actions have created the perfect villain. One that in the movies would fuck her and leave her crying— never looking back.

She pulls her knees into her chest and something in that deep cavernous place that lays dank and dormant, comes to life. "You should have told me."

"What difference would it make?" she asks. "If you

take my virginity here or in a bed? It's all the same to me. From the second I met you I knew I wanted it to be you."

Shaking my head, I let out a bitter laugh. "You don't want it to be me. This right here is testament." Gesturing to the truck cab, my face, and then to her timid, shaking body.

Caroline presses her lips together. "Let's do it right now. It's going to be you, Tahoe. Why not right now?" Instead of rattling off the many reasons I won't, I think about how I missed the signs. Dwell on mistakes. That's what type A folks do. It's how we better ourselves regardless of cost.

"Have you messed around with a guy before me?" I can't help the question. It's typically one my pride would never let me ask. Now, I need to connect the dots and I require her responses to help ease this pain.

She stays silent. "Have you kissed a man before me?" I ask, my voice cracking.

Caroline doesn't say a word. I swallow down the disbelief. "I'm getting the fuck out of here before I take anything else from you, Caroline. I'll catch a ride home with someone else. Take my truck and go home."

Her defiant reply comes, "No."

"I've taken a lot of things in my lifetime. I can't be the one to take this from you. I don't deserve it. You deserve someone who can give you the world—at the very least someone who can offer you a promise for a bright future." My future will sometimes involve trudging through gutters and subway tracks hunting bad people.

When you juxtapose me next to her, I can't understand how I could have been so blinded by our differences. Love. I was blinded by it. By the thought that maybe I deserved it. Could keep it. There was never any keeping it. Not in my world. There's only losing it slowly. Piece by piece. She's still whole–intact. I have to respect that.

Her jaw ticks. "Don't tell me what I want," she says. "You live in this insane utopia where you think everything needs to be perfect. Maybe I don't want perfect. Maybe I want to lose my virginity to you, drunk, in this truck. Maybe nothing else matters because I'm in love with you. Even despite you being completely out of your mind right now." What did I almost do? How did this happen? "Fine, if not tonight. Let's talk about this tomorrow when you're in your right mind." Her voice sounds desperate and it calls out my need to protect her. I can't protect her from this monster. I am what she needs protecting from.

With my hand on the handle, I survey my feelings using the part of my fuzzy brain that isn't completely wrecked by alcohol. "I'm not the man for that job. Never will be," I shake my head once. "Get home safe, alright?"

"Fuck you, Tyler Holiday. You really are an idiot!"

Gritting my teeth, I open the door and fall out. Blessedly landing on my feet in the pile of my own puke. My chest stings, and there's no way I can look at her right now. Turning around to survey what I've done would only drive the nail into my chest deeper—create more empty space, where she is. Where nothing else will ever be.

I close the door on her loud sob and trudge back to find someone to give me a ride home.

And another bottle of something to replace what I just lost.

This is one of my seconds. The seconds that change everything. The lonely, taking ones that will keep me company for the rest of my life.

Chapter Fifteen

Caroline

The thunder rolls, shaking the hangar all night long. In true Florida fashion, the storm hit unannounced on my drive home from the spot. I didn't want to follow his instructions, but my options were zilch. I didn't want to see him drown in a canoe. I also didn't want to face my peers with the strings of heartbreak scaring like shackles around every limb. It's all my fault. This is what men expect, and I was too scared to go with it. He was out of his mind drunk, and if he'd been a little more himself I would have had sex with him in that tiny cramped, smelly space.

I called Shirley on the way home and she confirmed I shouldn't have told him. Or waited until after. Even though that would have made it worse, she doesn't understand how Tahoe operates. This desire to perfect things he has no control over. Everything was exacerbated by the fact that he was drinking with his buddies in this odd environment that I was an outsider in.

I am delicate. He is a storm. Carnage was inevitable.

When the clock finally clicks to 5 a.m. I sigh in relief. I gave myself permission to a night filled with tears and feeling sorry, but now it's a new day and I have a shift at the diner. A master at hiding my emotions, I'm ready to put on a happy face.

I shower last night's mistakes and regrets from my body, letting the water scorch my body to a needling red color, and dress in the familiar, soft uniform my mom tailored to fit me perfectly. As I stare at my reflection, I tie my wet hair into a bun on top of my head and debate covering the dark circles haunting my under eyes. I decide to leave them there and make great time getting to work.

Everyone stares, the news from last night already trickling around the town like a lively case of bed bugs. Who knows what these people actually think they know. A lie. The truth. It doesn't matter. Not anymore. I'm numb to anything except what has always brought me happiness and comfort. The known entities.

I serve my usual customers at the bar, remembering their orders, filling coffee cups, and pretending better than I ever have.

"You doing okay today, Caroline May?" Bob asks. Maybe he's too old to be in the gossip loop.

I smile wide. "Of course. It's a beautiful day," I reply. Then I remember how wet and gross it is outside right now from the torrential downpour last night.

The smile he returns is sad. "You working by yourself

this morning?"

Raising my brows, I nod. "Giving Mama a break this morning." And Shirley, who is probably just now waking up in someone else's bed. After a night filled with what I couldn't bring myself to do once.

Caleb coughs from behind me in the kitchen. I've kept interaction with him to the bare, professional minimum. "Ketchup with your hash browns," I say, setting the bottle in front of his plate. "Let me know if you need anything else."

Bob winks at me, and I head over to a few of my other tables—all men, stopping in for an early breakfast before work. One tries to engage me in conversation. He asks me about my seashell bracelet, and smiles too wide as he listens to my curt reply.

I know what hides behind that smile. The lies. The games. I cut him off, "If you need anything else just let me know."

His false grin falls. I walk away knowing I'll never feel the same way about a man again. As if my thoughts alone could conjure him, Tahoe walks in, the bell jingling like a death sentence. A few of his teammates follow in behind him. His piercing blue-red gaze finds me immediately. The pain is etched in every feature— the guilt plainly visible.

Regardless, my pulse quickens and my whole body electrifies. "Take any seat," I call over to them as I head back to the kitchen. As I pass Tahoe I say, "You're alive.

Fantastic."

I don't look at him or wait for a response.

"I told you so," Caleb says as he pushes a plate through the window. His cocky grin boils my blood.

"Fuck you, Caleb." I grab the plate and spin on my heel.

Caleb doesn't respond, but when I glance at him as I set the plate down in front of a customer, he's wide-eye and gaping at me. Maybe he won't mess with me anymore. I should swear more often. I might be taken more seriously.

"What are you guys drinking?" I ask, standing in front of Tahoe's table.

His friends laugh and I'm reminded of the immature jerks I went to school with. "If drinks are funny then last night was a real roar of a time," I deadpan. "Water for the table then?" I meet their eyes one by one. "Or did you drink enough bay water last night, too?"

Their smiles vanish. I avoid looking at Tyler for fear of feeling anything except anger and misery. Leif replies, "Coffee for the table and a plate of regret for him." He tilts his head toward Tahoe.

"I'll be back with your coffees and his plate of chicken shit in a minute. Anything else while I'm here?" They laugh at my joke. Well Tahoe doesn't, but I didn't expect him to. Then again, I'm not sure what to expect from him.

"Fuck you guys. I'm outta' here," Tahoe growls,

standing from the table and blowing through the diner and out the front door.

Aidan looks smug. "We made him come here," he says.

"Why?"

"He said you broke up with him last night and we didn't believe him."

Leif cackles. "He also didn't think you were working this morning. You should have seen his face when he saw your bike outside." Their booth roars with laughter. These huge, burly men with their deep baritone voices echo the small space.

I place my hands on my hips, looking around at my tables to see if anyone is trying to get my attention. I'm okay for the moment. "Listen, he broke up with me," I say, placing a hand on my chest, over my heart. I think of Caleb's reaction to my cursing. Swallowing down the woman I used to be—the one who got burned. I have their attention, and I take full advantage of this moment. "It seems Tyler Holiday isn't good at everything," I say. "He doesn't even know how to take a woman's virginity."

Their smiles fall, and Leif's mouth hangs open. Aidan licks his lips. "Oh," Leif says, shaking off the shock of my unfiltered words. The silence turns awkward, overtaking every particle of oxygen. "It all makes sense now," he mutters, though I'm not sure he meant for me to hear.

"Maybe you boys can give him some pointers? I'll be back in a jiff," I say, scribbling the coffees down on the ticket.

Their gazes are boring into my back, I'm sure of it. Caleb's eyes look wary as I approach. "Don't say a word," I say, shaking my head. Leif exits the building, and comes back in a minute or two later, a grim expression on his face.

As I'm pouring coffee in their mugs, Leif clears his throat. "Uh, can you spare a second to chat with him? He's still outside. We all rode in together," he explains.

I shake my head. "Even if I wanted to, I'm waiting by myself today."

Aidan hops up. "Give me your apron. I have this. I've always wanted to live out a waitress fantasy."

Leif quirks one bushy brow. "You mean fuck a waitress in uniform. Not be one, right?" he asks, then realizes I'm standing right here. "Not you, though. I'm not suggesting he wants to fuck you." His face is horrified as he tries to talk around his blunder.

I grin. "Of course not. Why would anyone want to fuck me?"

Leif swallows hard. Aidan clears his throat awkwardly. "Go talk to him. Just thirty seconds. Aidan can pour coffee. I attest on his behalf. I'll supervise everything."

"I have nothing to say to him," I say, putting one hand on my hip.

Aidan ushers me to the front door, one arm on my shoulder. I ask Bob on my way by if he needs anything. He winks in response.

I hand Aidan the ticket book and tell him the guy in the suit needs his check. He smiles widely like I've entrusted him with a billion dollars. Tahoe is kicking the tires of the truck in the muddy parking lot.

"What do you want?" I call out.

At the sound of my voice, he hangs his head. "They told you to come out here?"

"Said you wanted to talk to me," I say.

He looks like crap. His face is haggard and his tan skin is a pallid color. "Tyler, I really don't have anything else to say to you."

"I fuck virgins," he says, a hint of meanness inside his words.

I raise my brows. "That's great. Just not me then. What a compliment. I didn't come out here to fight with you about your drunken declarations. Aidan is in there waiting my tables."

He kicks the chunks of wet mud with his big combat boots. "I fucked everything up, okay? Stay away from me and them," he says.

I laugh. "Don't tell me what to do."

"Caroline, I'm telling you for your own good. We aren't good men. I saved you. Stringing you along for all this time was one of the worst decisions I've ever made. I'm sorry for that. I am."

Frustration rears, leaving me furious. "I don't need a *good* man to take my virginity. At this point I just need someone who isn't afraid to do it. Aren't men supposed to want a virgin? I saw on the news one woman auctioned hers off. Maybe that's what I'll do. Get it over with so you'll find me attractive."

He spins, looking at me dead on for the first time since I came outside. "That's seriously what you fucking think? That I don't find you attractive enough?" He steps toward me. I look away, at the window where his friends are staring at us from their booth. The soft glow of the light behind them masking the expressions on their faces. "A war doesn't have anything on what you make me feel." He gets so close that I can feel the heat from his breaths.

I have to close my eyes. To get away from him in one way, because it's too much. Having him this close but not being able to touch him. "You are dangerous, Caroline," he says. I open my eyes as his flutter closed. "You threaten everything I've ever stood for. Everything I thought I needed. Wanted. I'm doing you a favor. Be reasonable please."

"That's it then?" I ask. "We'll just pretend there's nothing between us? This is a small town in case you haven't noticed." His B&B comes to mind and how entangled he is with my world now.

He backs away a step and inhales deeply. "Pretending is going to be hard for a while. I need to get the fuck away from you."

"How can you do this? I don't understand. How can you throw this away so easily? For something so trivial?"

Before it ever really started. Maybe my hesitance was warranted, maybe he was never that into me. Reading things this wrong is something I'll probably never recover from.

"You're asking the wrong questions," Tahoe replies. To his credit, he looks tortured and crestfallen. Like someone else made this decision for him and there's nothing he can do to change it.

Licking my lips, I take a step back toward the diner. "What a joke. Have fun in New York." All of it was too good to be true. Something picked from a movie and inserted in my life. The happily ever after doesn't transfer over in real life though. I'm not that naïve.

He raises his brows. "If I'm lucky I won't make it back." My stomach sinks at what he's insinuating. I can't have him, and I don't want anyone else to have him, but he needs to always exist. To prove what I felt, for even a small amount of time was real.

Shaking my head, I try to process that sober Tyler Holiday is saying the same things that drunk Tyler said last night. He stares at me. Hard. Like he's trying to figure me out. "You are something special."

"Not special enough, though. Too small town. Too simple." He watches my mouth as I speak.

He stalks toward me quickly and the sudden movement takes my breath away.

"Know that anytime you move your lips I want to be kissing them," he growls. This close I see everything he tries to hide. The specks of lighter blue in his eyes, the way his jaw ticks as he holds himself back. I know what it used to mean. Does it still mean the same thing now?

Blinking away tears, I enter the diner. Aidan has a tray of food haphazardly balancing on one hand, and Caleb is wearing a scowl fit for the Grinch.

One glance at the morose demeanor of Tahoe's table of friends tells me they watched the whole sad, sorry conversation deteriorate. Who knows, maybe they can read lips. I could punish them for their friend's behavior, but that would take more effort than I can muster at the moment. When Shirley joins me a few hours later, I give her the lowdown. She makes me feel better, because aftermath is what she's good at. I listen to her advice, forcing it to be applicable to me. She tells me men aren't worth it. They are only good for one thing. I tell her that one thing is why he decided I wasn't worth the effort and she does her best to conceal her confusion, but can't.

I shove my apron in the dirty clothing hamper near the kitchen. "You have to do it, Caroline. With anyone. It doesn't matter if they aren't up to your standards. Make him think he's a blip on your radar, not worth the dirt on the bottom of your shoe."

Swallowing hard, I think her advice through. "Isn't that kind of the opposite of what I want?"

"He is not a nice person, Care. Move on. With one of the Bronze Bay boys. They won't hurt you like that. I guarantee it. It sounds like he has some weird hang ups.

You're ready to settle down with someone?" Not with a Bronze Bay boy. I can't even fathom it now.

"I'm ready to lose my virginity," I reply.

Shirley smiles. "Let's focus on that."

I shrug.

Chapter Sixteen

Tahoe

There's a brunette in the kitchen when I walk out of the bedroom, a towel wrapped low around my waist. She's wearing a t-shirt, the curve of her naked ass peeking out of the bottom. Her legs are short and lean as she leans forward to look on a bottom shelf inside the fridge.

Aidan gallops into the room from the other bedroom. Gallops. Like a fucking horse. He blows a noisy breath through his mouth and nose before he neighs.

"Please take the pony play to the bedroom," I say, wincing. It's been a while since we've been in this kind of situation. Not since before Bronze Bay. To say the guys are going balls to the walls with the freedom in a big city is an understatement.

Aidan cackles and pulls the dark beauty into his arms. She leans back to kiss him and I have to look away. "You can come be a stallion in my stable if you want to," she says, breaking up their kiss to talk to me. The brunette winks.

"Yeah, man. I'll share," Aidan replies when I don't.

It's more of a growl. It doesn't tempt me in the least. Not anymore. I'm convinced the only things that do it for me are the ones I've sworn off.

Shaking my head, I brush past them to grab a bottle of water from the hotel fridge. "While it's an offer that's hard to refuse, I'm going to have to bow out gracefully," I say, making my way back to my room. "Use a saddle, Aidan," I call out before closing, and locking, my bedroom door behind me.

Their laughter carries through walls and it reinforces the lonely, awful feelings coursing through my body. I take a long swallow of the water, as sweat beads on my chest and arms. I just went for a run in the bustle of NYC and the shower didn't cool me down. It didn't do anything to clear my head either. My comrades are on a Tinder rage and I'm hung up on a woman, trying to come to terms with what that means.

Caroline was supposed to be here with me. This was supposed to be it. The time of my life. When I finally gave in and let myself have what I've been lusting after. Instead, I'm masturbating twice a day, in a penthouse suite while thinking about the woman who I'll never have. Not in the capacity that I thought I would. My brothers decided to come early with me because I wasn't able to cancel the hotel reservation, so they added several rooms. To fill the rest of the day, I'll need to distract myself. I need something. Want to forget that I fell so hard for a woman so effortlessly I didn't realize it until now. Until I couldn't call her mine.

A few loud raps sound on my door followed by Leif's baritone voice telling me to let him in. I throw on a pair of jeans that are on the floor next to my bed and slink over to let him in.

"You're a fuckin' mess, dude. Aidan is across the hall screwing a celebrity lookalike, my room looks like a brothel, and here you are," he says, waving his hand to my room, and then me. "Working out and moping like a sorry sack of shit."

I run my hands through my wet hair a few times to dry it. "I have to see her every day. It's a small, fucking town." Deviate from the real problem. My feelings. At any cost.

"Go back to San Diego. Ask for a transfer to another satellite base. They're popping up everywhere now. They wouldn't tell you no." The thought of moving makes my stomach sink.

Shaking my head, I say, "I like it there."

He comes in, and cracks open the mini bar and fishes for a bottle to down. "You need to get over the chick, then. You can't possibly be that hung up on her," he says. It's a question, though, not a statement. He's eyeing me in the way we look at bad guys we're questioning, trying to seek out truths inside blatant falsities. Without taking his gaze from mine, he screws off the top of a mini bottle of Jack and downs it.

"I'm in love with her," I reply. When it's this obvious how miserable I am, there's no sense lying about it.

"I thought you might say that," Leif says, setting the empty down on a dresser. "I called her."

Narrowing my eyes, I respond, "You called who?"

He shrugs, like it's just a mundane everyday occurrence, a wide grin playing across his chiseled, severe face. "The root of all of this unnecessary drama." Leif finds another bottle of the same, and tosses it to me.

"Stella."

My head swims and the jagged hole inside my chest feels a little wider. The sweat beads faster now, rolling down my chest and the sides of my face. "What the fuck are you talking about?" I ask.

A bang from Aidan's room ricochets throughout the suite. Then a loud neigh. I block it out in favor of fury. I step toward my friend. "Drink it. She's in the lobby waiting for you," Leif says, nodding at my hand. "Actually you should empty the mini bar as fast as you can. Don't look at me with that rage face and your balled up fists, man. You know as well as I do, that she's the hang-up. The reason you can't be happy. The ice bitch. The queen of blue ball happiness blocking. Instead of fighting me. Thank me."

Looking to the ceiling, I yell. It's a war cry of frustration. My breaths come quicker. "I'm not going down there." I drink the Jack.

Leif tsks. "She didn't want to see you either and she's still down there. Instead of fucking a redhead with the stage name of Jessica Rabbit, I've spent the past twelve hours tracking down Stella. Do us all a favor and at least speak your peace. We have to work tomorrow and we need you there with us." Leif taps the side of my head, and then wipes off my sweat on the side of his pants.

I drink another Jack, then another. I pace the room and Leif talks to me. About things I haven't brought up for half a decade. Horrible things that make me feel. Did I stop to consider the fact that Stella, and our past could be the hang-up preventing me from moving forward and taking what I want without thought for the future? Maybe for a half a second. Some memories are too painful to bring up even if they further the dissection of a current problem. What if Leif is right?

"Put on a fucking shirt," Leif says. I'm still sweating, but I pull on the first shirt I find on top of my bag. The mirror in front of me shows an image of a stranger. Sweat immediately bleeds through the black cotton fabric.

"I hate you so much," I tell him, shaking my head. "This is the last thing I need right now."

"It's one of the only things you need right now. Give me some credit. How long have I been your friend?" I shake off his fact. It doesn't matter right now.

Pacing once more to the window overlooking NYC, the place that stole her from me in the most dubious, sneaky way. There wasn't closure. There was a deployment the next day and a Dear John letter in the form of an email. I looked at the email every day for ten months. I woke up on the first of the eleventh month and instead of reading it, I deleted it. Buried it. Tried not to think about her or what I lost again. It worked on most days, and on others, I obsess over the failure.

At the thought of the failure, anger rises. Just enough to force my feet forward, one ahead of the other to the elevator and down to the lobby of the five-star hotel. I'm a fucking mess and the fact that this is happening right now, is hard to fucking swallow.

I see her from the back. She's sitting at the round bar in the center of the lounge, her blonde hair hitting just below her shoulder blades. It's shorter than it was the last time I saw her, but after spending years with her, she'll always be someone I recognize anywhere. She senses my presence, swiveling in her chair to face me.

She looks older, the skin on her face a little less

glowing than I last remembered. I swallow down the last of my hesitation and approach with leaden feet and a pounding heart."Stella," I say, my voice cracking.

She looks down at the gin and tonic in front of her instead of looking at me. "What is it, Tyler? I can't believe I'm here right now."

Okay. Patience. I won't kill Leif. Not today, anyways. He has my best interests at heart even if he's a fucking moron. Her cell phone beeps on the bar and she looks at it sighing. "My husband," she says, waving the screen at me. "Worried because I left the house to visit my ex-boyfriend." She waves an arm at me. "Why he's intimidated by you, I have no idea, but dear Lord, make this fast." She sips her favorite cocktail, sighing in annoyance.

I laugh. That's what you do during awkward pauses when you have no clue how to respond. "You wrote me a fucking email, Stella," I growl lowly. "Why?" Might as well get what I came for, right? The ten months of holding onto broken promises requires this to survive.

Her lips, ones I've kissed so many times in the past, purse. Looking at her doesn't feel like I thought it would. She's not some mirage, she's just a woman who I once loved, and it brings awareness to one fact, Stella doesn't hold a fucking candle to Caroline. My stomach drops. I brush my brow with the back of my hand.

The bartender catches my eye and I point to drink in front of her and hold up the number one with my finger. He squints his eyes and I remember my own messed up eyes. He nods and begins fixing me the drink I detest the most. "Is that really what you want to know? It was easier that way. We were so entwined that a clean break was needed. A new life presented itself in New York and you were always going to do…what you do," she explains, looking around to make sure we're out of earshot. "You can't possibly need closure. That email explained everything and then some. I'm not a woman to leave without cause. It was time to part ways."

Her tired eyes meet mine and I notice her exhaustion. It reminds me of the probable reason why. Her baby. "Why am I here?" she asks again. "Leif told me about your new base. I'm glad you're switching up your work pace. Maybe…it will be good for you." She has no clue. Leif didn't tell her anything. My drink arrives and I swallow down half of the nasty tasting liquid, and wince. "Still don't like a gin and tonic either. Your eyes are awful, by the way. I remember when Smith got a mask squeeze, so I won't ask how it happened. I'll just assume the drunken worst."

Sighing, I look away, trying to compile my thoughts. At least I don't have to worry about my demon eyes right now. "You're happy," I ask.

"Is that a question?" she narrows her eyes at the side of my face. "I'm happy," she says, when I don't answer. "My life is full. I love my husband and family. I would do the same thing all over again, Tyler. The same exact thing."

My jaw ticks, and I clasp my glass tightly in both of my hands. Looking at her, I let myself feel the pain from the past. The terror attacks changed everything. Perhaps that truly is why she wanted to move on from my life style. Not because of me. Maybe I didn't do anything horribly wrong. "I'm in love with a woman," I tell her.

She coughs. A nervous tick because I've surprised her.

"Oh," she says. "So this isn't some attempt to get back together?"That makes me laugh. "Fuck no, Stella. Fuck. No," I say. "After what you did?" She looks down and away. She should be ashamed of that fucking email. Of the no contact. Of the years wasted on our commitment to one another.

When she remains silent, it's my turn to tell her a truth bomb. "I love this woman more than I thought I was capable of."

Her gaze meets mine and I see tears shining—the hard facts surfacing. "Caroline reminds me of you in that one way that I've never been able to reconcile. This isn't me trying to get back together with a married woman, Stell. This is me trying to figure out if you're the one who blew my chances with the only woman I've ever truly loved."

She raises her brows. "Ouch," she says, smiling. "I'm glad you finally see. I'm sad this is what it took for you to realize you didn't love me in that forever kind of way, though." I down the rest of my drink while Stella sips hers, a thoughtful look on her face. Her eyes are narrowed, actually curious. She's relieved now that she knows what this is about. I grab a cocktail napkin and wipe my face and forearms, breathing deeply. "You look like shit, by the way," she adds. She's grinning when I meet her eyes. "You made a Tahoe sized mistake, huh?"

"Go big or go home, baby," I joke, using a phrase from our past. Her smile is wistful, but vanishes quickly.

"I need to know if you wanted to be with other men," I say, lowering my voice. "You know, other than me."

Her eyes widen, realization dawning. "I didn't break up with you because I wanted to sample the platter, Tyler. How could you think that?" she replies, looking left and right, and then meeting my eyes. "You literally stated, verbatim, why I ended our relationship. I loved you like water. Something required to survive. You couldn't be bottled. You slipped right thought my fingers." She pauses, her eyes glossing over. "Do you understand'?" She reaches out, her familiar hand seeking mine. I put my big one of top of hers. "You never needed me. Not like Harry needs me. Not like the baby needs me. I told you that in the email. It never had anything to do with wanting to try out other men before settling down forever with you. How I wish it could have been you!" She takes a few seconds to compose herself and it satisfies me in a cruel way to know I can cause her this obvious pain.

"She's a virgin, like I was?" she asks, pulling her hand back, to wrap around her glass.

I put my face in both of my hands and keep my mouth shut. "And you're afraid that she's going to run like I did," Stella says. "To make sure you're the one. In your selfishness to know you're the best, you think she can't decide for herself that you're the one without having been with other men?"

Groaning, I pick up my head and rub my tired eyes. There's no need to reply. This is where Stella is successful. I raise one finger to signal for another drink.

"How bad did you blow this, Tahoe?" she asks.

Turning, I look at her. What would it hurt to tell her? "I can't look at her without wanting her. I can't breathe without smelling her. Every single thing in my body wants her in every single way and I know I'll never be able to shake her," I admit. "She's perfect. I'm bound to the town. I bought property. I did all of these things because I convinced myself I loved Bronze Bay. When in actuality, I like Bronze Bay. I love Caroline."

"And," Stella prompts. She wants the gory details. The warm fuzzy facts don't help anyone. I want her advice so I have to crack open the dark spots.

"I didn't know she was a virgin and I almost fucked her in my truck cab, piss drunk, mind you. That's when she dropped the V bomb and I ghosted. I can't take that from her. I leave destruction in my wake," I say, letting my gaze flick from the top of Stella's head down to her waist, and back up.

Stella swallows hard. "I never thought I'd be giving you relationship advice," she says, calmly. "Does she love you? Like you love her?"

I run my hand through my hair. "I think so," I reply. She did. Maybe. Before I panicked—self-sabotaged, gave her every reason not to. "Probably not like I do. She makes me feel crazy. It was going to be perfect," I say. "I had it all planned out. This weekend in the city. I knew she was innocent. I did, but I had no clue. Blinded by everything else, I guess."

Stella shakes her head and reminds me of the story of how she told me she was a virgin. I wanted that back then—thought it was the greatest thing in the world to have a body untouched by any other cock.

"You have a type even if you don't want to admit it," She says. "She'd probably forgive you if you explain that a horrible virgin in your past burned you in the worst possible way."

I grin, and then down another drink. "Slow down on the drinks, buddy. Sounds like that's what got you into some of this mess." Nodding, I agree. "You were forever for me. The feelings weren't reciprocated," Stella says sadly.

"I can't apologize for something I didn't know," I say. "Had I never met Caroline I'd have thought you were it for me too."

Laughing, she shakes her head. "That is so offensive, but I get it. If it's real, she'll understand. I'm sorry, Tyler. For the email. For a lot of things. If you can salvage this with her, I feel like none of it will matter. Everything will work out the way it was supposed to. I'm glad Leif called me."

So am I. This was needed for so many reasons. The next drink we share is slow. Stella shows me photos of her baby on her phone and I tell her about Caroline. About Bronze Bay. About my home. When her husband calls, we end our meeting both feeling lighter. I walk her to the revolving door and follow her out onto the sidewalk.

She turns abruptly, and sets her gaze to meet mine. For a fleeting second, I miss our past, and everything comfortable we had together. Love isn't comfortable, though. It's a painful collapse of walls—a drifting into a place that feels like adventure and home at the same time. "Keep it," she says, smiling a familiar smile. "It's the only thing worth fighting for. Perfection is a mess, Tyler Holiday. Remember that." She spins on her heel and walks away, her blonde hair getting lost in a sea of meaningless people.

My feet don't move fast enough as I run through the lobby and back up to my room to make a phone call. Or seven.

Chapter Seventeen

Caroline

Not only has he broken my heart, he's cut me off from the rest of the world. Rather, all of the men in Bronze Bay. Shirley tried to get me a date with Buddy from the furniture store. Someone to pop my cherry and move on from the Tahoe sized hole in my chest, but he refused a date. So did Nathan from the body shop, Trey from the Bait and Tackle, and Rhett, the attorney in town. She opens her arms and talks loudly. "They all said you were Tahoe's property!" she exclaims.

I'm so furious, I'm crying. "How dare he!" I roar. The tears of frustration turn into sadness because as angry as I am, I'm also relieved.

I don't want Buddy. Or Nathan, or Trey, or Rhett. Not at all. Not even one tiny bit. I only want one man and that is absolutely infuriating. "He's already ruined everything with our relationship, but now he's all best buds with Bronze Bay residents."

"Caleb," Shirley says, ignoring my screams. "He would have sex with you."

I scoff. "You have sex with Caleb," I say, my mouth hanging open. "Are you out of your mind?" Leaning back in my desk chair, my friend perches at the edge of my desk, scrolling through her cell phone. "Are they back from New York yet?" I ask.

Shirley shakes her head. "I think they get home tomorrow or the next day though. I remember Aidan saying it should take a few weeks or so. I can't believe you didn't go to NYC without him. You don't need him to travel."

She's right. The thought did cross my mind. "What if I ran into him? I don't know where I'm going. As independent as I like to think I am, I'd need someone who knew where they're going."

"Hello! Take me. We could figure it out ourselves together. Let's finish planning your house warming with Malena and then we'll go to New York. We'll find men and have a lot of sex! That dude can't have reach up that far. There will be a man willing to take your virginity in the city. I've heard about these apps you use to find dates," Shirley explains, air quoting the last word. "You upload your picture and look at theirs and decide if you want to bang it out."

"You act like I'm a pariah and can't find anyone for myself," I exclaim. "I agree we should take a trip. Not to go man hunting, though. There's so much I want to see and do there."

Her thumb hovers over her cell. "Are you sure about Caleb though? You could be done with this tonight. He's really good at it, and everyone knows he holds a torch for you. I bet he'd be gentle and loving."

"Should I puke on your lap or hold it in my mouth?

I'm a grown woman. I refuse to share a man with my best friend. Why do you sleep with him if you know he holds a torch for me?"

She widens her eyes like I'm daft. "I just said, he's *really* good at it, Caroline."

"That's all it is then? Just sex for you? Has it ever been something more?" Merely kissing Tahoe electrifies my body. I thought that was normal. When his hands are on me, I forget planet earth exists. It's beyond a craving. The longing didn't disappear when his love did. There's no way I'd have that kind of luck. I dream about him touching me. Holding me. Kissing me. The dreams feel surreal and I always wake with frustration that morphs into sadness.

"Well, I guess it's for the company. I'm not like you. I'm not happy in a spinster tower all by myself with only airplanes on my brain. I like having someone to talk to."

"Why not a boyfriend, then?"

She hops down and dusts her palms on the sides of her jeans. "Too much work. I never said I want to be tied down."

I sort a stack of paperwork on the desk, completely distracted by my thoughts and tell Shirley to call Malena to finish the party planning. That's one good thing I have learned about a break up. Your friends feel bad for you so you can ask for things without having to reciprocate. I may have underestimated that facet in the past. She agrees, tells me she might have Caleb keep her company tonight and leaves the office. By the time I finish paying bills and returning emails I'm enraged with the thoughts racing back through my mind. How Tahoe barged in and took exactly what he wanted when he wanted it. He punched me where it hurt. My hometown. My life. The Homer property. Crick's Beach. Hangar five. My heart. I'm not sure which is more complicated. Losing yourself to a man or finding yourself because of one.

I've put on a good front for my parents, only telling them tiny bits of truth when asked point blank, but mamas always see the things we try to hide. She handed me half a pie, pulled out two forks and demanded to talk about airplanes. Using my love of airplanes as a distraction technique is one thing, but I know she hears more about aircrafts from my father so it clued me in to her intuition. She never did ask what happened between us. Maybe her super powers extend to that too and she already knows.

I make a visit to one of the hangars on the property that we do the large projects in. It has extra space for builds and rebuilds. It was decked to the nines for my high school graduation party, lights strung across the ceiling like wild stars in the sky. One Christmas long ago my daddy built a dollhouse in here. He thought he could hide it from me in the remote back corner, but even then I wanted to be exactly like him. I followed him, quiet as a field mouse, and snuck in behind him to find the glorious present. It was the last year I believed in Santa Claus. And the first year I realized just how much he loved me.

Sitting in a dusty wooden chair, I try to erase my current pain with happy memories of the past. It works for a little while, and no one would ever look for me here, but the loneliness gnaws at me. That might be the worst part of almost having something spectacular. Being a part of something. Having someone to share everything with. Never feeling alone even when you are. The worth in that is something no one appreciates until you've tasted it for yourself. And then lost it. When the nostalgia wears off and Tahoe fills all of my senses, I grab my bag and run to the closest aircraft. I need to fly. Get into the air—among the clouds. The technical aspect forces me to dwell on things that are easy for me. Gauges, wind speeds, and things that are second nature. It doesn't take me long to maneuver onto the wide runway and get the plane in the air. It might even be a record. I'm too upset to check. My mind is fixated on one thing: rewind and erase. Like those old VHS tapes you could record shows on. One accidental move and you'd clear the whole thing without the ability to recover. I'm begging whoever will listen for that accidental move.

Some might call what I'm doing running away. I always come back. The thought of leaving for good crosses my mind every time I reach the furthest peak of a short fly. It's almost as if I can feel my borders and boundaries even if I don't truly have any. He pressed me forward. Challenged me to look at things in a way I never considered. Nothing holds me back except myself.

It happens then. The stark realization of my inadequacy in checking and double checking everything. The clouds wrapping my airplane are a sinister hue, the wind a foe of the worst possible caliber. The sun, my only friend at the moment, even looks wrong. My stomach turns and flips as emergency procedures trickle into my awareness. It happened so quickly.

Then again, that's how all disasters happen, isn't it? I prayed for an accident, now I better start praying I live through it.

Chapter Eighteen

Tahoe

The phone call from Aidan is brusque, the information delivered in a matter-of-fact way. I'm used to that. Rarely does it affect me, but suddenly I can't breathe—my chest motionless because of the shock. The call for help came as we were unloading our gear from the airplane to the trucks. We flew back to Bronze Bay using our private plane. There's only one in which we can all fit. Now that we have a contract with May's Airfield we flew straight here. I was on pins and needles with the intent of going to see Caroline the second I stepped on land. Support staff carry cumbersome pelican cases from the hold and stack them in the truck beds as I take stock of my own bags.

Aidan was loading up his stuff when he received the phone call from our base. An airplane crash. It landed on an island off the coast of Bronze Bay and the SOS system is down with a clear visual of smoke rising at the place of impact. It's her. I know it is. Even if they didn't say names, they mentioned the type of aircraft that was missing from the airport, and connecting the dots was easy after that. The rain falls down in an angry tirade, the drops pelting the side of my face. Why would she fly in this? Where was she going?

"Tahoe you stay here. We'll take the boats from the base over to the island with the fire department," Leif says, overhearing the conversation that is spreading like wildfire among our surly, tired pack. It's been one hell of a mission. Admitting to being out of practice would be the same as admitting defeat. My muscles are coiled with annoyed rage, and I'm pretty sure even my bones are crying out in protest. All of this doesn't touch the drowning sense of dread I feel right now. Caroline. My cell rings in my pocket. It's Shirley. She's squealing into the phone, her voice a panicked version of a hysterical cat. "I just landed," I state calmly, trying to let her know I can't solve anything that quickly. "It's going to be okay. I'll figure it out," I reply, trying to keep my voice even. "We're getting all of the information right now." I cover the mouthpiece of my cell while she cries in the background.

"I'm not staying here," I respond to Leif. "There's no fucking way I'm staying back." Does he know me at all? "You don't even know if it's her," he replies, slinging the response over his shoulder as he organizes the masses in front of us, doling out instructions and tasks.

I shrug. "If it's not her it's even more reason for me to come. You're not keeping me here," I say, shaking my head. I let go of the mouthpiece to talk to Shirley who finally mentioned something that piqued my interest. "What did you say?" I ask.

"She texted me. It only said Shell Island. It is her," Shirley says in between sobs. I ask when she heard from Caroline last and she says she was at the airport with her earlier today and then just the text message. I ask a few more questions, and I promise to take care of everything. Even if it's the hugest lie in the history of deceit.

My focus shifts. Caroline is okay. She made it if she could send a text message. She has to be okay. I've made my decision. The only decision that matters. One of the trucks is in my line of vision. Without thinking twice, I hop into the cab and tear out of there as quickly as humanly possible, skidding around on the dirt road like one of those assholes in the drifting movies.

All caution is thrown to the wind as I dismantle every rule I've ever formed for myself. Always use care and caution. Nope. Don't take anything too seriously. That's out the window too. Keep it light. Nothing has ever felt heavier. I just returned from weeks of hunting bad guys. A task that is just as complicated as it is difficult. SEALs are tapped to do these types of jobs for a reason. We're the best at it. The irony that I suck harder than a hoover vacuum in my personal life would be funny if it wasn't so awful. I see two other trucks in my rearview driving just as reckless as I am. The rain tames the dust making the visibility better. By muscle memory, I pull into my usual parking spot and throw the truck in park. I jog through the parking lot to the office, the rain soaking the rest of my uniform. It's torrential at this point so even my boots are sloshing each step I take.

Aidan greets me as I blaze into the doorway. "The boats are started. They're waiting for men," he says coolly, his palms outstretched. He's trying to pacify the beast.

"Anything else? Any other updates?" I ask.

He shakes his head. "The fire department loaded their equipment and they are ready. The rain will work to our advantage. Hop on the second boat, brother," Aidan says.

His tone tells me he knows how important this is. I'm not saying my life is worth more than someone else's, but hers is. He knows it. You can only take so much good out of the world. The scales will tilt in the favor of evil. That's what happened with the terror attacks. Dirty facts of life.

"You aren't going to try to keep me back here?" I snarl, ambling to my desk to pull on my worn out ball cap from a bottom drawer. "Leif thought to try," I add.

Aidan's footsteps are loud and his voice carries as he greets more men who enter the building. The same status is given to them, and he turns to face me. "Go find your fucking puppy," he growls. The grin tells me he's being kind, a fact no one else in their right mind would understand. He slaps me on the back. I force a smile as reply.

Wet from the rain and sweating from the unknown, I jog down to the docks. My muscles protest, and it gives me something to focus on instead of thinking about the alternative. The searing selfish pain of my mistake. All of them, actually. Harboring so much resentment from a past relationship, I let it affect a new one. The only one that matters. Trying to control every aspect backfired.

Boarding the boat, we set off at a breakneck pace, pounding on the choppy wake as we travel toward Shell

Island. The smoke is pouring into the dark sky, a signal we're traveling in the correct direction. We've passed the island while going out to sea for fishing and training so I know exactly where it is. I thought it was pretty. It's too small for houses and doesn't have the infrastructure to have buildings of any sort. I've seen colorful tents so I know it's a popular camping spot. There are shells bleached white from the sun that line the coast and trees of varying sizes. I can't recall the shape of the island even though I've seen it bird's eye on a map. The motors are too loud and the chop to rough to ask questions, or else I would be pestering everyone around me. The driver of the boat is stoic, a steely take no shit mask on his face. He's a guy from another Team who got transferred to Bronze Bay against his desires.

The mangled, fiery wreckage comes into view as we approach and I'm pretty certain it matches my insides right now. The time to be cool, calm, and collected is long gone. Now, the time has come to panic like a mother fucking, raging idiot.

I bellow as we slow down and the side comes into view. I know every one of the airplanes that belong to May's Airport by heart. I memorized them when I was trying not to obsess over Caroline and what that meant for my street cred. Even though I already knew it was her, and Shirley told me as much, seeing it in front of me in living color is a page from my worst nightmare playbook.

Someone puts their hand on my shoulder, but I can't turn my gaze away from the wreckage to acknowledge the gesture. It takes multiple seconds to swallow, another few to realize I need to take a breath, and then several more to shuffle my feet as the boat hits land.

Men pour off the first boat and the portable water system shoots water onto the flames, while others approach a wing of the airplane that has been torn off. It's obvious it exploded after it landed, and not on approach, small indicators giving away gruesome clues.

My gaze scans the beach surrounding the aircraft, hopeful to find what I'm looking for. My hand rests on my side arm even though this isn't a time for guns. It shows how desperate and disheveled I am in this moment. Orders are being followed and my feet refuse to move.

Another matte black boat rolls onto the beach, and I know Leif must be on it. A silence transcends all that is happening, the business of everyone working as a team as I finally trudge through the rain towards the plane.

Voices cut through my self-imposed deafness. Words like *empty cockpit, no human remains, must have escaped before the explosion,* make my heart hammer along faster than the rain stinging my skin.

The sight of the blackened cockpit speeds my breathing. "She wasn't in there," Leif says, walking past me. "Come on," he says. His lips are moving and although I hear his words, it feels like a slow-mo movie. I can't fully comprehend. "Come on, Tahoe," Leif repeats. "You're okay. We've got this." He nods a few times until I nod back.

Shaking it off is difficult. "Take that section over there," he says, pointing left, further from the wreckage. "Guy and Taz are over there combing the brush. Help them search."

I take my orders and start for the section of island, but someone yells, voice booming, in the opposite direction. That's when I run. A haphazard staggering on top of the shells and sand. More voices echo off the trees, and my soaked ball cap feels like it weighs a thousand pounds.

"She's over here! Medic! Medic!" It's Aidan's voice.

When I make it to huddle of people, I throw a few men out of my way to get a visual. They have a makeshift tarp propped up shielding the top half of her body from the rain. I'd recognize those bare legs anywhere. The shade of tan. The curve of her knee. I try to ignore the burn marks as I survey her body. My gaze travels up further to her bare stomach as the medic rushes in to perform CPR.

The three freckles.

Connect the dots.

He breaks her ribs with a hard compression, the slicing crunch and crack prickles my skin. Someone tries to pull me back, but I turn with a hard, right hook to a face. No one fucks with me after that.

I drop to my knees when I'm next to her and lay my hand on her stomach, keeping those three marks hidden. They're mine. Removing my hat, I bow my head. I'm not the praying type. When you've seen what I've seen, you have to doubt God exists. I'd sell my soul to the devil with a firm handshake if it means Caroline pulling through. So, I do pray. Hard. Mercilessly. With every fiber of my being. I ask for healing.

I ask for a miracle.

Perfection is messy, but I guarantee it never looks like this.

Chapter Nineteen

Caroline

Even if I had checked the radar before I left, I wouldn't have anticipated how furious the storm that took my plane down would turn out to be. For all intents and purposes it was the perfect Florida storm. Gory and treacherous, wild with surprise, and mild in warning. It took no prisoners. I spent four months recovering in St. Mary's Hospital. Months that were brutal for many different reasons. My body and mind will never be quite the same, ever again. The hospital is inland several miles and I swear to God, you can't smell the sea air that far away. It was like being trapped in another dimension. One in which a fern named Beatrice kept me company during the lonely night hours. I kept the plant alive. When everything hurt and tears were pouring down my face as I sat up in bed, watering that plant gave me a purpose. Water the fern. Eat. Water the fern. Sleep. Water the fern. Breath. Water the fern. It was the only mantra I lived by, watering that fern kept me alive.

Friends came and went, but after such a long time,

the visits dwindled down. Aside from my mama bringing in lunches and dinners for the hospital staff a few times a week when she visited me, I was alone but for my beeping monitors and a night nurse named Felicia.

One person who wanted to be there daily wasn't, because I wrote his name on the do not visit list. There's really no such thing in a small-town hospital, but I made Felicia promise me she'd tell the office girls to make sure he didn't get up those stairs to see me. I envisioned the employees swooning instead of obeying my wishes, but I haven't seen him. Not even since I've been home. I only know he wanted to visit because my daddy told me so.

I moved in with my parents so they could help me maneuver around with the crutches, and if I'm being perfectly honest, I can't bear being that close to the airport. The house up on the hill gives me the distance I need and assures me I won't run into him. Or any of the memories that used to bring me happiness.

It's the middle of the day on a Wednesday when my mama knocks softly on my door. I'm staying in my childhood room, the walls a soft blue, the color of the sky—the color it's been since I was old enough to have an opinion. At the moment if they were black, they wouldn't be dark enough for my tastes. I call out, "Come on in." She does, slipping inside with a hot mug of water and a canister of loose leaf tea on a small tray.

Smiling, she puts it on a table across from my bed. "Whatch ya' reading?" she asks, seating herself next to me.

"I really don't feel like talking right now, mama. I know you don't care what novel I'm reading right now, and it's just your opening introduction to today's pep talk. I'm going to be okay. I promise."

She sighs, and the guilt hits me square in the chest. She's worried about me and only wants to help. Logically, I know she's just being a good mom. "A month tomorrow, darling. Since you've needed the crutches. Dr. Taylor says you're as good as healed. It's not getting any better. When do you want to try on your old life again, honey?"

There it is. The annoying pep talk. "You don't want me here anymore?"

Mama looks thoughtful for a second, her gaze reaching away from me. "I don't," she deadpans.

"What?" My tone is shrill, the worn paperback that smells like an old friend falls to my lap.

She shrugs. "It's the only way to get you out of here and back to your life. Daddy told me you don't want to fly. Caroline, I love you, but you're an adult now and Mays pick themselves up by their bootstraps and get on with it." Her hand shakes between us, but she decides to lay her hand on my calf, in the end. "People are... talking," she adds. "You say you don't care, but you still live here so you must, in some way, care what your friends think."

Do I love flying? Yes. Will I always love it? Probably. Do I want to fly? No. A million times no. Who knows how long I'll feel that way. What if that happens again? I was told a dozen times how lucky I was that Shell Island existed, that otherwise I would have never made it out alive.

Leaning my head back against the wall I contemplate the way this conversation is going to go. "Fine. If you want me out, I'll go back home."

An annoyed noise escapes her. "Did you hear anything else I said?"

"Yes, yes. I need to go on with my life and pretend I didn't almost die. Check. Thanks, mama. That tidbit was su-per helpful. Not like that's something I'd do if I could, or anything." I groan, and face my mother. Living in this house makes me feel like a teenager.

She squeezes my calf. Hard. "I know you may not be healed all the way," she says, her gaze dipping to the center of my chest. "You march on anyways. There's a party," she says, turning away.

"I cancelled my housewarming party the first time Malena visited me in the hospital. There's no party I have to attend."

"It's not for you, darling," she quips, a sparkle in her eye. "The world has moved on without you in it." The thought slices me, but I can handle the truth. Especially when it hurts. That's when it means the most. "The B&B is opening for business this weekend. The whole town is invited. It's going to be a great time. I'm helping cater, though it's so big June Bug from the Italian restaurant is also providing food and drinks. It's in three days, figured if you had a few you could get yourself ready." She leans over and picks up a limp, dingy strand of my hair. "Or at the very least wash your hair."

Firstly, I'm irritated. Why didn't Shirley mention this when she stopped by yesterday? Why didn't Malena text me. Or call me. It's a one-two gut punch to know I'm not that important anymore. How come no one told me he was going to open it as a B&B? I've been swallowed whole by the accident and my decisions following it. "Oh, please. I haven't left the house in weeks and you think the best way to reintroduce myself into society is by going to a party where every single person I've ever known will be in attendance? No pressure." I cross my arms, and turn to the side. The blue walls comfort me even if they haunt me at night. "No one even told me," I say, sniffling once. Mama stays silent. "I don't even have a thing to wear, anyways. I'd need something prettier than a sundress if I'm rising from the dead." I shuffle my feet, but her hand stays firmly on my leg. "It would be awful. I'd have to make small talk and heaven knows I'd have to relive the accident at least a hundred times."

When the silence between us grows to be too much, she whispers, "And?"

I meet her worried gaze. "And he'll be there," I say, bottom lip trembling.

She pats me a few times. "And you have to get used to that. It's always easier to tear off the bandage quick. You know that."

"Does he even ask about me?" I ask, voice low, offending every drop of pride I have left.

Mama stands, moves to the table and begins fixing my tea. The light shining in the window showcases the thick silver streaking through her hair. It reminds me how much time has passed us by. How much time we have left. The finite seconds that leave before we have barely welcomed them.

She sighs as she stirs, the tinging of the brass spoon on the inside of the mug. "Caroline, this isn't a game of telephone. You aren't sixteen. Go talk to the man. I know he's respecting your wishes by staying away, but who knows what's running through his mind. You're healed," she says, her eyes narrow, "You're have to move on. This is it. The moment that you can define, or let the accident define. It's your decision, honey." She offers me the warm cup without averting her gaze. I can't help but shrink back into myself a touch as I accept the cup. She's using her firm voice. The one that let me know how much trouble I was in as a child.

She's right.

Shirley said the same thing. Malena did, too. Daddy just looks at me with sad eyes and I know he's thinking what everyone else is. *Will Caroline recover?*

I nod my head, and she leaves, closing the door behind her. It wasn't just about recovering from the accident. This recovery was something deeper. Something far more painful than broken ribs and a burned body. Over the rim of my mug, I eye my open closet door. The tea, sweetened to perfection, sears down my throat. Maybe I'm not ready to fly, but I am ready for this. I have to reclaim a slice of my life back. It's time. Standing, I walk to my closet. I'll pack my things and go back to my hangar. I touch the fabric on one side of the wall. All sundresses I haven't so much as looked at in half a year. I'll relieve my daddy of the airport duties. My hand stops on one, particular piece of clothing. I'll go to this party and face down my demons.

And I'll wear the white dress.

As soon as I step out of my Daddy's truck, I'm convinced this is an awful idea. The whole town is here. Cars are lining either side of the road and we have to walk about a half a mile to the main entrance of the Homer property. When we are finally standing in front of the new white picket fence, Daddy pats me on the shoulder and heads toward the gaggle of catering tents off by the water in search of mama.

People are mulling about as far as the eye can see, the lush green grass is manicured to perfection on all sides of the large house. Ladies are wearing their bright dresses, and men have donned their fanciest khaki shorts and polo shirts. The scent of Chanel No. 5 hits the salty breeze like a Bronze Bay calling card. It's one of the only fragrances carried at the general store so almost everyone wears it. I'm so busy trying to avoid eye contact that I missed the large sign hanging above the tree-lined drive. Easy Days Inn & Bar. It's wrought iron with a sun setting behind the words.

The whole thing looks like a completely different place—something out of a storybook, a venture that doesn't look suited for a town so small. So much work has been done it's hard to tell what hasn't been touched.

"Caroline May!"

With a sigh, and a silent prayer, I turn toward the sound of my name. "Malena!" I return, with a little less enthusiasm than she used.

"I thought that was you. You look beautiful. I'm so glad you decided to show up," she says, stepping into my personal bubble.

Backing away a touch, with a smile on my face, I reply, "It's time I got out of the house. I'm feeling so much better now. This place looks amazing." I swallow hard, thinking about how much time has passed since I stepped foot in the foyer here.

"I know, right? Tahoe did such a fantastic job," Malena coos. My stomach sinks at both her casual use of his nickname and the fact she knows something I don't. "He's been working like a madman on it so it's not that surprising," she adds, tossing her long hair over one shoulder. Even the sun decided to play nice for the occasion. It's not blaring down on us relentlessly today.

I raise my eyebrows and try nonchalance. "Yeah? He did this all by himself?" I ask, waving an arm around. There's a flower garden with a sitting area in the distance and the dock has been extended to wrap around the property on both sides. Now boats can tie off and frequent the bar. Get too drunk, and then stay the night. It's a genius idea.

"He did. I know Leif and the boys helped with some of the manual labor, but this is Tahoe's brain child. When you refused to talk to him, I mean, after the accident and you needed to recover," she says, opening and closing her mouth when she realizes her blunder. "He was upset, Caroline," Malena decides on. "This is the product of that. You should see the inside."

My heart squeezes. The smile I offer is weak, something in absence of words. "He's inside greeting guests. Go say hi," Malena says, grinning. "I know he'd love to see you."

I'm rubbing the sides of my dress between my fingers—nervous, scared, excited to finally lay eyes on the man that ripped my heart wide open and stepped inside like he'd always lived there.

"I'll go see if mama needs my help first," I say.

Malena clears her throat. "No. She's fine. I was just there."

I quirk one brow. "Oh?"

She nods quickly. "Go inside. They have your favorite profiteroles on a table in the foyer. The ones we were going to have at your house warming party. Remember?" Her face falls. Malena does love to plan a party. I'll have to let her plan something again.

She is trying too hard, but I can't deny that I'm anxious to see the inside. If the outside looks this amazing, the inside must be top notch. She pats me on my back and I take my leave, trying to keep my head down as I approach the front of the Inn.

A few older ladies who are friends with my mama say hello. Their faces are friendly, but I see the pity in their kohl rimmed eyes. It's the same look my mother wore when she told me to move out and get my life together. I rub the numb spot on my leg. One of the reminders of my accident. The burns on my leg were bad enough that I had to endure multiple skin grafts. I'm lucky my leg healed as much as it did. I should feel lucky for a million reasons, apparently. Right now, I feel anything but. I move on from the latest person who feels bad for me, with a new sense of purpose. Everyone is giving me exactly what I need without realizing it.

The stairs leading up to the porch and front door are stained a dark walnut, and the new double doors are a vivid blue adorned with a skeleton of a frog etched in the glass panel. One side is open, so as quietly as I can, I slip inside.

There are just as many people in here, so I'm safe, undetectable, for at least another moment or two while I take in everything. He redid almost everything, but the staircases are still the same. He left those intact. The walls are a bright white and the beachy feel meshes with the masculinity of the dark, sleek décor. It's an odd combination I wouldn't have put together, but it works well. It's Tahoe. I close my eyes and take in a breath. This is my new reality. One I need to take control over regardless of how much it hurts. He is integrated into my world. In my absence, even more so. SEALs are around, chatting, drinking, being friendly. I haven't recognized any of them as Tahoe's friends. They're just another indicator of my new reality.

Spotting the profiteroles, I grab one and a small plate and head for the stairs. When I'm at the top, my breath catches. "How much money did he throw at this thing?" I gasp. There's a huge bay window that overlooks the bar, the docks, and the bay in the distance. The view is something from a beautiful painting. I look down and see the terrace that he left untouched, where Tahoe first kissed me.

I take a bite of the confection as I let the memory play softly in the background.

"It's rude to ask prices. Where did you learn your manners anyways?"

With a mouth full of sugar and cream, I let the voice, his voice, soak in. I knew I missed him, but I didn't realize how much. I avert my gaze from the window, to him. Nope. The mere sight of him makes me weak in my knees. There's no way I'll be able to coexist with this man. The town is too small. I hate it. I despise myself for this flaw, knowing it will be the greatest challenge I'll face in this lifetime.

He smiles. It's crooked. A dimple pops. His gaze dips to my body, the dress I picked out specifically for this reason. His gaze lands back on my face and holds. He heaves a long breath. "Caroline," he says, voice cracking. He swallows hard. "You came." Relief washes over him, his shoulders rising and lowering in a deep breath.

I set my plate down on a small console table next to the window. This is why I came here, right? To get this over with. "It looks fantastic, Tyler," I say. His eyes narrow. Suspicion. "This is something to be proud of. It will be great for tourism and Bronze Bay residents alike." The panty scorching smile drops from his face. At least this will be easier now. "Thank you for all that you've done for our small town." Polite. Concise. Everything a southern woman should be. "We appreciate it."

"Caroline," he repeats. "Say something."

I clear my throat, and turn my gaze to the hardwood floor. "I just said multiple things, Mr. Holiday."

"Mr. Fucking. Holiday? What the fuck are you playing at?" he growls. "You avoided me for months. Half a year I tried to talk to you. Tried to see you. You're finally here, finally. And you're going to pretend we're strangers?"

I shake a finger at him. "Not strangers. Friends. You broke up with me. I'm just trying to get on with it. You're living here for the foreseeable future?" I ask.

"Of course. You knew that," he replies, waving a big arm to the Inn.

"So am I. Let's be civil to each other." I make a move to leave, but he blocks the stairs with his body—his sheer size a deterrent to any further movement forward.

"Talk to me. Please, God. I've waited so long for this. You're killing me here. Please," he pleads. I see the desperation in his eyes and I want to erase it, but then

I'm reminded of how quickly he threw everything we had away.

Folding my arms across my chest, I say, "Talk to me then." I meet his blue eyes and it's a mistake. My insides quake back to life, calling out for him.

"Will you come with me?" he asks. "Somewhere private?"

My traitorous body answers for me, walking past the stairwell toward the rooms. He calls from behind me, "Last on the left."

I walk in. It's a white room and it's decorated in the fashion one might find in an inn, but it has personal items draped here and there. A black shirt hanging on the back of the desk chair, a uniform hanging in the open wardrobe. Man products on the counter in the bathroom. It's his room. The king-sized bed looms large to my right and I bypass it to sit at the table under a large window. The door clicks closed, and I hear the deadbolt slide home. My pulse speeds, and my stomach swirls with the unknown. As he approaches his footsteps reverberate, vibrating a vase on the bedside table. It reminds me of jack and the beanstalk. The giant is coming. He's coming for me. I'm defenseless, armed only with my feelings.

I keep my gaze focused out the window to control my thoughts. He sits in front of me and waits. I stay silent. He waits some more.

Sighing, I blink slowly, and look at him. "What? What can you possibly have to say?"

His eyes are sad. "I have everything to say to you. You

gave me months and months to concoct the perfect thing to say to you, Caroline. When you wouldn't see me, I didn't blame you. At first. I did a bad thing, said awful fucking things, but I told you I wasn't a good person. You knew it the whole time. Then, after a few months went by and you didn't return any of my calls or letters I got angry. So angry that I thought I might torch Bronze Bay to the ground." Tahoe pauses, breathing heavy through his nostrils. His rage permeates the air. "I didn't deserve that."

I want to tell him he did. He broke my heart and acted like an immature jackass, but I can tell he's not finished yet, so I let him continue. "I threw myself into the Inn, hoping I could distract myself from you, our past, and your accident, but that didn't work. After all of this time has passed I look at you and I never want to look away. I've missed your sun so much and I am so, so sorry."

An apology. I never expected that from a prideful man. "You hurt me," I reply.

"And you hurt yourself," he says, looking me over, shaking his head. "I thought you weren't going to make it. I was there, you know? At the site. I'd just gotten home from New York when it happened. It was the last time I saw you." He closes his eyes and he's taken back to that dark, rainy day when Caroline May did something stupid.

I knew he was there. My friends told me as much, but I didn't think about it much after that. Or how it would affect him. "Don't remind me of my mistake please. Now

I look at you and think about the accident. You left me here. We had plans, Tyler. I gave you everything despite having reservations and you threw it back in my face. Your motives were questioned for good reason. Look what you did." A tear slips and I wipe it away with the back of my hand. "I do have a question for you."

He makes a grab for my hands in the center of the table. I fold mine in my lap. Touching him will be a mistake. Shaking my head, I close my eyes. "Why? The real reason you freaked out that night and ran away."

He runs his hands through his hair, his biceps bulging with the movement. "It was because I thought I couldn't be with a virgin."

"That's lame," I reply. He smirks, shaking his head. "If I never told you, you would have fucked me to next Friday," I continue.

He clears his throat, his posture changing. I chose my words very methodically. "Don't swear," he chastens.

Laughing, it's my turn to shake my head. "You're going to have to tell me more. What's wrong with me? It's not because I'm a virgin."

"So you still are?" he asks, eyes lighting.

Scoffing, I quirk one brow. "You're serious? Of course I am. Men don't find a hospital bed the best place to have sex. I could be wrong though. Maybe I should have tried a bit harder with my physical therapist. Those exercise balls are quite the rage in the bedroom, aren't they?"

He looks at the table, embarrassed. "I heard you were trying to date guys so I couldn't be sure. I'm glad you didn't do anything out of spite." Of course he heard. He's the one who reverse cock-blocked me.

"Do you even know me at all? Don't be my superhero. Keep your goals obtainable, Tahoe. Save the world. Not my virginity."

He stands. "I do know you. And what if I can save both?"

My mouth is open, ready to retort, but his question takes me aback, and I don't have a quick reply. "What is that supposed to mean? How do you propose you save my virginity?"

He paces to his bed, picks something up, and strides back in front of me. "You didn't want to see me so I wasn't sure this was ever going to happen. I had a perfect plan, you see? But I feel like if I don't do this right now. Right this second, too much time will have passed. In my quest for perfection, I realized that sometimes perfection can be defined in different ways." His words are passionate, and my heart wants to leap out of my chest when his gaze scans my body. "Caroline, you are perfection and it scares me that I'll never be able to live up to those kinds of standards. You deserve the best. Perfection as defined by the *Merriam Webster Dictionary*. While you were avoiding me all of these months, I came to the conclusion that it doesn't matter." He shakes his head. "Because no one is going to love you as perfectly as I do. That's what matters. I was scared of my feelings before. If I did one wrong thing I'd scare you away, so I left before I could fuck it up."

I turn in my chair to face him, tears pricking my eyes as the emotions he's speaking hit me square in the chest. Tahoe clears his throat. "I'm sorry for being scared. I'm sorry for not defining my love for you earlier, Caroline. I love you more than anything. I'll always love you more than anything. Even if you say no. Even if I sit in this house by myself for the rest of my life and watch you find happiness with someone else. It's only going to be you for me. I know that now."

"Say no to what?" I ask.

His lips press in a firm line, as his gaze darts to the side. "Whatever it takes. I'm willing to do whatever it takes to have you. I've never been more certain about anything in my entire life." In a life-sized move, most only dream about, Tahoe drops to one knee, a red velvet box in one hand.

"I can save both, to answer your question. Your response to my question decides one fate."

I'm too shocked to say anything, to even move an inch. He must sense my confusion, because he takes my left hand into his right and works the box open against his chest.

"Marry me, Caroline? Will you be mine forever?"

A tear rolls down my cheek. "You realize you could have just asked for my virginity," I reply, smiling through the barrage of wetness flowing down my face. "I probably would have told you yes. No one else in this town will take it." I wipe at the tears, while laughing.

His confidence bolstered, he slides closer, the square

diamond sparkling against the dark velvet. He pulls it from the box and slides it on my finger. "I want you. All of you. Every single part. Forever. I never want to wake up without knowing you're mine in all ways. I can live without you. I've done it for a while now. I checked my pride at the door when I fell for you, because I know without a doubt, and against all odds, I don't *want* to live without you." He shakes his head, and moves in closer. "Love is a luxury men like me don't indulge in. You've made it essential. I need it to live."

I think of all the things left unsaid, all of the sadness and grief after my accident. How angry I was with him for breaking my heart. He's mending it, or at least trying to. He's dangling an olive branch in front of me in the form of a lifetime commitment. I blink a few times to make sure I'm not dreaming, and he's still there, still as handsome as ever, and still holding my hand. As I look at the beautiful diamond on my finger, and then his eyes as he awaits my response, I know that I feel the same way as he does. My fresh start doesn't look the way I thought it would. It looks like something out of my dreams. A kiss the sky, blue hue, dream come true. "This isn't just a grand gesture to apologize?" I ask, my voice wavering.

He sighs, then grimaces. "Would sky writers be too grand?"

I widen my eyes, horrified. "I'm joking, I'm joking," Tahoe says, laying a hand on my knee. "I wasn't even sure you'd show up today. I hoped you would." He rubs the bare skin on my thigh, and a shiver hits me, reminding me of the monster in the room. Unchecked Desire. "Marry me and let's define happily ever after for ourselves," he says.

"You're sure?" I ask. I've loved him in every way you can possibly love a human. I think I've also hated him in every possible way you can hate a human. "I love you, Tahoe, and while this is probably the best way to earn my parents' love and respect back," I say, pausing, trying to think of how best to phrase what I want to say.

In the pause, he slides forward, between my knees and pulls me forward for a kiss. My eyes flutter closed as every sense in my body is wracked with Tyler Holiday. With one hand, he works my head, to tilt toward him, slanting his lips over mine. After feeling nothing for so long, feeling everything is almost too much to bear. I can't control anything except my need for him, and it's peak. Prime. I break the kiss to utter, "I love you so much."

My confession sends him into primal mode. He grabs me under my ass and picks me up from the chair. A second later, I'm on my back on his bed, the coolness of the duvet in stark contrast to the fire raging from my face down to my toes. My flip flops fall to the floor, as I scoot back on the bed. "I couldn't wait another second to taste you," he says, brushing my blonde tangle of hair from my face. "I'm sorry."

"Don't apologize for that," I reply. "Kiss me more," I say, mesmerized by the ethereal quality of the moment. I love this man so much.

I lift my head, seeking his mouth, but he leans away. "You didn't answer my question." There's a sly hint to his voice.

Can it really be that simple? I say yes, and everything unfolds the way I imagined six months ago, minus a veil? Would everything work out? Running my hands down his face and neck, I relish the feel of him under my palms. I wasn't okay living without him. Even if I convinced myself my misery wasn't tied to him, my happiness rests next to him. I'm sure of that, and it's a start. "Will I marry you and let you save my virginity from the dark corners of Bronze Bay?" I ask.

"If you want me to take it now, I will," he says, his smile falling. "Whatever you want, Caroline. Say the word. I'll take it." He leans down, and drags his lips across my neck. He's tense now—body rigid, and he wasn't before. It means something to him.

It. Means. Something. To. Him.

I never considered that before. My virginity means something special to him. His kiss on my neck is tender and molten at the same time. I take his face in my hand and shift him so he's looking down at me, his blue eyes hesitant and turned on. I lean up and kiss him gently on his mouth. Neither of us close our eyes. We watch this magic moment. A moment that when you consider all things, shouldn't be happening.

"Save it for our wedding night, big man."

I'll never forget his smile, that particular one, for as long as I live.

Or the orgasms he gave me with his tongue directly following.

Chapter twenty

Tahoe

Caroline is naked in my bed. I can die a happy man. If today is the last day earth exists, I'd smile and wave on my way out. She makes me deliriously happy and I'm almost shocked at how seamlessly the proposal went. She walked right into it. Her hand, the one with my diamond on it, is resting on my chest, and it feels like my heart has finally found its lost rhythm. She said yes. Caroline is mine. If I could, I'd throw her over my shoulder, take her out to the docks and marry her this instant, just so I can be sure she won't change her mind. A sweet sigh escapes and my thoughts switch. We have to do this right. The proper way. Get one thing right in the sea of fucking disasters I created in my quest for perfection.

"Was Malena supposed to send me inside when she did?" Caroline says.

Chuckling under my breath, I let her take from that what she will.

"This whole thing? The party? Was it to get me here?" Now she sits up, propping her head on her hand. Caroline strokes me, her finger nails cutting figure eights across my chest. I have to hold my breath. Her touch feels like a fire on a cold day. Like coming home after a brutal deployment. The safe place I always wanted. Holding her close would be my dying wish. "Well, the party was the mayor's idea, and I did go along with it because I knew if everyone was here, maybe you'd show up."

"My parents were in on it, too," she says, growling while she pinches one of my nipples.

"Ouch!" I bite. "I asked them to tell you about it and coaxed them to get you here any chance I could, but I didn't expect you to listen to them. Your mom said you were worse off than you've been in a while. It truly was a surprise to see you walking up the drive." I watched, from one of the upstairs windows as each person walked through the entrance of the property.

She's thoughtful, her blue eyes downturned, and her bottom lip caught between her teeth. "But you had this ring," she says, looking at her hand. "How long have you had it? If you didn't plan on asking me today?"

I swallow hard. "Since New York."

Her face drops, and I know I've surprised her. "Why didn't you call me or text me from New York? What changed? You broke up with me before you left!"

Deciding how much to tell her is tricky. The very last thing I want right now is the ruin the moment. I also don't want to lie in any shape or form. "I found closure in New York, and I guess you could say, it took a little distance to realize what I wanted. Caroline," I say, using one finger on her chin to direct her gaze to mine. She raises her brows. "When I want something and make a decision, that's it. I'm not changing my mind, and this wasn't some spur of the moment proposal. I asked you to marry me because I'm certain there's no one else I want to spend the rest of my life with."

She smiles, and it warms the icy confines of my heart. There was a point when I was so angry I thought I might not ever be able to look at Caroline May again. Or if I did see her, I'd feel nothing but bitter rage. She did what no other woman had done. Ignored me. Let me stew in my bad decisions. I found myself outside of my career again, without any interruptions except the Caroline sized hole in my heart.

I should have known better, I'll never look at her with anything except love. And respect. And with the fucking desire of a thousand suns. Her beauty stuns me—forces me to accept how delicate I've become outside of the SEAL arena.

She gazes at her hand, turning it so the stone catches the light. "Never would have imagined I'd be in your bed wearing an engagement ring today. I came here today to try to start my life. After the accident," she says, pausing and swallowing hard. "I thought I'd lost everything. They weren't sure I'd be able to walk without a cane, or if my body would heal the way it was supposed to." Her eyes meet mine. "And that terrified me, because I have no clue who I am outside of the persona I created for myself. Throw in a breakup and I was floundering to understand the point of everything."

Clearing my throat, I slide one hand down her bare

arm. "You healed fine and you don't have to worry about that. Don't think of it anymore. You did start a new life today," I say. "Our life."

"I didn't read the letters," she admits, watching my hand. I stop at her elbow, and wait. "Well, I read the first one and assumed the rest would be of the same, and I couldn't be persuaded out of feeling sorry for myself. I'm sorry," she whispers. "I'm glad you waited for me."

As if I had any option. "I visited the hospital every single day you were there. I brought coffees to the ladies at the front desk and they gave me your updates."

"Doesn't that go against some privacy law?" she says, quirking one brow. "I knew it. They never told me, and that's probably why. They were afraid I'd get them fired."

"Why did you keep me away? Even if you were upset, I still can't understand why you wouldn't see me at least once to speak your peace," I say. "I thought you'd written me off for life." And it hurt more than a million Stella breakups.

Her eyes turn down in the corner. "I didn't want you to see me like that. After such a stupid decision. You pride yourself on perfection, and look at me. I'm such a mess." She shrugs. "I didn't think you cared, either. With how fast you took off."

I shake my head. "I make mistakes every fucking day. A mistake is what lead me here to Bronze Bay. To you," I explain. "I get to have this perfect life that I didn't even know existed because I got my buddy shot." I cringe, but at least I'm able to talk about it now. "That was a mess, Caroline. Not an accident."

"And now I know you obviously did care. The whole time," she replies, shaking her head. "I still can't believe it."

"You would have known sooner had you read all the letters," I say, smiling. She throws one naked leg over my midsection and I hold my breath and watch her cautiously. Her lithe body appearing from under the bed sheets. Those three freckles on her mid-section calling *my* name.

I take a few deep breaths to control my fucking libido as her wet pussy presses against my lower abs. I have on a pair of boxer briefs and they might as well be our chastity belt, because they are the only safe guard we're using to keep my dick out of her vagina. "If I read those letters maybe we wouldn't be here today," she says. Caroline leans over, and her long, wavy hair hits my shoulders and shrouds our kiss. My thumbs hold her hip bones and my pinky fingers rest on the top swell of her ass. She teases with her tongue as she circles her hips. I flex my abs, mostly because my whole body is tense, but also because she's working her clit against me and I want her to come—to see her face as she takes her pleasure. The kiss deepens and I open my eyes to watch.

Her face transforms, and although she keeps her mouth against mine, she's panting. These tiny, moan inducing breaths as she presses against me harder. In response, I stop breathing and listen. Her wetness sliding against my stomach, her breathing inside my mouth, the faint sounds of the party out on the lawn. I watch her face as her eyelashes flutter, and her tongue slides across her bottom lip. She grimaces, and then she comes, her mouth opening and her features softening. The squeezing of her orgasm can be felt, and for a moment, I close my eyes and imagine what it will feel like to be inside her while she comes. That first time. And every time after.

Caroline presses her wet lips against mine in a smile. "I'm going to like having you around all the time," she says, breathing hard. "You're like my playground."

Oh, this woman. What she does to me with mere words. I turn my head away from her and make a groan that ends in a laugh. "You know just what to say, Caroline May."

"You made a rhyme," she replies. After a beat or two, she lays her head on my chest. "I can't wait to marry you."

"So you can have the full Monty slide instead of my abs seesaw?" I tease. Taking her face in my hands, I stare into her deep blue eyes. "I can't wait to make you my wife and keep you forever."

Her smile in reply is so big and beautiful that I melt a little. Caroline tucks herself back beside me and asks me a million questions about the time she spent away. We talk about the Inn and work, she asks me about the guys and future plans for missions. I tell her what I can. Then we talk about the wedding logistics and we agree, in unison, that it should be an intimate affair on the water and as soon as humanly possible.

After that's out of the way, we delve into the harder topics. The ones that have to be broached. She's pulling her dress over her head. "Where will we live?" she asks, looking out of the window and then back to me.

I swallow, and raise one brow. "Where do you want to live?"

She paces to the window. "Here, probably."

Narrowing my eyes, I approach her from behind and pull her against the bulge in my shorts. "You love the hangar," I say, nuzzling into her ear. "Why don't you want to live there?"

She clears her throat and answers without missing a beat. "I'm not sure I'll fly again. I can still run the airport, though. I can help here, too. I can tend at the bar or run things downstairs. That will take up my time."

Avoidance. I know this tactic all too well. One of my buddies didn't deploy for a few years after his buddy got killed on a mission. He was right beside him and there was nothing he could do to save his life. He blamed himself and spiraled for a long time. His story is told as a SEAL history lesson in the Teams now. "You have to get back up," I tell her. I didn't realize she hadn't flown since the accident. "As soon as possible." My mind starts concocting a plan—one she won't be able to refuse.

Caroline shakes her head. "I think that was just a part of my life, a hobby, Tahoe." She turns to face me, her arms draped on my shoulders. "Some things you're meant to do for a period of time and others are lifers. Maybe flying wasn't supposed to be forever for me." Her eyes gloss over.

Kissing the top of her head, I pull her close. "I get it. I do. But you have to fly again. At least once, and then you can decide if you're a lifer or not. Okay?"

keeping it

She cries a little and I know she's thinking about the accident, her lack of control over the one thing she's always controlled. "I can't," she whispers. "I'm not good at it."

I push her away so I can look at her face. "You aren't good at it," I exclaim.

Her brows draw together and she tilts her head.

"Because you're amazing at it. Perfect at it, even."

"Stop it," she replies. "You're just saying that to make me feel better."

Shaking my head I say, "I'm not. Plus, I need you to fly us to New York for our bachelor party."

She smirks. "Don't you mean bachelorette party?" Her eyes light. "Or a joint party?" Ah, I got her interest. "Like all of us together? In N.Y.C?"

I smile back. "Only if you fly us there."

Her lips curl down. "I don't know if I can risk it," she says. "Not you."

"So fly yourself there and I'll meet you?"

She hits my chest playfully. "I'll think about it. When?"

"Next weekend?" I shrug. Leif won't care. He'll love it. He'll close the whole entire base for a week if it means he'll get some time alone with Malena. His pursuit is relentless. "In an effort to get this marriage ball rolling as soon as possible. Let's plan it."

"Oh, Malena will freak out if I tell her this. I'll let her plan it all." She pulls on her bottom lip, her gaze far away in planning land. "And she can put the wedding together." Now she claps her hands. "I won't have to do

310

a thing!"

I laugh. "You really don't like this stuff, do you? We could elope? In New York? No one would know except us?" As much as I don't like the idea of her not getting a proper wedding, I wasn't lying when I said I would do anything to make her happy. My motto has transformed from "Keep It Simple," to "Whatever It Takes."

She shakes her head. "No, I think we should have a wedding for sure. A small one. Do you need to get back to your party?"

I take her by the left hand. "It's our party now," I coo. "Happy Engagement Party!"

Her eyes widen. "Oh dear," she replies.

Chapter twenty-One

Caroline

I did it. I flew that stupid plane all the way to the private airport outside of Manhattan. Tahoe kept a straight face, trying to hide his phobia of flying in small planes. I was grateful if only for having one less thing to deal with. I was on alert the entire time, using more caution than I've used since I was a flight student. It was a smooth ride and everything went as planned. I spent all of Wednesday and Thursday tracking weather patterns and studying air traffic patterns outside of the area.

"Wear the green one, Caroline," Malena hollers from the other side of the suite. "I'm going to wear the lilac one. Britt is wearing the champagne colored skirt and black blouse," she adds. I do have my own room here at this beautiful hotel, but everyone is getting ready here because there's more space. Tahoe is one floor down and seven doors to the right. On the corner. I've seen New York in movies, but I never expected it to be so busy. In real life, it is so grand. There's no grass save for squares here and there, and in Central Park. The buildings take up all the space where sky should be. The city has a way of making you feel small and insignificant, but it's an experience I'm happy to be having. An outlook I never considered.

Tahoe took me to breakfast and then after a make out session in his room, he took me to lunch, and now we're in our separate quarters getting ready for the festivities tonight.

His friends have promised debauchery and the finest strip clubs money can buy, and my friends, or rather Malena, by herself, has lined up the best restaurant, and bars. She did it all on the crazy time crunch of a week that we gave her, and she did it happily, without asking me too many questions. Though, I have a sneaking suspicion she probably pestered Tahoe with most of her concerns in an effort to keep me from freaking out and calling the whole thing off.

I finger the green dress in my hands and shake my head. This is going to make for an interesting evening. Britt, who only came because Malena begged, has been on full on jealous mode because not only am I getting married before her, we're in a big city celebrating my union. Not in a dirty bar sipping old, foamy beer while feeding a juke box. She didn't cancel her wedding to Whit, but they did pause it. I'm not even sure what that means, or how it's any different, but that's what she's been saying to anyone who asks.

Shirley hangs up her cell behind me with a curt goodbye. "Caroline, it's going to look amazing. Put the damn dress on and let's get this party started." I sip the champagne, my third glass since I started getting ready. Someone came to the room and did our makeup and hair, and I've never felt so fancy in my entire life. "I won't even look like this on my wedding day, Shirley. Isn't it," I say, slurring a bit. "All too much?"

She laughs and lays her hands on my shoulders. "All women need to feel like a princess once in their life. Put it on," she orders. I do, and she zips me up, moving my cascade of curls to one shoulder. "You look like a blonde Princess Kate," Shirley drawls. "He knew what he was doing."

"What do you mean he knew? He chose this?" I run my hands down the sleek fabric as I stare in the mirror.

"Of course he did." I knew he was footing the bill for this weekend, and I was hesitant to let him, but I never would imagine his duties involved selecting fashion for his bride.

"I love it," I say.

"Now you love it," Shirley says, rolling her eyes. She's wearing a black number complimented with thick, dark eye makeup. 'A 90's grunge dream come to life' she proclaimed after the makeup artist completed her look.

I turn to view the back of the dress, eyeing the detail more thoroughly. "Of course I love it more now that I know he likes it. Take a photo and send it to mama," I say. I pose with my hands on my hips and it feels awkward. "Wait, wait. Take another one. How should I pose?" I ask my friend.

She tilts her head, surveying me. "Cross your ankles. One hand on your hip. Turn to the side a little. Hair over that shoulder," she orders, as I try my best to follow along. "A little bit more twist. Yes. Like that."

Her cell phone camera flashes and she squints her eyes as she appraises the image. "Perfect."

"Let me see," I say, teetering on my heels to stand next to her. It is a good photo. I look like a totally different person. Everything polished and preened to city shine. Shirley presses a few buttons and proclaims it's been sent. To both my mama and to Tahoe.

My cell phone, the new one, that has a touch screen front and more features than I know what to do with rings on the night stand. Tahoe's text reads, "You look beautiful. I can't wait until you're my wife." He ends it with a smirking smiley face.

"So you can take the dress off?" I fire back.

His reply is swift. "No, I'll be taking it off tonight regardless of your marital status."

My stomach flutters with excitement. As hard as it's been to stave off the sexual act that has caused so much strife in our lives, the anticipation is something that should seriously be written down in history books. We have done every non-penetrating act of foreplay you can possible do in every position that is humanly possible. He's frustrated. I cannot wait. There is a tension that crackles in the air when we're together. Those around us feel it, and despite our best efforts, a lot of time the elephant in the room is the topic of conversation.

Another text pings. "I can't stop staring at the photo." I blush.

"Oh my gosh, would you guys get it over with already?

What's it matter if you do it tonight or next weekend? It's obvious to anyone in a seven-hundred-mile radius how mad in love you are with each other." Shirley exclaims as I smile at my phone.

I've explained the reasons a dozen times, but no one seems to understand. Sometimes, when having sex feels like the natural next step when we're messing around and we're both so fucking mad with lust, I think it doesn't matter, but our definition is written in ink and we both are holding strong to that belief. We're together in this. In the decision. "I don't expect you to understand," I say.

"Why? Because I'm a whore?" she jokes.

Sighing, I say, "No, because I've already tried to explain it to you still continue to ask me. It's important to us."

She shakes her head, tells everyone we're ready and we set off, a tribe of champagne drunk girls as we ride down the elevator. I refused all of the typical bachelorette party fanfare, the mere thought of a penis hat causing me actual stomach cramps. Malena rolled her eyes, Britt got offended, and Shirley changed the subject to dinner. Something we all agreed would be the best experience of our lives.

When the elevator doors ping open in the lobby, he's there. Standing against a column, wearing a white button up shirt, gray fitted slacks, and dress shoes. Pinching my lips together, I try not to scream like a fan girl seeing her favorite celebrity. He looks delicious in every way. His hair is done, and he's wearing *that smile*, with *that dimple*, and if I wasn't wearing heels I would sprint at him like a cheetah. One hand is in his pocket like he doesn't give a shit, and the other hangs by his side so he can be ready at the drop of a hat.

When I finally reach him, he grabs at me, "Come here you." His growl is a rough timbre, that rolls over me ending between my legs. "It's almost a crime other men get to see you look like this when I want you all for myself."

I turn my head to whisper, "I am all yours. And you're all mine. You look like a movie star."

"An action star I hope?" he replies, leaning his head onto mine. "One with a big cock and the stamina of Rambo?"

I giggle. A noise that surprises even me. I feel his dick harden against my stomach even further. "Of course, Rambo. The hottest most alpha movie star in the history of Hollywood. One more week," I remind him. He kisses my head, and steps out of my embrace.

"These two. Ugh," Britt whines. "You can't do that all night long you know?"

Malena clacks up to our group and Leif eyes her like she's dinner. And dessert. "I asked if you guys would be into a Killing Kittens Party and everyone said no," she says, raising her brows like we're petulant children. "They could have shagged all night there. I bet her virginity would make for the main attraction."

"Killing Kittens was on the table," Aidan barks. "How come no one told me?"

"Killing Kittens was never on the table," Tahoe growls. "This isn't about that. This is about having a good night out with our friends in a beautiful city."

Aidan sighs. "It would have been fun." "I know, right?" Malena says, folding her arms across her chest. "No one wants to listen to me. I know how to have a good time." Leif looks completely pissed that Malena and Aidan are discussing a sex party. His eyes narrow at his friend and Aidan gets the message quickly, excusing himself to grab a quick drink from the lobby bar.

Dinner is fabulous and the alcohol flows copiously around us. I try to stick to champagne until someone buys shots at the second bar and I'm told it is bad luck to turn it down. Tahoe sips water in between his drinks, mindful of every aspect of the dynamic happening tonight. The last time I was with him and he drank too much, everything went to hell. Aidan and a few of the other SEALs left the first bar to head to the strip club instead of sticking to Malena's schedule.

She wasn't bothered. She's boobs deep in Leif's arms with hooded eyes and a thick agenda for the night.

Shirley is dancing on top of the bar with Britt and I'm sitting in our booth wrapped in Tahoe's arms. He's staring at me—an intense look that lets me know exactly what he's thinking. The music is loud, and it's reverberating inside my chest as I let everything wash over me. The whirlwind happened so quickly. I thumb the back of my engagement ring to remind myself it's real. I'm in this big city, for the first time in my life, taking in everything, with the man that I will love for the rest of time. The drinks go to my head and I lean in to kiss him. My intent is just a peck, but because we're starved for each other, it ends up being more. He pulls away from me when his breathing speeds and his hands wander where they shouldn't be in public.

The music lulls into a quieter slow song and the bodies on the dance floor begin to sway in time. "Are you having a good time?" he asks, using distraction to halt the truth. We both want to tear off our clothes and go at it in this leather booth. "I know it's a lot," he adds, raising his brows at the fanfare surrounding us. "But you have to please everyone. Weddings are never about the bride and groom anyways." He grins.

"How did you get so smart?" I ask, scooting away from him. I need a breather and I know he does too if the bulge in his pants is any indication. "Maybe for us, it can be about us," I say. "It's going to be small, and the reception will just be dinner. Then the rest of the night is ours alone."

He sighs, fisting his hands by his sides. "I wish that was right now instead of next weekend."

"Me too."

Tahoe's phone lights up on the table in front of us and he leans over to look. I assume it's just one of the guys trying to lure him to the strip club, but he grimaces, and flips it so the screen is on the table. "I need to be honest with you about something, Caroline. Before you get worried, it's nothing that I think is huge, but it's something you should know."

My mood shifts a bit, but the alcohol helps keep me from spinning into a fear tirade. "Oh, okay. Do you want to go outside to talk? It's important?" I ask. "I've had a lot to drink," I admit. "But I'm sure I'll remember it in the morning."

His face goes solemn. "Stella wants to talk to you, Sunny. She's here," he says, and my heart sinks down to the floor. Through it, actually. It's probably halfway to China right now. "Well, she lives here. But she's coming here because Leif invited her, but I didn't say no either. It might be a good thing if you talked to her."

The closure. Stella. I should have known, yet it still hurts. "I don't think that's a good idea, Tyler."

"Don't call me Tyler. Come on. It makes me uncomfortable even asking, but that's because she knows the man I was before there was you. That's why I'm not scared. I'm that confident in my convictions, and my decisions, and my love for you."

"Why does she want to talk to me?" It comes out in a rushed panic.

Before he can answer, I see her. What I assume is her, even in my drunken state, because she's looking for someone, her eyes scanning the crowd and the booths, until she finally spots ours...and then me. Stella is blonde and tall, and as beautiful as you'd expect. "She's here," I tell Tahoe. His gaze traces mine and I can see his chest heave a huge sigh next to me. Stella walks toward our table, a small smile on her face, and for some reason my fear vanishes. She's married, Tahoe said. She has a baby, a family. He said she's happy. This woman is not a threat. She was never a threat if what Tahoe says is true.

Tahoe stands to greet her, and helps me stand. "Caroline, this is my old friend, Stella. Stella, meet my fiancée, Caroline."

Stella shakes my hand, and eyes my ring. "You lucky dog," Stella says, winking at Tahoe. "It's so nice to meet you, Caroline. Tyler has told me so much about you." He has? "Only the best of things. It's like I'm looking at a legend right now," she adds, eyeing me up and down. It's not malicious or catty in the way that Britt sometimes regards me, it's her taking stock of me. It's curious and confusing.

"I wish I could say the same," I return. "It is great to meet you. Any friend of Tahoe's is a friend of mine. Would you like to sit? Have a drink?" I ask, southern manners dictating I host, even when I'm not really hosting.

"I just wanted to stop in and give you both my congratulations. I wouldn't intrude on your special night," Stella replies. Leif pulls himself away from Malena to greet Stella and I can see the daggers in my friend's eyes. Aimed directly at her current threat. Stella. If I could will her cattiness away for a minute, I would. Right now. Because she has no clue.

"Stella," I interrupt. "Tahoe mentioned you'd like to chat with me for a bit. What do you say? They have a table in the other room we could sit at for a moment or two?" Leif pulls away, some other sense telling him to back away from the woman and return to the drunken one jockeying for his affection. Stella wishes Leif a goodnight, waves at Malena to show no ill will, and agrees to talk to me.

"Are you sure?" Tahoe asks, seeing the exchange

and understanding I only offered to save my friend from embarrassing herself.

"Sure. It's just a talk, right? What can she possibly say? I love you, Tahoe. Nothing will change that."

His gaze turns worried as he walks me around the table and all the way into a private room. When it is just the three of us, he kisses my cheek, walks out, and closes the door. The silence is the first thing I notice. "Gosh, I wonder what these rooms are actually for," I exclaim. "You could kill someone in here and no one would know!" I steady myself on one of the plush chairs.

Stella laughs. "You don't want to know," she says. Her smile is friendly and there's no malice behind it. "Not for killing people, though."

I blush. "I probably don't want to know, do I?"

"You really are more beautiful than he let on. The innocence box was checked the second you said hello. You know what I think Caroline, flyer of planes and slayer of beastly hearts?"

I grin. "Huh?" I ask.

"That if one person was created for everyone, you were made for him. A few years ago I'd be upset about that, but now that I've found my own happiness outside of him, I couldn't be more thrilled. He deserves to be happy, you know?" Her eyes glass over. "He's had a really hard life. Had to make some tough decisions." She looks away, almost as if she's talking directly to him instead of to me. "He's the best friend everyone hopes to have. I think losing him as a best friend was the hardest part for me."

My stomach sinks. I am Stella's overdue closure. I am the walking talking happily ever after she didn't get. "He is a great man. No one goes without flaws, but his are of the most forgivable variety. He makes mistakes, but his heart is big. He loves me more than I deserve," I say. "I'm sorry you lost him as a friend, Stella. But didn't you leave him?"

"Sit down. Please. Should we grab that drink?" she asks. Suddenly, there's nowhere else I'd rather be. She has information about the man I'm about to marry. With her, she carries a perspective no one else on this entire earth will have. I'd be a fool to act like a jealous fiancée and turn this opportunity down. We both know I've already won. There's no sense to be bitter about it. She's not. I won't be.

We start with small talk about her husband and baby and I find myself engrossed with her life. The life she could have had with Tahoe if she hadn't broken it off, right? But it doesn't take long for her to veer back to our initial conversation. "Caroline, I broke up with Tahoe, because he didn't…love me. Not like he loves you. The way you're supposed to love a person you're meant to be with forever."

I widen my eyes. "Oh." It's the only response I can muster.

She smiles sadly. "It's obvious how much he loves you. He told me he blew it with you. The whole drunken, truck cab incident," she says, her voice trailing off. She's embarrassed for him. For me. For having to bring it up. "He thought he'd lost you for good. Do you know what he told me?"

Sighing, I take a sip of my water. "I'm not sure I want to know," I reply, honestly.

"You do," she says, eyes twinkling. "That you were too perfect for him."

I laugh at that. "I'm not even close to perfect," I muse, mostly for my own benefit. "He sees me in some alien light, I think." We both make a joke about his obsession with perfection, and it's easy. She knows him. It's a strange sensation, but not wholly unwelcome.

"That's it. That's what love is. What the real stuff is made of. Seeing through your person." Her eyes light. "I just want you to know how much you mean to him because I know what it feels like to not mean that much." Her voice catches. "Your innocence doesn't play into this."

"How much did he tell you?" I ask, clearing my throat.

"He took my virginity. It was awful," she says, a smile playing on her lips.

I choke on a sip of water. "Oh my God!" I laugh.

She snickers. "Don't worry. He got better at it," she says. "Wait, that's awkward. I'm sorry."

Well, he certainly brushed up on foreplay. I have to squeeze my legs together at the reminder of being naked with him. "I hope so."

She hides her surprise with a sip of her drink, but ignores my admission. "He's attracted to the opposite of what his life is surrounded with. The death. The destruction. War. Blood. Fighting. Politics. His reprieve is loving, wanting that good inside the untouchable part of his world. He'll do anything for you. I know he's going to be the best daddy, too. I wanted you to know that despite any horribly stupid things he might have said and done that the man is worth it. One hundred percent worth it. I wasn't as lucky as you are and I need to you know that."

Tears prick my eyes, because I know she's right. My dreams are made of Tahoe holding our baby, kissing baby toes, being the kind of brave, strong father that I had growing up.

"There wasn't any hesitation before, but I have to say thank you for telling me this. Your perspective means everything to me. I'm sure it costs you to be honest like this and I appreciate it. So much," I admit, taking her hands in the center of the small table.

She looks down and thumbs my engagement ring. "He did good, girl."

Wiping at an errant tear, I laugh. "I know. It's so beautiful." The ring in question never was a big deal to me. The idea behind it was everything. He chose it for me. An object of his affection he wants me to wear for the rest of my life.

"You're welcome, Caroline."

After she finishes her drink we walk back into the bustling club. Tahoe is pacing next to the booth, the rest of our surly group nowhere in sight. They must have hit the next spot on Malena's list.

"Are you okay?" Tahoe asks, rushing me. "Everything fine?" he asks Stella when I don't respond.

"We're fine, Tyler. We did a little reminiscing," Stella

calls out over the music.

I'm staring. Because I just found another side of the man I love without knowing it. I'll never question his love for me again. Not after tonight and the things Stella told me.

"I love you," I say, throwing myself into his arms. Tentatively I feel his arms close around my body.

"Told you," Stella croons. "You two enjoy the rest of your night. I'm meeting my husband at the bar across the street, we have a sitter until midnight!"

Tahoe peels me away from his body. "You're sure you're okay? I love you, too."

I nod, happy tears spilling down my face. I hug Stella good bye, and she leaves, her light blonde hair disappearing into the crowd. I'll probably never see her again. The woman he didn't love enough. The one that happened so he could know I was what true love felt like. Does that eat at her like a disease? To be that close to having something spectacular and having it snatched away? I have to believe she's happy now. With her life and her choices. It's the only way I can be thankful and not sad.

Commitment

Tahoe

Camaraderie and Commitment. The two words in my life that mean the most. To me, they can be exchanged as definitions for one another. Today I gained both in the form of a radiant bride. She's twirling around the wooden dance floor under the starlight with her father leading. Her smile is huge and her laughter could be the only music I hear for the rest of my life and I'd be perfectly content. Her gaze catches mine, and I see more of her teeth. She's breathtaking in every sense of the word. Her wedding dress is lace and modest, and her face isn't painted like it was in New York.

This is my Caroline.

Her hair a tangle of waves, is pulled away from her face, but a few strands tugged free and cut across her face as she spins. Slow motion. Pause. Rewind. I want to do all of these during this moment. The camera flashes and I'm thankful the photographer saw what I just did and was wise enough to capture it.

My chest aches. The love I have for her so

encompassing, I'm not sure she'll ever truly know how much she means to me or how far I'll go to make her happy. Finally. Finally. I have what I desire most in this crazy world. My very own sunshine. Even on those days when I'm thinking about dark things, I know that by walking into the room she'll steal those thoughts away.

How do I tell Caroline she's saving me without telling her why?

"Tahoe," Caroline calls. Her mouth grinning around my name. "Come here."

Standing from our little table, I approach her and her dad. The blush of her cheeks and the sheen on her neck call out to the beast that lies dormant. I finally get to tap him on the shoulder. Tonight. Our wedding night is here.

"The band is playing our song next. Are you ready?"

I grin, and her gaze darts to my lips. The dimple she loves. "I'm never not ready," I reply. May shakes my hand and kisses her on the cheek and heads back to Mrs. May who is crying and laughing in the same measure. She knew all along. Or so she told me when I asked them both for permission to marry Caroline. They were both overzealous in their acceptance of my offer, even going as far as telling me I needed to propose as soon as possible. That was when she was recovering, though. I think we all thought her acceptance or refusal was a shot in the dark.

I was the one to get her back in a plane. I think that's when they knew she'd be back to her old self in no time. I was fucking petrified we would crash. Not because she was piloting, but because that's what happens anytime you hear about an airplane crash on the news. You wonder if yours is going down next. The fact that I saw her fiery wreckage didn't help my phobia either.

"Have I told you how ravishing you look tonight?" I take her into my arms and the camera flashes.

"Only about a thousand times," she replies. "How are we going to do this dance? Malena was probably right. We should have practiced or something, right?"

Malena did an awesome job. But I think most of this wedding came together because of the small town of Bronze Bay. They drop everything to help one of their own, and the fact is we didn't want anything fancy.

The band came from the next town over and we have the restaurant hook up already. I'm wearing my uniform, and Caroline's dress is a remake of her mother's that the town seamstress updated for this decade. For something so impossible, it came together effortlessly, like this was how it was always supposed to happen.

My buddies shout out from the corner bar when the band starts the familiar twang of our song. She wraps her hands around my neck and presses her lips into a thin line. Someone is clinking their glasses, signaling they want us to kiss. I lean down and give her a chaste peck and she narrows her eyes.

I laugh. "We can't give them too much. That's ours, remember? After we finish up here?"

The reminder sets her on fire. I know what to say and it thrills me to no end. "Mrs. Holiday."

"I'm like Mrs. Claus now," Caroline jokes.

I lean over and lean into her ear. "Ho. Ho. Ho."

She gasps. "You're Mr. Holiday, tonight."

I swallow hard. "*You're my wife*. Thank you, Caroline. Thank you."

The music slows. "Thank you for loving me."

"I never had a choice in that," I reply. "First, I took over the beach. The one you took your first steps on. Then I took over your airport. The one your family owns. The next logical step was to love you. For the rest of my life."

Holding her face with my left hand, I hope she feels the platinum band rest on her cheekbone. "You're so suave sometimes," she says. Resting the side of her face on my chest, she stays that way for a few moments.

"Sometimes?" I mock. "I feel like you're shortchanging me."

"All the time. Fine. When you're not being silent and stoic, that is."

"That's a defense mechanism," I argue. "It's how I try not to fall in love."

"Remind me of that when you're being stoic with your friends," she says, smirking.

I laugh. "You're feeling frisky tonight."

"In more ways than one."

I glance at my watch. "Not long now," I soothe. Rubbing her exposed back.

The moment crystalizes as my time in Bronze Bay comes together. The utter awful feeling of being sent to a satellite base, to the sheer joy of exploring the small town, to falling in love. With not just Caroline May, but with this this place, my new home. The people surrounding us have played a part in our relationship in some form.

My buddies from San Diego flew in for the occasion, and seeing them and their wives gives me more than hope, it gives me proof that real love survives anything.

It has to.

Because I won't survive without her.

Not without her friendship, and surely not without the commitment we made today.

Chapter twenty-two

Caroline

The suite in the Inn is something out of my wildest dreams. One of his friends from San Diego stopped him in the hall. Several of them are staying here tonight. We had the extra space so it was perfect, even if right now, it's inconvenient. They were bro hugging and talking about something related to guns and bad guys, so I smiled politely and took my leave. This isn't the room that Tahoe was staying in when he asked me to marry him, this is a few rooms that were renovated into a gargantuan room that overlooks the bay. It was far later than we wanted it to be when our guests started dispersing, so the late hour lends a blueish tint to everything it hits.

The ceremony was beautifully simple. We exchanged vows on the dock. I teared up, and staying true to character, Tahoe was serene and well spoken. There were cheers, and wild shouts when we kissed, and for that one second, all was right in our world. There was nothing on my mind but the love we shared. My cheeks, honest to goodness, hurt from smiling so much. We finally snuck away when the rental company arrived to tear down the big, white tents. Now there's electricity running through my veins where blood once raced. I'm buzzing with excitement and anticipation—the anxiety I feel at finally knowing what it feels like to have Tahoe in all ways.

There are white candles scattered everywhere. White lilies are in vases, covering every surface, even a few bouquets in large displays on the floor next to the arched window. It takes my breath away. It's so eloquent. It's so special. But I knew he wouldn't treat this any other way, not after all we went through to keep this moment intact.

I sense rather than hear, when he's behind me in the doorway. "What do you think? Do you like it?"

"It's perfect, Tahoe. I can't believe you did all this for me."

He drops a kiss on my shoulder. "I did it for us," he corrects. "I want this to be perfect."

Just this once. I agree with his definition of perfection. "It already is. Today was the most magical day of my life. I couldn't picture anything differently. I'm so happy you're my husband." The last word is new, so I smile like an idiot when I say it.

He walks in and shuts the door. The resounding lock follows. "Yes, wife. I agree. What should we do first?" He uses his cell phone to play music through a wireless speaker. He turns it up. "Need some background noise, I think."

My heart races. "Yes. Of course. What should we do first?"

He works the buttons on his uniform and I watch in awe. "I'll make the plan then. It's not the most comfortable uniform. I'll probably get comfortable. If you don't mind. *Wife*?"

I nod. Like a meek child. Him naked is my favorite sight, better than a million sunrises or sunsets from the air. Better than a cloudy sky in mid-July.

He hangs up his shirt, a careful maneuver, and unzips his pants. Tahoe meets my eyes. "Then you should probably get out of that dress. It can't be comfortable either." His pants fall to the floor. He's controlling this atmosphere completely and I'm eating it up in the wildest way possible.

"It's not. It's absolutely horrid," I deadpan.

He holds his dominance, but I see a hint of smile in his eyes. He grabs the collar of his white undershirt and pulls it over his head in a brusque maneuver. Running his hands through his hair he rakes my body with his gaze. "Shame. I don't think you've ever worn anything that makes me want to fuck you more."

I gulp, losing my breath. "Not even my white sundress," I counter.

He shakes his head. "Nope. Not even close."

"Why?" I raise my chin, and step toward him.

He tilts his head and narrows his eyes. "Because this dress means your mine."

"Remember that time in the diner? You sat in Shirley's section and barely noticed me?"

That memory takes him out of character—a slight grin pulling up his lips. "That wasn't the first time I noticed you. That was the first time I let you see me noticing you."

"I wanted you even then. When I thought I had no

right to like a man as faultless as you. Even when you hassled me the month we worked on my house. I never admitted it to myself but I was yours even then, Tahoe. A dress doesn't make me yours," I say, crossing to where he stands in a pair of dark boxer briefs. Slowly, I raise my left hand to his chest, right above his heart. "This makes me yours."

His hand encircles my wrist and it's warm, a soothing touch.

"What comes next in the plan?" I ask softly. The moonlight makes his eyes glow even bluer than they are in natural light. Every muscle is shadowed and lit in perfect harmony. "I want to touch every single part of my husband," I admit. "Can that be part of the plan?" I ask.

He shakes his head. "Turn around."

I do, showing him my bare back and the hidden zipper the seamstress worked so tirelessly on. It's a work of art and it honors my parents' marriage in the best possible way. I was grateful to be able to have this from my mama on our wedding day. Tahoe kisses the middle of my back and then pauses to blow a cool breath on my spine.

My skin prickles, and I close my eyes to the sensation sliding over my whole body. He blows again on the back of my neck, and while I'm distracted by the brush of his exhale, he slides the zipper down over my backside, until the dress is released. It falls off my shoulders and turns into a billowy puddle around my feet. I inhale sharply as his fingers slice down the sides of my body, brushing the sides of my exposed breasts, and against the nip of my waist. "I like the dress on the floor even more than on your body," he says, mouthing the words on my arm as he drags his lips from one shoulder blade to the other. "Any last words?" his voice is strained, and the sound travels down as he kneels behind me to drag my white panties down my legs.

I sigh, and look up to the ceiling to catch my breath.

He kisses, and then licks the back of my thigh right where my ass meets my leg. "I might not live through your seduction," I say, breathing out violently. My hands are in tight fists by my sides, unable to touch him.

"You'll live," he whispers. He brushes the insides of my thighs with one hand, until he finally gives a gentle caress at my core—wet and waiting. At the first touch, my knees buckle and I lean forward, palms on the edge of the bed. "And you'll be better for it. Stay still, Caroline," Tahoe urges.

We've never played games like this, he's never been this person when we mess around. "You've been holding out on me," I say.

He doesn't respond. All I hear are his sharp intakes and exhales as he rubs between my legs. When I'm about to come, because he's a master at playing me, I feel both hands on my ass cheeks. He spreads them wide.

I gasp, but he quiets me with a hum of a noise. Intuitively, I know what's coming next. His tongue is lapping at me and while the rest of my body is as cool as the night air, everything below my waist is fire, lighting up with each stroke of his tongue, or suck of his lips.

I call out in a muffled scream and can't stay upright another second, my stomach collapsing on the bed.

Tahoe wipes his mouth on my right ass cheek, and

then growls, "Not yet. I've waited too long for this."

"Why don't you just stick it in and then we can reset?" I say, flipping on the bed keeping my knees open to give him a view of which I speak. "Let me come at least a few times first. You're so good at it," I plead. "Husband," I add. "I won't suck your cock or anything. Only sex for Monty tonight. Okay?"

His gaze turns feral as it alternates between my face and in between my legs. "Say suck your cock one more time and I'll fill your mouth quicker than you can say *please*."

Smirking, I scoot back until my head hits the pillow. "Suck my pussy until I come," I say instead.

Tahoe puts his hands together like he's praying, and looks up. He doesn't say another word, he eats me out so furiously, I come back to back with barely a pause between. This is the part of the night where we normally retreat to our respective sides of the bed and pray our subconscious personalities don't come out while we're sleeping and fuck each other rotten.

I'm fingering my hair, coming down from the orgasms and he's panting with pleased exertion, chin resting on my pubic bone. "Twice?" he asks, impressed.

I nod. "That felt amazing. It wouldn't stop. Only one thing would have made it better?"

He quirks one brow, wary of any criticism in the bedroom. I decide to put him out of his misery quickly. "If your dick was inside me while I was coming."

"Oh," he says, taking a page out of my shocked playbook. He's still wearing his boxer briefs, our M.O. still in play due to brutal habit.

"What next then?" My heart rattles against my rib cage. I'm already turned on and ready. I can tell just by looking at his face, he wants to come. This is the game changer. The moment we've been saving all of our self-control points for. Why we fought with our friends and broke up in a panicked haste.

I lean over and slide the stretchy fabric down his thick thighs. He bends over and takes them the rest of the way off. When he stands up, his tattoos shaded in the candlelight glowing from the nightstand, I can see his hesitation. In the twinc of his muscles and the set of his jaw. "They are all the way off," he says. His chest heaves as he looks at me. "Caroline, I love you so much." Tahoe's voice shakes at his admission.

"Like I love you," I reply, making a reach for his steely hard cock. He shakes his head softly, but the smile on his face tells me he's not telling me not to touch, he's telling me he doesn't believe we love each other equally. "It's going to fit," I remark, when I wrap my hand around it and my fingers don't meet. "We've had this conversation before, but I want to ask now that it's going in there. Preliminary reassurance," I say. "Don't get me wrong, I want it inside me more than anything else, I'm just talking logistics right now." He joins me on the bed, on his knees in front of me.

I rise up to meet him. One naked body pressed against the other. Heart to heart.

I slide my hand up and down the large shaft, and he reaches between my legs once more. This time, he doesn't rub my clit, he spreads the entrance open with his pointer and ring finger and slides his middle finger inside me.

His eyes flare open. I see the surprise. "It's going to be a tight fit," he admits, clearing his throat. He moves his finger inside of me and my eyes actually roll back in my head. "Oh my god," I moan. "What is that?" I lean my head against his chest.

"Eyes up, Sunny," he orders. "I want to try something." As he speaks, he keeps moving his finger in that come hither tempo that is seriously boggling my mind, and turning my legs to jelly.

I open my eyes. "Try it. Try anything," I breathe. "Please. It feels so good."

I've forgotten his dick in my hand for the moment, at the gentle surge in my hand, I work it a little more. He closes his eyes with pleasure. "Stop for a second. I need you to focus," he says. "Better yet, I need to focus." I refuse not to touch it, but I stop pumping my fist.

He stops moving his finger and presses the same spot hard. There's no way I can keep my eyes open. The pleasure is seated too deep. When I open them, he's smiling. "I got two in," he says, biting his lip. "One more, and you might not tear when I fuck you." He swallows, and runs his lips and nose against my neck. The full sensation is fucking brilliant. "I want you to enjoy this. I should have been fingering you the whole time. I feel like an idiot."

He licks my neck and I forget to breathe. "There's nothing you can do that will hurt me right now, Tahoe. Absolutely nothing. Your touch only makes me feel good."

I spread my knees apart a little further to give him

better access and I feel it more—his fingers slip deeper. Tahoe stars moving his fingers again in that same rhythmic motion, and I toss my head back.

"Lay down," Tahoe says. He takes my body weight in one arm and lowers me like I'm a feather, until I'm resting on the mattress. His skill is top notch because his working hand is still making me feel light headed—turning everything I thought I knew about an orgasm on its head. He kisses me, his lips a whisper touch against my neck. My ear. My mouth. With both of my hands free, I let my fingers roam his body. The contour of his hips where his sculpted ass starts has mostly been hidden from view unless I was giving him a blow job. The warmth of his body on the inside of my thighs is another new sensation.

"I think I'm going to come," I say, arching my back so my breasts press against his chest.

He stops moving. "No, don't. Not yet. You're feeling good?" he asks, eyes vivid and assessing.

I groan. "Look at me, do I look like I'm feeling good?" He lets his gaze wander over my body—my hardened nipples, my hips working his fingers, and my flushed, excited physique.

He scoots forward, and removes his fingers in a slow, deliberate move that has me feeling cold and empty. I hiss out a frustrated breath. "That doesn't feel good."

"It will soon," he replies. "I hope," he adds in a lower voice. His hand shakes a bit as he lines up his throbbing shaft to where it's never been before. He swallows hard as he watches his body and mine.

His gaze flicks up to meet mine, and there aren't any

words left to say. I feel the head as he pushes it in. While it's bigger than his fingers, I'm so wet and ready to receive him, it makes me delirious with lust. Here's this big, beautiful man trying to be careful with me. Because he loves me. Tahoe is watching my face for any sign of discomfort. "I'm okay. Give me more," I say.

He hisses out a breath. "You have no idea how badly I want to give you all of it. Right now, Caroline." His words are a feral growl, and they send a shockwave to my core. The very place that needs the pep talk. "Can you raise your hips? You're so fucking tight. So tight."

I raise my hips a touch, and I realize why he asked, it slides his cock in a bit more at the same angle so it's less jarring. I back my hips to bed the bed and rock into him again, going a little further this time.

"I feel so full," I admit, moaning when it rubs just the right way. He takes this as his cue to work my clit as I try out my new superpower.

He sighs, "I'm not even half in yet, Sunny. Your game is fun, but can I give it a go now?"

I moan when he flicks my clit with his thumb back and forth. "Yes," I reply. "Fuck me, Tyler Holiday and never stop."

He leans in and kisses my mouth. His body shakes, and he leans back up, with one hand on my hip and the other firmly on clit duty, he drives his hips forward. He stops and kisses me again. "Okay?" he rasps, putting both hands beside my head to hold himself up.

"Half in?" I ask, grimacing a little. "It stings a bit, but it still feels more good than anything else."

He grins against my lips. "That's as far in as I can

go," he replies, jutting his hips forward to make his point obvious.

"You're in me," I exclaim, biting his bottom lip.

He exhales. "I'm all up in you and it feels better than in my dreams."

"Make love to me now. That's the plan."

He withdraws his dick and pushes forward again. I make a loud noise and he stops short. "Did I hurt you?"

With both hands, I grab his ass. "Yes, by stopping. Don't stop. Keep filling me," I command. "If you want to please your *wife*."

He does exactly that. He keeps kissing my lips, and listening to every moan and sigh I make, but he's moving against me, with me, inside of me, all over me. We're connected at the basest level, and every time he thrusts deep, I can't control my screams. It's his name. Or something that makes zero sense, or it's prayers that it never stops, that every moment feels just like this. His lips taste like me mixed with our wedding cake, and while our bodies find their perfect harmonies together in this new act, it still feels familiar. Right.

Tahoe's neck tightens. "I'm going to come," he says. "Should I slow down?" I love that he's controlling this, trying to let me have the best experience possible. His pumps grow deeper, and slower as he waits for me reply.

"Like that," I say. "Slow and deep."

He nods, and I can see the resolve in his eyes right before I shut mine to lose myself to the building orgasm. "Fuck me. Just like that," I say. "It's hitting the spot," I tell him, louder than I intended.

"When you talk like that it makes me come quicker,"

he says, taking my earlobe in between his teeth. He pumps deliberately now that he knows I'm almost there. "Come," he says, his breath tickling my ear. "Come now."

My body tightens and then I come, right on cue. The waves of pleasure concentrated where our bodies are connected. It's not a blip of an orgasm, it's a massive, world shaking orgasm. I hold him to my chest and relish this new connection, this new way of expressing just how much we love each other.

"I need to come, Sunny," he says, reminding me with a gentle nudge. "Where do you want it."

I remember how he told me he's never come inside a woman. It's something he told me when we were painting the hangar. To think, I was shocked by that tidbit back then, and now I'm about to beg him to leak as deep inside me as he can.

"Inside me," I say.

He closes his eyes on a satisfied smile and begins a comfortable, scorching pace again. It doesn't take long now that he's concentrating. He tucks his head into the crook of my neck and his body goes rigid. I'm amazed to feel him flex with each hot burst inside me. It goes on and on for longer than it ever has when I've given him blow jobs.

We stay connected, him inside me, while we both catch our breath. It happened. I can't even begin to process how good it feels. What a different sensation it is to have his big, stunning cock in my body. "I'm going to pull out now and it might hurt a bit. Ready?"

"I'm not made of glass, Holiday."

He smiles a knowing smile and slides out of me in one swoop. "Ow," I say, automatically grabbing my vagina with a cupped hand.

He leans up on his knees and looks down at me. "I told you," he chastens. "How was it? Are you scared of me now?" He takes his dick in his hand and shakes it a couple of times. "Was it what you hoped it would be? That's a lot of pressure. I thought I was going to blow my load the second I got all the way in there."

I let my fingers glide over the tender, wet skin as he watches. "I'm surveying the damage to see if there's any possible way we can do it again right now. I'm glad you held out. It felt so good. I can't believe I've been missing out on that. I feel empty now."

"We have the rest of our lives to play fill the hole. I want to make sure you're not going to walk funny tomorrow."

"You came in me," I remark, grinning. "You've never done that before."

"It's a day of firsts isn't it?" he replies. "It felt so good coming inside your tight body. I'm getting hard again just thinking about it." He does too, his dick growing back to full tilt right before my eyes. "That, I want to do every single day."

Instead of focusing on the sensitive skin, I rub my clit instead. Tahoe watches, stroking himself as he does. "This marks the best day of my life," he says, eyes lowered in a mask of lust. "One I don't want to end. I want to keep it forever."

"It doesn't have to end," I reply. "We're defining everything from now on. Today doesn't end. Let's repeat this every single day for the rest of our lives."

He grins. "Every single day?" I nod. Tahoe lays next to me on the bed, his hand still on his dick, my slickness still coating him, making his hand slide easily. "That thing you did before. On my abs," he says, slanting his gaze my way. "Except on this, instead." Pushing down until it's standing straight in the air, he sighs. "If you're up for it, that is. Basically I want to replay every time we ever messed around, except ending it with me inside you."

"You're up for it. So am I," I coo, slinging my leg over his wide hips. I take over holding, and have to lean to one side to position him where I think he's supposed to be. From this angle, actually seeing it, the size looks harrowing. "Tell me if I'm doing it wrong," I say, meeting his eyes.

He shakes his head. "You can't do this wrong. If it's in you, it will always be right. Always."

I sit down, and to the side and suck in a sharp breath when his head opens me wide. "Right. That's right. That's right," he hisses. "Nothing has ever been more right. Keep going," he urges.

He closes his eyes and wets his bottom lip. His chest and stomach are rippled to perfection and it seems every muscle in his body is textbook perfect. Looking at him, piece by piece, underneath me, gives me a power I didn't know I had. He's mine.

I sit down further, and feel a throbbing jerk deep inside me. I lean over and put my hands on his sculpted midsection and ride him up and down. This feels like a different pleasure, another angle that rubs me just the right way, and I can't escape the moans of pleasure I know are coming. My clit slides against him, and his huge girth brushes me.

When I meet his gaze, he gives me a lopsided grin. "Every day, yeah?"

"Oh, fuck yes, every day," I cry out.

"Say fuck again," he says, narrowing his candlelit eyes.

Riding him, I crawl forward until my lips are balancing just above his. "Fuck *me*," I tease, mouth barely brushing his. "I never was good at being your girlfriend," I breathe, grinding on him in a slow tempo.

He catches my bottom lip between his teeth and pulls. "Because you were always meant to be my *wife*."

He said the word. I kiss him hard, and his hands slide from the sides of my face down my body to land on my hips. He guides me to our orgasms, the waves tearing through us at the same exact time.

I lay on top of his chest, listening to his heartbeat for what feels like forever. Though I know it can't possibly be that long because forever is what you ask for, and right now is all you're promised.

For us, our love was destined, a mark in time that came hurtling toward us without our consent. Found and lost. Love and loss. Promises and lies. Floating and falling. Forever and never.

Defined simply: happily ever after.

Epilogue

Caroline

Three years later

I found him there. In between who I was and who I wanted to be. In the place I've always been, the same small town I grew up in, surrounded by the people who love and loathe me in equal measure. And he stayed. And he loves me more than I knew a human could love another human. I love him more than that. The relationship is existential—existing in its very own realm of love.

The airport is my second love, still. The accident served as only a roadblock to finding my happiness in all ways instead of in merely one. Still to this day, I consider the healing process my rebirth, the thing that shaped me into a person willing to accept faults, wary, but strong. From the ashes rose a woman desperately wild, capable of loving, and forgiveness, seeking adventure, with the ability to take mistakes and learn from them instead of letting them crush me.

"You better get that ass in here and help me get these

dishes out on the lawn, Caroline May Holiday Bae," Shirley hollers from across my kitchen at the Inn. I'm washing dishes at the sink, my mind a million miles away as I study Tahoe and his friends chatting in a circle.

I pop my ass out so she can swat it on the way by. "Do not call me that. Bae is the Danish word for poop. How many times do we have to go over this?"

She shrugs. "The Kardashians say it, so it's usable. Turn on a television every once in a while!"

I wipe my hands on a dishtowel, and refuse to reply to my friend. Caleb and Shirley have been going steady for about a year and I can't say I'm surprised. She seems happy, and Caleb seems less…bitter. Grabbing a tray, I follow her out. It's my parent's wedding anniversary and we're hosting a big party. It reminds me of my wedding and I'm feeling nostalgic.

My mama comes up beside me as I'm heading toward a tent, her white apron a gleaming white. "What can I help with?"

"Nothing. This is your day. Take off the apron. We don't need your help today," I say, swatting her away from trying to remove the tray from my hands. "Seriously. Go have one of those cranberry juice drinks. Tahoe was up late working on the recipe. They taste like candy. Go. Shoo," I say.

"I love you, baby," Mama drawls, giving me that sweet smile. "I'm so proud of you." I grin in response. I did have to quit waitressing to help at the Inn, but I don't think anyone was more pleased with that decision than my parents. I think they viewed it as me finally growing up and taking a life of my choosing. The airport is still my haunt and that's my first and favorite job, but with the few employees I have, it's not so much work that I feel overwhelmed. Six days a week I'm busy, but Sunday? Sundays are for my two favorite S words. Snuggling and sex. Not necessarily in that order. Tahoe has had to go on a few missions here and there, but for the most part the terrorists are controlled. Or so the government has made it seem. They're still opening bases all over the U.S. Every once in a while, I say a little prayer and thank him for sending Tyler Holiday to this small town. And that he loves it as much as I do.

When desires and dreams collide, magical things happen. My current location as proof.

I'm sliding the tray of side salads onto the table when I feel him behind me.

"Mrs. Holiday, are you almost finished in the kitchen?"

I lean back, and he catches me against his chest, his big arms cradling my body. Sighing, I say, "There's a joke in there somewhere, but I'm going to let it go because you're hugging me."

He tightens his arms. "Everything is going so smoothly. I told you Malena wasn't the only one who could pull something like this off. Your Dad is hitting the cranberry drink hard," he says. Malena had a trip to the city planned forever, and couldn't help as much as she wanted to. I freaked at first, but I'm glad it turned out as well as it has. Stick a feather in my hat, I can plan a party. His hands slide a little lower to rest on the bottom my stomach. He leans his head down to whisper in my ear. "When do you want to tell them? Still after dinner? Or now? Or now?" The second or now asked with even more excitement than the first. He is so excited. Granted it's been weeks of keeping my pregnancy a secret, so the relief of everyone finally knowing will be great, but I wanted to wait until their milestone anniversary to let the cat out of the bag. I don't think my mama will want for another thing as long as she lives when she finds out she's going to be a Grandma.

"Are you saying we need to announce it before my daddy gets tanked on your juice concoction? Or are you just so stoked," I say, using his west coast friend's word, "that you literally won't be able to keep your mouth shut a minute longer?"

He laughs, and kisses the side of my head. It gives me butterflies. Not baby's fluttering kicks, either. The love tinged madness of him affecting me so fully that I have no control over my own body. "A little of both. What do you say?" Tahoe bounces from one foot to the other.

"Oh, goodness, go get the present already!"

"Yes!" he shouts. When people glance his way, he tries to hide his excitement. "Be right back," he says, clearing his throat.

Hands on my hips, I watch him go, and skip a little as he tries not to sprint into the Inn for their gift. I walk toward where my parents are sitting at a table when I see Tahoe exit the house with the medium sized box.

It's as good a time as any. Friends are mulling around the bar, and some couples are already dancing, or sitting down and eating. Tahoe's parents weren't able to make it tonight, but they will be here early next week to stay for an entire month. They haven't been here since the wedding. We visited them last summer for a couple weeks and it was easy for me to see why Tahoe is so amazing. They are loving parents. His dad has blue eyes and a dimpled smile, and his mother has blonde hair and an understanding way. We're going to wait to tell them until they arrive, but tonight is the night for everyone else. The Bronze Bay gossip column is about to be flooded with predictions.

Tahoe wraps an arm around me and pulls me close. "We got you a gift," he exclaims, extending the box to my mama.

She takes it, wearing a warm thankful smile. "Go on. Open it now," I urge, when she goes to set it aside. Manners dictate one should wait until guests leave to open gifts so no one gets their feelings hurt if one present is obviously nicer than another. It was the same when I was a child. I remember having a big birthday party with a dozen friends and staring at the present table with longing. She'd say, "When everyone leaves you can open them all. I'll make notes of who got what and we can write our thank you notes. Be polite. Use patience, Caroline May."

"You're sure?" Mama asks, tilting her head in confusion.

Tahoe clears his throat, and nods. "We're sure. Open it now."

My daddy looks at the box as my mom tears into it and starts unwrapping the layers and layers of white tissue paper. She finally gets to the little notecard. It explains what it is. Tahoe helped, but it was mostly my idea. It's a metal starfish I made from scraps of an airplane. The airplane that almost killed me, if I'm being perfectly honest. On the starfish is an engraving. "A kiss the sky, blue hue, dream come true."

Her eyes water and I know she's connecting the dots. It's our saying. The one they coined when I was born. "You're going to be grandparents," I say softly. Dad hugs mama, a one-armed lopsided hug. "It's a boy. He's due on daddy's birthday."

"Well that's something, isn't it?" Daddy says, "This is some anniversary gift! Anyone top this? I'm going to be a Grandpa!" he roars, standing to hug Tahoe and then he envelops me in a bear hug. "Oh, Caroline. Way to make your old man cry." Those around us are clapping, and shouting. Tahoe's friends are roaring with shouts and cheers, Shirley screams, and looks horrified I hadn't told her. Britt, off in a corner, fakes a smile and nods in my direction.

Daddy sniffles a bit, and Mama looks on with loving, tear filled eyes. "Thank you," she mouths, holding up the starfish. One of the arm points is blackened. I didn't want to use a charred piece, but it happened to work out best with the design I planned, so I went with it. Symbolism be damned.

"Happy Anniversary, Grandpa and Grandma!" I say. Tahoe places his hand on my lower back.

My Mama finally pulls herself together enough to hug me. "I had a feeling, baby. I'm so happy for you and

Tahoe. This is best gift you could have given us. Thank you so much." She tightens her arms around my neck, and releases me to hug my husband. When she leaves to accept congratulations from their friends, I link hands with Tahoe and meet his loving, searing gaze. My eyes leak.

Not because I'm sad.

Not because I'm happy.

Just because I am here.

Being where you are is a gift others will never have. Bloom where you're planted. Love when it's offered. And keep it at all costs.

International Bestselling Author
RACHEL ROBINSON

Rachel Robinson grew up in a small, quiet town full of loud talkers. Her words were always only loud on paper. She has been writing stories and creating characters for as long as she can remember. After living on the west coast for many years, she now resides in Virginia with her husband and two children.

racheljrobinson.com
Facebook: racheljeanrobinson
Twitter: @rachelgrobinson

Made in the USA
Columbia, SC
07 February 2018